1. farm in Vermont
raise a family.
2. return to school
to follow up on
ideas of expression
modes for frustrated
children.
3. die happy

Such was the plan that my mama had
scrawled out on a scrap of paper
when she and my dad first got married.
But one July day
they took a detour and ventured off
into the Alaskan backwoods . . .

*The road widened out at a farmyard
that reminded Kate of the elephant burial ground in "Tarzan."*

I was born in Sleeping Moose, Alaska.

When I was young, my mama used to tell me stories about things that happened while we were living out in the Alaska bush. She said they were all pretty much true.

This creative narrative is my best effort to fictionalize my mama's reflections of actual incidents so as to protect every last soul.

The town names, characters, and some chronological details have been reconstituted in order to make this story comfortable to tell.

"No sense in getting shot over a couple of stories," as Mama would say.

Atwood Cutting

"I have not seen the 'Elephant.'
I am told, however, that he is ahead, and
—if I live—
I am determined to see him."

*From the diary of a soul unknown to me,
but quoted in Merril J Mattes, ed., Platte River Road Narratives (Urbana:
University of Illinois Press, 1988), 62. Platte River Road Narratives: A
Descriptive Bibliography of Travel Over the Great Central Overland Route to
Oregon, California, Utah, Colorado, Montana, and Other Western States and
Territories, 1812-1866." The Annals of Iowa 50 (1989),309-309. Available at:
http://ir.uiowa.edu/annals-of-iowa/vol50/iss2/28*

WHERE THE MOOSE SLEPT

An account of two late-20th century pioneers
who "saw the elephant" on the Last Frontier.

SLEEPING MOOSE SAGA
PART ONE

Told by Atwood Cutting

WHERE THE MOOSE SLEPT

An account of two late-20th Century pioneers who "saw the elephant" on the Last Frontier.
Sleeping Moose Saga Part One. Told by Atwood Cutting

Cutting/Echo Hill Arts Press, LLC. Colorado Springs, CO
https://www.atwoodutting.com

Publisher's Cataloging-In-Publication Data
(Prepared by The Donohue Group, Inc.)

Names: Cutting, Atwood. | Cutting, Atwood. Tales from Sleeping Moose. Volumes 1-2.

Title: Where the moose slept: an account of two late-20th century pioneers who 'saw the elephant' on the last frontier / told by Atwood Cutting.

Description: Colorado Springs, CO: Cutting/Echo Hill Arts Press, LLC, [2016] | Series: Sleeping Moose saga; part 1 | Substantial revision of Tales from Sleeping Moose, Volumes 1-2, which were originally released in 2015.

Identifiers: LCCN 2016909024 | ISBN 978-0-9975819-0-4

Subjects: LCSH: Frontier and pioneer life—Alaska—History—20th century—Fiction. | Adventure and adventurers—Alaska—History— 20th century—Fiction.

| Families—Alaska—History—20th century—Fiction. | Alaska— Social life and customs—20th century—Fiction. | LCGFT: Historical fiction.

Classification:
LCC PS3603.U88 W44 2016 | DDC 813/.6—dc23
ISBN-978-0-9975819-0-4

Both Atwood and Kate
wish to express gratitude for the support of so many.

Thank you, April. You were instrumental in my decision to
publish this story.

Buck, Ann Ely, Cecil, Dave, Paula, Lynn, Leo, Cynthia, Suze,
Fred, Brandon, Ann Wood, Christa, Karen, MMAT, Brandon,
Dick and Bob, we love you for making the pilgrimage to
"Victory Garden." It meant a lot to us.

Lisa Marvel at "The Book Haven" in Salida, Colorado, thank you
for sponsoring delightful Dies Librorum book-signing events for
local bibliophiles, for having my early editions on your
bookshelves. I wish you every success.

Anya Nelsestuen (at age nine, my youngest fan),
Marion Cutting, Ann McEachern, Marjorie Yates, Lisa Bentz,
Gene Martin, Vickie Urban, Richard Hinebaugh, Jacqueline
Keller and Rebecca Sangueza, thank you for your
emotional support during this project.

Tracy Fischer, Sasha Lee, Anika Nelsestuen, Evelyn Hollowell,
Kaye Brabec, George Read and Dee Dee Fischer—You were all
very helpful with your proofing and editing suggestions.
Thank you so much!

Thank you, also to Lily Donelson and Maryam Negm, Jay
Polmar and Liliana Garcia at ipublicidades.com for your patient
assistance in producing this original and
"nearly true" life story.

Thank you all.

This Memoir of
our Alaskan Pioneering Adventure
is Dedicated to:

John and Angeline,
Windsor and Mary,
Elvin and Lorene,
Ralph Waldo Emerson,
Webster Caye,
and David.

Living the Dream

Building the Dream

Table of Contents

Some Alaskan Terminology

Prove up - To fulfill the requirements of homesteading, and receive 160 acres of raw land.

Bush - Wilderness, back woods, raw land.

Cheechakos - Newcomers to Alaska.

Sourdough - Someone who's been in Alaska long enough to have grown sour on the place, but doesn't have the dough to get out.

Jack Mormon – Born Mormon, but no longer practicing.

End of the roaders - Folks who eschew normal society for a variety of reasons, choosing instead to live as far away from people as they can get.

Arctic Entryway - A small anteroom that protects a warm house from being blasted with frigid air each time the front door is opened.

Breakup – Spring thaw and permafrost melt. Very long and messy.

Snow-machine - The Alaskan bush family car.

Go-molly - To hide the dirty dishes until later.

Woody – A style of station wagon with wooden side panels that was popular in the 1940s and '50s.

The Slope – The north slope of Alaska, home of Prudhoe Bay oil production.

Union call - Union halls "call out" the open jobs daily.

Drag up - Pipeline camp talk for "quit."

The Lower Forty-Eight - The 48 contiguous states.

Outside - Same as above.

Outside - Where bush folks go to the bathroom.

Going outside - Leaving the bush for winter jobs.

Mamasan - Japanese-Hawaiian for Mother.

Tutu - Hawaiian for "Grandma."

Mahalo nui loa – "Thank you very much" in Hawaiian, the newly adopted language of many an old sourdough.

Moose Creek meandered through Moose Flat.
The starry-eyed honeymooners decided to build their house
on the very spot where a moose had slept, at the back of
a field of wildflowers on the far end of the flat.

A Preface of Pure Fiction

AT THE FIRST sound of gunfire Ruth grabbed Jimmy and dragged him into a windowless corner of the shack. They huddled there, flinching and ducking as each new gunshot rang out. Then the valley grew quiet.

Frampton let out his breath. "I gotta go out an' check on the hogs. You two stay put," the squatter told the hunkered pair. Then he went outside to gather his litter.

"So-oie!" He produced the conventional high-pitched hog call and waited to hear the crunching of brush being trampled by a sounder of swine. But no pigs appeared. He gave out one more shout between megaphone-cupped hands. "So-oie!" Not one sow came out of the woods to see what he had to offer.

"Dammit!" Snyder spat, and his fists balled up in response to the rage that was now building in his gut. "Dang that Bill O'Leary!" he hissed. Frampton wheeled around and stormed back toward the shack, burying his boot in a deep pile of pig poop somewhere along the way. When he got to the door, he kicked open the plywood panel and made straight for his gun.

Ruth and little Jimmy were still cowering in the corner, but Frampton Snyder had more important things on his mind than their feelings. He ripped the rifle from its hooks and started back for the gaping exit, pausing just long enough to issue one order. "Don't you two go nowhere!"

"But where are you goin'?" Ruth risked asking, even though she knew better than to try stopping him.

"I got business down the road," he snarled over his shoulder.

Trouble had been brewing in the neighborhood ever since Frampton's animals had moved in. Now things had come to a head. That morning he'd turned his drove of hogs out to forage and watched them meander off in the direction of O'Leary's. And now there'd been gunshots. It could only mean trouble.

"They's gonna be more trouble over there where them shots came from," the free-range rancher warned his wife. He grabbed up some ammunition, tucked his gun under his arm, and stomped out through the wide-open door, leaving a trail of boot-shaped dung patches behind him.

Ruth and Jimmy helplessly watched him go, and waited for the next volley of gunfire.

Chapter One
Summer, 1976

To What?

KATE INSTANTLY FELL in love with the Kenai River. When the highway they were traveling first brushed against it, she saw water so turquoise that the short glimpse gave her a thrill. "Oh Tim, look!"

The highway afforded them several more heart-stopping views of flowing aquamarine glacial melt as they descended from Cooper Landing into the flattening terrain of the central Kenai Peninsula.

They were headed to Homer to catch the ferry to Kodiak. Kate wanted to see a Kodiak brown bear before they left the 49th state forever.

After several miles, the meandering honeymooners entered a little settlement, slowed to a stop and got out of the car. It was a hamlet with a handful of houses, a Tesoro gas station, and one small general store built of logs. There was a flagpole out front with a sign nailed above the door that read, "Sleeping Moose Post Office."

"What a charming spot," Kate said.

Across the road from the post office a dirt lane shot up the hill and headed into the woods. To what? There was a makeshift sign posted beside it that had "Land for Sale, 5 miles" hand-painted on it.

Why not go up and have a look? Maybe they might want to buy land right there in Alaska, instead of moving to Vermont, which—up to that very moment—had been their plan.

It was a long, sunny day in July and they were in no hurry. Tim turned up the unmarked trail and headed away from the tiny outpost sitting on the edge of civilization. On a simple whim, they set off on a detour that was to become the adventure of their lifetime.

Rooster tails of dust lingered behind their car as the pair drove with gusto for a half-mile. But when the earth began shifting and sagged with increasing dampness, Tim had to slow down to navigate a series of mud holes pockmarking the path. His bride held onto the dashboard and leaned with every swerve of the car.

After about a mile of puddle maneuvering, the casual explorers came to a fork in the road. They took the one that had a second "land for sale" sign pointing toward a wooden bridge that crossed over a small creek.

Tim drove down toward the creek, stopping just before going out onto the bridge.

He turned to Kate. "Shall we find out what's on the other side?"

The old trestle looked rotten and the co-pilot had her doubts. "Do you think it's safe to drive across? I can see holes right through in some places."

"Let's find out," the handsome driver said. He hopped down out of their shiny new four-wheel-drive car and turned the hubs on both front wheels. He got back in, shifted a floor gear labeled "4WD," and slowly edged the rig out onto planks that had been laid across supports barely scanning the gap.

Kate looked out her window down over the side of the car and studied the water they were crossing. She was staring straight through large gaps in the planks and seeing lazy swirls and eddies curling away downstream. The crossing looked precarious. She held her breath and pulled up on the edge of her window, as if this might keep them from falling into the creek below.

Then . . . they were safely on the other bank.

Tim gave the engine gas and steered the little car around a particularly slippery corner, and lost speed again as they plunged into more trees and even softer earth on the far side. The mud got deep as the road took them through a flat, soggy section of woods nearly a hundred yards long. There was something made of lumber lodged in a ditch along the side of the road.

Most of it lay buried, but there was still enough of the thing poking out of the mud to make a person curious.

"Okay," Kate said, "I give up. What is that?"

"It looks like a homemade road grader that someone uses to drag the road smooth and drain it."

"I don't think it works all that well," Kate observed dryly.

The next moment, they bottomed out in a deceptively deep mud hole.

"Still, it's intriguing to think that whoever lives up here fends for himself . . . It'd be nice to have that kind of privacy," Tim dreamed aloud.

Kate agreed. Having long ago embraced Emerson and his belief in self-reliance, she subconsciously harbored a "Brook Farm" fantasy. "Yes, it would," she murmured. "It's really beautiful up here."

The road wound through many more spruce trees and muddy patches before it started to climb a straight grade. Now it paralleled a wire fence that bordered the edge of a pasture. The mud dried as they left the marsh behind and began to gain altitude. The possibility of an unobstructed view on top had both explorers leaning forward, eager to see.

When they popped up onto a flat space, Tim took his foot off the accelerator. They had entered a functioning "bush" farmyard.

The sight of several ancient tractors and pieces of rusting equipment lying around somehow reminded Kate of the sacred elephant burial ground in the movie "Tarzan:"

There were several big, rusting forms lying in the grass. Why was there so much old equipment lying around? A big silver cargo truck seemed to be serving as a fence across one end of the yard. A long red cattle trailer parked between the barn and the pasture closed another gap. There was an older-looking outhouse sitting next to a newer-looking chicken house. A few hens scratched at the dirt in front of both structures. Behind the privy stood a paddock where a small flock of sheep that had been grazing now cast startled stares at the recent arrivals.

There was a big barn near a small stand of trees, and nestled in the trees was a little house. Its shape was a dead ringer for a Hostess Twinkie. And a stovepipe sticking out of one sloping sidewall sent little puffs of smoke up into periwinkle and sunshine.

This was a fairy tale setting, for sure.

The two visitors stood looking around at miles of untamed Alaskan wilderness. Kate turned full circle, taking in the waves of uninhabited hills and several distant glaciers shining bright turquoise following the recent eruption of Augustine volcano across the inlet. Gorgeous. A single, rounded mountain rose like a dome up ahead. It was dazzling. Pure untouched Alaska. An old man opened the antique-glass-paneled door and stepped outside. He looked his visitors over for a second, and then he smiled and stepped forward.

Tim and Kate did the same.

This fellow had to be at least sixty, which seemed practically ancient. He was bowlegged, like maybe he'd done a lot of horse riding. And his silvered head fit perfectly into a big, white cowboy hat. Dressed in Levi's, boots, and a plaid shirt with abalone-snap breast pockets, he appeared to be the genuine article. His eyes were a pale, pure blue. The way they shone when he smiled made Kate want to like this fellow from the get-go.

"Howdy," the man said. He gave a nod and touched the brim of his Stetson. "Can I help you folks?" He sounded like a real cowboy, talking slowly and relaxed, as if he had all day.

Tim stretched out his hand and they shook. When he stepped back, Kate did the same.

"The name's Goodman," the cowboy said.

"Peters," Tim responded.

Right away the man invited the couple inside to meet his wife.

Their home was a simple World War II Quonset hut. It had a window in each end and the one glass door, through which they had just entered. A long kitchen counter skirted with wooden cupboards and two matching dish shelves, took up most of one side. The front end of the room housed a mid-century tin sink-unit. A vintage Formica table separated the kitchen area rom the living room area and there were four bent-steel chairs positioned around it. The whole place couldn't have measured more than twelve by twenty feet— maybe less. An old double bed was positioned against the far end, and extra sets of Levi's and shirts hung on a row of nails protruding from the back wall. Two easy chairs and a reading light near the furnace completed the living room section of their compact house. That was the whole mountain home. Kate didn't see any side doors in the room. She guessed these folks still used the privy across the yard.

"This here's my other half, Elsie," the cowboy said. "We came up here and homesteaded in '58."

Apparently, a homesteader's work was never done, since the fellow admitted he hadn't gotten around to building a real house for Elsie yet. They'd been living in this tiny shack for the last eighteen years. Remarkably, they both looked happy.

The four talked for a few minutes before Tim inquired about the land for sale.

Goodman smiled. "I've got plenty of land back here that you might like," he said. "The road stops at the top of our homestead. Nothing beyond there but wilderness," he told them. "We hold the grazing leases all the way to the river. It's raw nature back there, and lots of it. There's a good house site at the top of the road, if you're of a mind to build." They looked "of a mind," so he continued. "Say, how would you two like to go see the best building site on this mountain?"

Tim and Kate were captivated. The view was so good from where they were right then—how much better would it be higher up? With no plan or preconceptions, they accepted the cowboy's "invite" to see what they could see.

Elsie said, "You three go ahead. I'll stay here and wash the dishes. I don't like to go-molly 'em."

At a questioning look from Kate, she explained. "That's a trick the church folks use. They like to hide their dishes to be washed later, so they can get to their activities in a hurry. But I can't see doing that," she concluded.

The trio went outside and climbed into Goodman's Jeep pickup. They bounced out of the yard and continued across another rough pasture, down into more woods, and up again through another meadow before arriving at the very top of the one-hundred-sixty-acre homestead.

The panorama rivaled that colossal view of Yosemite Valley from Glacier Point, a sight she would never forget.

A gnarly bear trail wound away into the trees. And there was nothing but uninhabited land beyond. "No one lives back there?" Tim sounded incredulous.

"Indians might have once, I suppose. But no one lives there now," Goodman assured him.

Tim smiled broadly. Kate was entranced. With one look, the newlyweds decided—right then and there—to spend their nest egg on this precise parcel of paradise. Their wonderful dream would blossom out right from this spot. They clasped hands excitedly and stepped up to Goodman. "We'll take it!"

* * *

"Have you got a calculator?" Tim was asking as the three entered the Quonset hut through the glass front door.

"No, but I've got a pencil and paper," the silver-haired cowboy said. "Have a seat, why don't you?" He gestured toward the table. "Say, Elsie let's have some of that pie. We're celebrating! The Peterses here are buying the back forty!"

Mrs. Goodman smiled. "Oh, my goodness! Well, welcome to Round Top Mountain! We'll have pie soon. It's about ready to come out of the oven."

"Please call me 'Kate,'" the young Mrs. Peters said as she chose the smallest of the bent steel chairs and sat. Kate found that her chair sort of rocked and she liked it.

Mrs. Goodman set out saucers and forks while the two men sat at the other end of the table and began scratching out some mathematical equations to figure up a payment schedule.

"Okay. Let's get your full names," Goodman said. He had started writing up a formal agreement on a clean sheet of paper.

"Timothy David Peters and Katherine Cutting Peters," Tim replied solemnly.

"And you're buying four ten-acre parcels, at $2000 an acre?"

"That's right." The two newlyweds nodded and grinned. Neil Goodman carefully lettered out all the information, folded up the paper, and stuffed it into his shirtfront pocket. "We can go on into town later to record the deed. But right now, this pie of Elsie's is a-callin' to us, don't you reckon?"

"Definitely!" Kate blurted. She had been happily rocking and drinking-in an aroma she hadn't come across since she was a little girl. "I think I smell rhubarb," she said, turning to Mrs. Goodman who was crossing over to the range. "My mama used to bake rhubarb pies. Some people put strawberries in them but she never did."

"It so happens, this is plain rhubarb," the cook said, as she took the pie from the oven and set it on the long plank counter. It was still steaming when she started carving four big pieces out of her work of art.

"Plain rhubarb is my very favorite!" Kate exclaimed. The young bride rocked in her springy chair and looked around with pleasure at the utilitarian and extremely inviting home they had discovered at the end of a little road. It was perfect.

* * *

While they ate pie, Neil answered their questions about homesteading and told them a bit about the area. He explained how they'd had to *prove up* by putting five acres into cultivation. "To do that," he said, "we needed a barn. And to build a barn we needed a saw mill, so we had to build that first," . . . and so on until here they were, eighteen years later, with a lot of dusty furniture still waiting for a living room to live in. For now, the couch sat in the barn while Neil and Elsie Goodman shared this cozy, if tight house. Neil said maybe one day they might hook up hot water. But by 1976, cold running water was as far as they'd gotten.

Elsie looked content. "I wouldn't mind having a second room someday," she quietly admitted to Kate. "So's I could go to bed while Neil's visiting with the neighbors."

Kate was surprised at the mention of neighbors. "We only passed one house on the way up here and that was about five miles down the road."

"Oh there's a few. One couple lives over on the next ridge there." Elsie said, pointing east. "They homesteaded like us. We usually get together before we leave for the lumber camps, and again whenever we get back. Neil likes to talk politics with Charlie Myers. And then there's a nice couple down close to the highway. You drove past their place on your way in."

"We did see one little farm," Kate remembered. "It had a nice garden with goats."

"Yup that's it. Young folks like you. And there's a couple more locals that live out past the fork in the road at the bridge. You'll likely meet 'em one day."

This is how the Peterses' grand adventure kicked off. It was a sunny day. Tim and Kate were eating pie in that little Twinkie-shaped hut and everything felt right.

* * *

They visited the Goodmans many times over the next two years until the old timers moved away. Kate always sat in the bouncy chair and delighted in the rustic comfort of their place. That first conversation over a warm piece of pie had launched a friendship that Kate still talked about years later, long after their dear friends Neil and Elsie Goodman had left the state. Despite the road and the rain and a few questionable neighbors, she vowed as how those memories of meals at the Twinkie were some of the happiest of her life.

Good times at the Twinkie.

Getting Comfortable

THEY PLANNED TO build a cabin. They planned it on a napkin. It would be a small house with a little window in the back wall so Kate could watch the squirrels playing outside in the alder grove.

She thought she could make do with a campfire on the dirt floor just inside the door and an opening in the ceiling for smoke to escape. After all, they would only be living in it until they had the big house built, which they figured would take about a year.

Kate had discovered a pressed-down patch of grass in the exact shape of a cow moose.

You could see the perfect outline of her body with the head and neck stretched out full length. And it didn't hurt that the settlement below was called Sleeping Moose. "If this isn't a sign, I don't know what is," she'd told Tim. That smart moose had chosen the perfect spot; with a nice windbreak to the north and a panoramic view of the Chugach Range, Skilak Lake, and the ice-capped Kenai Fjords to the south. Kate said she wanted to build their home right where the moose had slept.

"General Delivery" would be their address for now, and the Goodmans, three-quarters of a mile below, would be their closest neighbors. Their next human neighbors were four miles away by dirt road. You could take a snow-machine over the flat in winter, but it wouldn't be easy to walk across that muskeg. Good and private. Kate, a true nature lover, could already picture herself dancing naked in the summer sunshine out in front of their little cabin.

Meanwhile, Tim was envisioning himself as Jack London, who'd built a house to winter in until he could sail down the Yukon to the Klondike and mine a lot of rich lore for *Call of the Wild* and his other books. That sounded fun too.

"Do you think we can really do that?" the bride queried.

She suspected that any construction project she undertook was likely to end up looking like, and lasting about as long as, a tree house.

"If anyone can do it—we can," Tim assured her. And that was how they would play it.

That night they slept out under the stars.

* * *

"It's time to go shopping. Let's head down to Footprint. Hopefully they'll have a hardware store there," Tim suggested. "Hopefully there'll be a bigger grocery store too. The selection here is pretty disappointing," Kate said.

Their new hometown wasn't much of a town really: just a mom-and-pop grocery store/post office and two Tesoro gas pumps. Footprint, located twenty miles southwest of Sleeping Moose, was the biggest town around. It sat all alone in the middle of a million lake-strewn-miles of moose-filled marshland. Footprint wasn't huge, but Neil Goodman had assured them it had more to offer than Sleeping Moose.

Soldotna, another twenty miles further west, was the next town. If they couldn't find what they needed in Footprint, a supply run to Soldotna might take all day.

List in hand, Kate had written "water cans" at the top of their list of supplies needed. There was a lot of permafrost around and very few houses outside of town had running water. The perpetually frozen soil plagued underground pipes in all but the sunniest of southern exposures making plumbing a troublesome enterprise. Most folks took their empty cans along with them whenever they went into town and filled them from the public spigot outside the grocery store. Thus, backwoods living quickly distilled a person's requirements down to basics. In the bush, survival was the overriding concern; transportation was a strong second. No one cared much if your house was dirty since everyone's house was dirty. Kate was not interested in housekeeping, so she appreciated the Alaskan idiosyncrasy.

* * *

"Have you got time for some coffee?" Neil Goodman had just intercepted them as they drove through his farmyard on their way to town. The two had a thousand plans for the day. But the older couple probably didn't get much company up that far. So, why not?

"Sure," Tim said. "That'd be great." They got out of their rig and followed Neil inside. "We can only stay for a few minutes though."

"Uh-huh," Neil said. He called in as he opened the door, "Look here Elsie. We've got company!" Elsie glanced up from tending the furnace as they entered. "Have you got any of that apple pie left?" he asked her.

"No," she said. She smiled right at Kate. "But I did bake a rhubarb pie this morning just in case these two were to stop by." Elsie finished rearranging the coal embers, shut the furnace door, washed her hands in the chilly water, and started cutting up the warm pie.

Kate studied the aging cowgirl's back as she fixed the plates, noting first the back brace she wore, then the cowboy shirt and Levi's, and on down to the western boots that held her leggings tight against her ankles. She studied the woman's raven black hair. It was cut short in the back like a man's, but two little twirls of hair wrapped forward around her ears. Kate homed in on Elsie's dangly turquoise earrings and—the cowgirl turned to face her—red lipstick!

"Welcome to the Last Frontier," Kate thought to herself, "where men are men and women wear pants. And one or two actually wear lipstick."

Elsie sank into a chair across the table from Kate and took a bite of pie. Kate asked, "How did you folks get supplies up here in the old days? It can't have been easy."

"We used to pack the groceries up on snowshoes or drag big loads up behind the tractor," Elsie said in a pleasant baritone. The woman gave no indication that their life had been unusually difficult or the least bit out-of-the-ordinary.

"I guess you were glad when you got snowmobiles," Kate ventured.

"Oh, my yes!" Elsie assured her. "That made things a lot easier I'll tell you."

"Where did you two come from before you homesteaded here in Alaska?" Tim asked Neil.

"Arizona," Neil said. "Elsie's dad was a cattle rancher and so was mine. When we hitched up, we started our own cattle operation there. Did fine too, 'til the government took it all away with some eminent domain malarkey." Kate was listening to the cowboy but her thoughts were still on Elsie. There wasn't a gray streak anywhere on her head even though she looked older than Kate's own mother in Hawaii. The settler's eyes were grayish blue. Her skin was fair. Could she be part Indian? The earrings looked to be Native-made. One day, Kate would have to ask.

Elsie was wearing lipstick and earrings. Why? Had she gotten dressed up just for them? It was possible. After nearly two decades the woman might be excited to have some neighbors close by.

In fact, how had Elsie avoided cabin fever and lonesomeness all this time?

Kate wondered how she might fare in a similar situation. She had always been free-spirited and artistically expressive. But she'd never tackled anything as wild as this. Was she independent enough and smart enough to survive on an isolated mountaintop? In the absence of her own Mamasan Kate decided she'd do well to take a few lessons from Elsie.

This homesteader's wife was a perfect role model for the bush life.

After two pieces of pie and three cups of coffee each the young couple inched their way out the door and recommenced their journey into town. By the time they'd returned home and unloaded all their new gear it was starting to drizzle so they opted to bed down in the back of their water-tight covered wagon instead of sleeping in the rain.

* * *

The next morning the newlyweds painfully unfolded their knees and uncurled their crumpled bodies and slowly emerged from the Toyota's cramped cargo area. The rain had stopped and they were met by a glorious new day.

"Today we start to build our house," Tim announced with a huge smile.

Kate was making oatmeal on the shiny new Coleman stove they'd purchased in Footprint. Neil Goodman had been right. There were plenty of stores in Footprint. They'd also bought two spoons, two metal bowls, two tin cups, a speckled blue coffee pot, a small white ceramic cooking pan, and five surplus G.I. water cans. Each one would hold five-gallons. And now they had plenty of water that they'd gotten from the public spigot in front of the Super Grocery. What more could a bride ask?

Luckily Tim was turning out to be quite a handy fellow. After returning from the jungles of Vietnam he had worked construction and maintenance outside of Boston before heading north to Alaska.

He brought a lot of practical experience to the table, which was good since Kate had absolutely no affinity for mechanical matters. She joked that her greatest contribution could be lifting heavy things. She had been a performing artist, a singer and a dancer up until the day she'd quit show business and gone to Alaska to see a winter.

"Oh, Katie you're 'going to see the elephant,'" is what her mother—instantly thrilled by Kate's description of their impulsive purchase—had said.

Now Kate was resting her trust in this man and his dream, hoping that together they would make a strong and eminently successful team, and foster a peaceful and perfect colony amid the wildflowers.

Tim pulled off the tarp that protected their tools, picked up his new chainsaw, and began wiggling the chain back and forth filing one of the teeth from time to time and giving the whole thing a tweak every so often.

"Let's hope we don't get any more rain until we've finished the cabin," he said.

"Yeah. That was hard last night," Kate agreed, "sleeping all scrunched up in the car. I couldn't straighten my legs all night. And now I can hardly squat down to cook breakfast."

She was stirring the oatmeal on the new camp stove that rested on two low flat stones.

"Maybe we can make a little table for you today," Tim suggested.

"That would be good. And the sooner this cabin is done, the better," Kate threw in.

When breakfast was ready, they gulped down the oatmeal, had a cup of coffee, rinsed out their bowls and their mouths, because they were gritty after "cowboy" coffee, and gathered up all the tools they'd be using for a day of cabin building.

"Let's do it!" Tim said.

"I'm ready!" Kate cheered.

Off they went in search of a few square rocks and a couple dozen straight trees.

By evening they had four good-sized cornerstones set plus two more to hold up the doorframe. The cabin would rest on these boulders that they had dropped down into the subsoil and wrestled flat into the mud. Tomorrow they would start cutting trees for the log walls of their first home. "We also need to build an outhouse," Kate added.

"Huh?"

"We're gonna need an outhouse," she repeated.

"Let's get ourselves a house first. We can go in the alder grove for a while."

"I suppose, but at least let's designate a specific spot to use. I don't want to step in anything in the dark."

That night a hard rain fell. But the next morning they went out anyway to scout for and cut down some trees. Home at dusk with four trees chained behind their little green tank, they were jubilant. The newlyweds had really begun to build their cabin.

As soon as they had four logs limbed and hauled up to the site Tim used chainsaw and chisel to notch the ends. Then Kate helped him lift and set the logs on top of the corner-stones.

The next day they logged and bucked and set the second round of logs on top of the first. Every day after that they repeated the sequence. When their day's work was done, they'd rest on a couple of stumps set out under the sky or in the car if it was raining and dine on Kate's new one-pot specialty, corned beef hash. When they'd finished supper, Tim would make sure the tools were covered and Kate would rinse out the pan, spoons, and bowls. After a last visit to the alder grove, they'd accordion themselves into the back of their little car and try to get a good night's sleep.

* * *

It rained solidly for the next ten days and nights but Tim and Kate worked regardless. They wrestled in the woods all day logging, bucking, and dragging the day's harvest back to the cabin site and setting another layer of logs in the wall. After that they ate and crawled into their four-foot-square luggage area for another miserably cramped and sleepless night.

One thing the Toyota was good for was dragging home the cut and readied logs. One thing it was bad for was *sleeping.*

They went to bed exhausted every night and woke up with painful joints every morning. Having seen inside one of the old four masters on exhibit in the Honolulu Harbor,

Kate couldn't imagine how the sailors had slept in those tiny bunks. As for her, she couldn't wait for that wonderful day when they would be able to move out of the car and finally unfold themselves inside a real cabin.

After five hard days, the walls were almost waist high. Tim cut a doorway into the south side and they stood back to admire their progress. It looked good. The logs wouldn't need peeling since this would be their home for such a short time. But chinking might help to keep the wind out. Kate was reliving those days of pioneer women building their sod huts out on the prairie. So far, she was enjoying the whole adventure.

She figured she could stuff wads of moss in between the logs for insulation. A little creek they had discovered down in the woods was loaded with mossy rocks so as soon as the rain let up Tim and Kate went moss collecting. Tim stood guard in the mist with the shotgun tucked under his slicker while Kate plucked and stuffed big wads of moss into a plastic bag. Whenever the saturated mist gathered together and dribbled off the end of her chin, she used her flannel sleeve to wipe her nose. The wolves and ravens wouldn't tell.

* * *

It took another three days to get the walls up to armpit-height. This made a total of eight rainy nights eating and sleeping in their miniature wagon.

They joked that they might look like a pair of jack-in-the-boxes by the time they finally got to sleep stretched out straight again.

On the ninth day Tim had a brainstorm. "Why don't we make the roof take off in a slant right from here and call it done," he suggested.

"Wouldn't that look funny?"

"Who cares? At this moment, it just needs to be dry."

Kate agreed with that and they switched to vertical log poles and finished the place in two more days. Who would care if it looked like half a cabin? It could be slept in and that was what really mattered. Besides they'd be moving up into a real house soon enough.

The minute Tim had a layer of green roofing paper tacked on top they constructed a hasty bed of plywood-on-cinder blocks. Two quilts later and "ta-da," they'd be stretching out straight tonight!

Tim was on a roll. He built a triangular shelf in the corner for the Coleman camp stove and another shelf underneath for the bowls and cups and all their food: peanut butter, jelly, bread, canned corned beef, instant potatoes, onions, oatmeal, raisins, brown sugar, coffee, powdered lemonade, and powdered milk.

By now they had two additional white enameled saucepans and one well-used cast-iron frying pan. Cooper Landing, a few miles north had lots of garage sales. Kate decorated her new kitchen by hanging all four pans in descending sizes from nails in the slanting wall.

Next, they ran a couple of clothing shelves along the back wall just above the bed. Carpentry tools would get the whole end wall and Neil's G.I. stove would take up the last corner. That bare metal firebox had been a surprise housewarming-gift from Neil. He'd had it sitting out behind the barn for a decade or two waiting for the new house. He'd dug it out and given to them saying he thought the two might be needing it sooner or later.

Kate had resisted his gift for a half second because it wasn't the fire pit in the dirt she'd been picturing. But Tim said, "Yes," right away and installed it in the corner between the bed and the door. He cut a hole in the highest corner of the steep roof and stuck a length of stovepipe up through it. Now they had a living room.

Kate wedged two concrete blocks between the wood stove and the bed and hoped they would prevent any spontaneous combustion. It was close quarters in there.

The last home improvement Tim made was to pound a pair of spikes into the lintel over the door. He twisted a sock around each peg and rested the shotgun on them. Kate had fainted the day she was holding up that lintel waiting while Tim labored to get it attached to something. "Tim, I feel . . ." Boom! She'd been on the ground before she knew it.

And now Tim was hanging their means of protection from that lintel. They had really arrived!

The young wife wrote to Hawaii updating her mother with the highlights of their exciting quest. Her early notes home mirrored those of Lucy Rutledge Cooke. Kate had read one of her letters in a book about crossing the west in a covered wagon back in the 1850s. Cooke had written, "Oh the pleasures of going to see the Elephant!!"

Now, a century later Kate was showing that same gusto—and perhaps the same romantic naivety.

August 3, 1976 - Dear Mamasan,

You'd love this place. I've been gathering moss and chinking the walls with it like a pioneer woman in a sod house out on the plains. Tim gave me a hatchet lesson the other day. Slipped and could have cut off his leg in the process. (Not a deep cut but we both got an idea of how careful we need to be way out here.)

We're sleeping in our car until we get the cabin finished. Luckily, we've got a Toyota with 4x4 knobs on the wheel hubs and a heavy-duty winch on the front bumper. I call it the "impregnable rolling fortress" because it'll go anywhere and never get stuck. Also, we can jump into it in case a grizzly should happen to stroll by. Don't worry Mom. We bought a shotgun so we don't have to be overly concerned about the bears.

Oh, but this is all so much fun!

Love, Kate and Tim

P.S. What did you mean when I told you we were going to build a log cabin in the wilderness and you said that we were "going to see the elephant?"

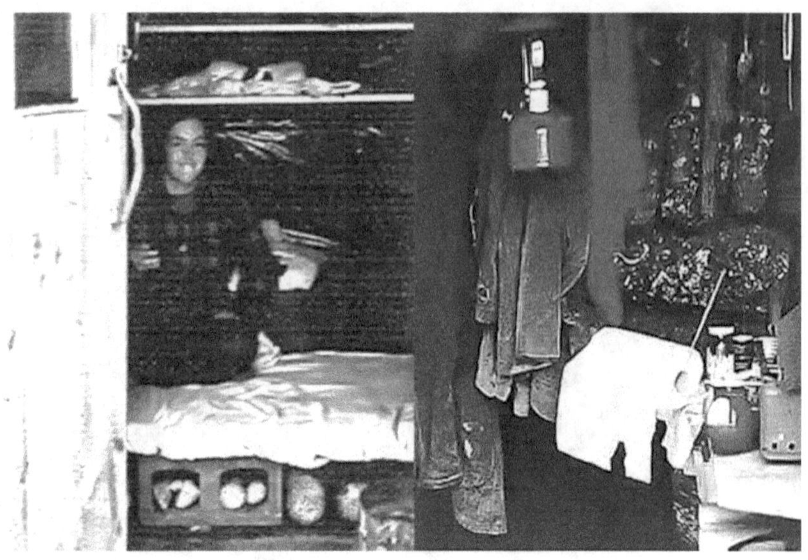

"It's not as big as I thought it would be," Tim admitted. They were standing inside the fully appointed cabin with the door shut. "I guess we should have cut the logs a little longer to allow for the notching."

There wasn't room for one more thing inside that little cabin. If one of them wanted to go outside the other one was obliged to step onto the bed so the opening door would clear.

It was dark inside too. The plywood door with insulation stapled to it allowed no light. In fact, the only place they could see light was through the four-by-twelve-inch squirrel window in the back and some sparsely chinked spaces that left gaps in the vertical log walls.

"Maybe we can cut a window in the door," Kate suggested. "More light might help."

"Yeah I'll do that as soon as we get some more Plexiglas. But this'll do for now. At least we'll be sleeping out straight."

"That's right partner. We'll sleep like kings!" Kate began chattering with excitement. "It's our very first home and we built it ourselves. Don't you just love it? *I* do! What shall we name it? How about 'Half Dome?' It kind of reminds me of Half Dome. Or maybe someday we'll add the other half and call it 'The Lodge.' That would look nice from farther up the hill, where our house will be."

"I'd like to call it 'Honeymoon Cottage,'" Tim said.

"That's a fine name," Kate agreed. And it really was.

Measuring the dimensions, they found that their little honeymoon estate measured just shy of eight-feet-by-eight feet. "It's a perfect starter home," Kate declared, sounding truly delighted.

They took turns dragging each other over the threshold, and then they bedded down for their first good sleep in ages. Heaven.

House-warming

AS THEY SLEPT in their new cottage on that first night the temperature outside stealthily dropped, steadily approaching the freezing point the way a heating kettle sneaks up on an unsuspecting frog.

Long before dawn the rain switched from gray sleet into white snow and heavy flakes set about feverishly erasing the road and covering all the supplies the inexperienced pioneers had stored outside.

When Kate woke in the morning and pulled open the big winter door there was nothing to be seen outside; nothing at all. She stared at a blank screen.

Only ten hours earlier the friendly fireweeds had been their guests. Now the entire landscape looked barren and bitter. Their glorious view was eerily vacant. That spectacular horizon had vaporized. There was nothing to see but a milky galaxy swirling under blustery winds. She stood for a while staring out at nothing. "It's too bad we didn't get around to gathering up some firewood before now," the homesteading wife thought.

Tim rolled off the plywood platform and pushed the door closed. He gave his woman a confident grin. "We need wood," he said. "No problem. I saw some dead wood up in the windbreak. Let's go."

The man was indomitable.

"Okay that sounds good. But let's have some oatmeal before we go out in that cold. We need something in our stomachs and I need to try out my new kitchen."

Tim sat back down on the bed and leaned against the clothing shelf. He folded his hands behind his head. "Perfect. I can sharpen the saw while you cook the oatmeal."

"Deal." Kate took a pan off its nail and opened the door (with Tim swiveling his legs out of the way). She stepped out over the threshold and poured some water from the can sitting on a shelf outside. She had to break it away from its mooring and chunks of ice banged together inside as the can came loose. She poured out a trickle of water, just enough to fill the white saucepan and half of the blue coffeepot.

"Where are we gonna store our water to keep it from freezing? Under the bed?" Kate asked when she was back inside.

"Let's just worry about getting some firewood now."

And that made Kate start wondering where they were going to store the firewood, too.

Ten minutes later, with hands warmed from the camp stove they sat on the front edge of their bed staring at the inside of their silver-foiled insulation-puffed front door and ate hot mush.

Suddenly Kate sat up straight. ". . . Do you hear something?" Tim stopped eating, and the pair listened to a growling noise that was loud enough to cut through the gusting winds. "That's not a bear, is it?" she asked her husband who had been born and raised near Boston and knew no more about the man-eaters than she did.

"No," Tim said. "It's something mechanical. I think it's coming closer." He stood up to crack open the big door and peek out.

Kate rose and stood behind her protector. The growling sounded closer, all right. It was clearly a clanking, grinding, mechanical sound. Kate squinted to look over Tim's shoulder. She saw a plume of black smoke swirling up out of the opaque wall in front of them as a gargantuan yellow monster emerged from the void.

"It's a bulldozer!" Tim cried. Indeed, a giant earthmover was chewing its way steadily toward them, etching out a new road where the surprise blizzard had taken away their old one. "It's Neil!" Tim cried, recognizing their good-hearted neighbor despite the unfamiliar winter hat he now wore.

Neil brought his D-6 Caterpillar to a halt and waved down at the amazed pair. "Good morning!" he shouted against the wind. "I thought you two might be ready for the other half of your housewarming gift." He gestured back over his shoulder toward a silvery dead spruce tree chained to the back of his puffing machine.

"Oh gosh Neil you brought us firewood!"

"How perfect!"

"Thank you so much!"

"Come on in. We've got coffee!"

They were both talking to him at once and the roaring wind carried their words away to oblivion, but he seemed to get the idea. "Sure, for a minute."

The sourdough left his diesel cat idling and climbed down off the dozer. He and Tim broke snow over to the dragging tree. The chain had tightened during the trip and they wrangled with it for a while before they got the choke hold loose and the silvery skeleton rested comfortably in the snow. His delivery complete Neil now ducked under their low lintel and entered the tiny abode.

Kate poured some cowboy coffee into a freshly rinsed cup, handed it to Neil and sat down on the edge of the bed beside him. Tim had gone outside with the chain saw to make firewood out of the dead tree.

Kate, ever a Girl Scout at heart, grabbed up some paper and wood splinters and laid a fire on the grate in the wood stove. She wanted to have a little flame burning by the time Tim came back in with the real firewood.

* * *

"How can we thank you enough?" Kate gushed. The three were now standing in a tight circle staring straight down into the open G.I. stove watching the thin flames begin to catch on the seasoned wood.

"Yeah you really saved us today," Tim reflected. He slid the round stove lid back on top of the barrel and bent to adjust a little air door at the bottom.

"No need to thank me," Neil said. "It's good to have some nice young neighbors to move in."

He stayed for a few more minutes talking mostly about the weather, the neighbors, and the grizzlies. "They come right through here every spring and fall."

Neil invited the cheechakos to come down for dinner—which turned out to be lunch—at one o'clock. "Steak and biscuits," is how he described it.

He stood up to leave. "You just watch out for 'em. They're out there all right. But they won't bother you if you stay out o' their way."

Their generous neighbor stood and zipped up his work coveralls, adjusted his earflap hat and mittens, and ducked out of the cabin. He climbed up onto his bulldozer, pulled the lever to swing it into gear and headed home. For the second time that day he plowed out the three-quarters of a mile of drifting driveway between their two houses as he went.

Kate pictured Elsie waiting for her partner with a warming cup of Ovaltine when he emerged from the tempest. You needed a good partner out in the wilderness. And you needed to be a good partner. Kate and Tim were total opposites and sometimes they joked that if they stood back-to-back, they could probably fight off or solve just about any problem.

Her mind traveled back to what the sourdough had said just before he left. "They won't bother you if you just stay out of their way." Had he been talking about bears—or the neighbors?

Without a timepiece in the new cabin they estimated when it might be one o'clock and headed down to the Goodman's' place. The snow berm was shoulder-high and the roadbed was choppy but their forest green mini-tank was handling the rough terrain well. Getting home in winter wouldn't be a problem, as long as Neil kept the road plowed.

When their rig cleared the last spruce tree and entered the wide space in front of the Twinkie house someone appeared at the glass door. Which rancher was it? They both dressed pretty much the same. When the door opened it turned out to be Neil and he beckoned them inside.

The young couple entered, took off their Carhartt canvas coats and wool hats and sat down at the table. Kate sat on the bouncy chair and started rocking comfortably, as had become her custom.

The whole house smelled wonderful. There was something with cinnamon and sugar baking in the oven that made the two guests grow hungry in a hurry.

That first dinner Elsie cooked up for them was a feast of pork chops, potatoes, home canned tomatoes, peas, corn, hot gravy, applesauce, biscuits with butter and honey, and cinnamon turnovers for dessert.

When everyone was stuffed Neil rubbed his barrel chest and uncapped a bottle of Rolaids, which looked totally at home sitting on the kitchen table, and offered them around. Nobody took one.

He popped a handful of the calcium pills into his mouth and chewed them up. Now he was ready for one last cup of tea and a little neighborly talk.

Goodman, who called himself a "Jack Mormon," was a bona fide member of the John Birch Society. He wanted his young neighbors to know about the recently exposed Rockefeller conspiracy that he and the Birchers were worried about. Elsie got out a big aluminum kettle and started heating water to do the dishes. Kate offered to help. The two women stood side by side at the sink washing and drying, looking out the window at raw nature, and passively listening to Neil's conspiracy argument.

This was all new information for Kate, but she figured Elsie had heard it a few times before. It was no wonder that she wanted a house with a second room.

The Peterses left the Goodman's' quite a while later all informed about the alarming fact that the world was being manipulated politically by the helpful-sounding but insidiously-intentioned "Tri-Lateral Commission."

They got home just in time to stoke the cooling fire with an infusion of dry wood.

* * *

September 1, 1976 - Dear Mamasan,

After sleeping cramped up in the car for almost two weeks we finally got to sleep in our new log cabin! Just in time too, because it snowed that night! We plan to live here until we have our big house built farther up the hill. We figure we'll be done with that sometime next year. But for now, we're happy to be warm and dry. We still need to build a place to store our water and our firewood. And we need an outhouse. But things are getting more comfortable around here each day. The folks that we bought our land from are so nice! Wait 'til you meet them.

By the way, when can you come up to visit?

Love, your silly backwoods maid

* * *

The next gift from Neil and Elsie was a load of coal that they delivered two days later. They claimed that most of the locals gathered their coal right off the beaches near Anchor Point. "It's free for the taking," Neil assured them. "We'll show you where it floats ashore."

That sounded easy.

Three generations of Goodmans posed for a photo in the Twinkie.

CHAPTER TWO
Early Fall, 1976

Meet the Neighbors

"ARE YOU ABOUT ready?" Tim had his hand on the door latch. This was the day of Clem Curd's going away party and Tim and Kate, the newest residents on Round Top Mountain, had been invited to join the affair right along with everyone who'd lived up Round Top Road for years.

"Okay I'm ready. Let's go," she said as she zipped up a down vest, slipped into felt-lined boots, and grabbed her green wool hat. They loaded into the car and started off for the party at the other end of the road.

"I hope we don't stink so badly that we scare everyone off," Kate said. They hadn't showered for a few days. There was a laundry and shower house down in Footprint and they'd showered there less than a week back, but they'd been working hard and sweating a lot, since then.

It was a long way to go to town just to wash up for a party, so today they'd be meeting folks as they really were: dirty. Kate looked outside and saw Tim getting into their new Toyota, all relaxed. He was right; they probably didn't need to get too dressed up for this thing. She went outside and climbed into the passenger's seat.

Tim put the four-wheel-drive in gear and they headed for the shindig. This would be a rare opportunity to meet all their reclusive neighbors and they wouldn't have missed it. The hosts of the parting event were Clem's cousins Greg and Craig Curd, two brothers who lived over across the flat.

A moose probably could have crossed that muskeg in half an hour, but with all the rain they'd had since July the road would be eight choppy, sloppy miles each way. And if they got stuck, they might have to winch themselves out.

Their new best friends, Neil and Elsie Goodman were waiting for them when Tim and Kate pulled into the old farmstead. From there the Goodmans led the convoy down to the Curd brothers' place, ready to introduce the newcomers around.

A handful of tractors and trucks filled the open space in front of the house when they arrived. Tim parked their own off-road rig with nose and winch facing outward—in case the road got even worse before it was time to get out of there—and they followed their guides out of the rain and into the little shake house. It was time to meet the neighbors.

They entered through a typical Alaskan arctic entryway lined with slickers and coats hanging on hooks. From the raucous sounds coming out of the main room it looked like the party was in full swing. Most of the partygoers took little notice of the arriving newcomers since they were already well into their revelry. Boosted by some deceptively strong colorless liquor called Everclear, they were engaged in several spirited conversations about everything from cattle to Congress.

Kate looked around at the rough furnishings: a simple kitchen work surface with a wood cook stove at one end of the room, some chairs and benches, and one long table near a Round Oak stove at the other end. The closed door on the north side probably led to sleeping quarters. Both stoves were putting out heat and the space was plenty warm. An opening off the kitchen led to a pantry and everyone who came out of that closet had a full mug in his hand.

The newcomers stood in the entryway waiting to see if someone was going to welcome them. No one did, so they finally edged into the din and made their way over to a little knot of men and women gathered near the cylindrical wood stove. That's where Neil and Elsie were visiting.

Elsie introduced the new folks to three other couples who lived on the mountain. The oldest two at the gathering were named Myers, and they were homesteader friends of Neil and Elsie's. The four had known each other for nearly two decades. Neil steered Mr. Myers over to the corner so they could share the latest conspiracy news.

There was a much younger-looking couple sitting against the wall at the far side of the long table.

"Brian and Anna Tanner, this here is Tim and Kate Peters. They bought our back forty last summer and they're fixing to settle here," Elsie said.

Soon she moved over to talk with Augusta Myers about one of their mutual interests, food processing, and left Kate and Tim to their own devices.

With a handshake and a smile Brian Tanner squeezed out from behind the table and went to get drinks for his new neighbors. Young Mrs. Tanner bent down behind the table and tended to something at the base of the wall. There was a lot of noise going on and that seemed to concern Anna Tanner.

Kate glanced around at the sparse cabin again. The place looked like it was being run by a couple of bachelors. Was there a Mrs. Curd somewhere in this group? There were only five women at this party, including Kate. And men outnumbered the gals two to one. The new bride tried to imagine being married to any of the unattached men gathered at the other end of the room. Every one of them was dirtier than Kate and Tim put together and she decided she wouldn't want to climb into bed with any of them—Ugh!

Most of these fellows would probably have trouble finding a woman to put up with them, which meant that any female who lived up here might be like a lone heifer in a herd of bulls. She'd have to watch herself.

Elsie and Mrs. Myers were talking about baking now, so Kate sat down and smiled across the table at Anna. Anna smiled back and Kate soon confirmed that she and Brian were the ones who lived at the "vegetable garden and goats place" with the lovely view. It also turned out that Anna and Brian had a baby girl tucked in the corner behind the table. That was why most of Anna's attention was centered there, but she did share that she had a potting wheel and threw pots. She said she had sold some of her bowls in Anchorage.

Kate gasped at the pleasure of finding a fellow artist in their remote enclave. "Maybe our children can be playmates."

"That would be great."

The last woman in the clutch looked old enough to be Kate's grandmother. She seemed very friendly. Her name was Pat and she said she was married to the old codger over there in the liquor room. Their place was the first one this side of the bridge.

Kate said she had seen their house off in the trees on the way to the party. Pat's husband, Bill came out of the pantry talking with a short, wiry fellow whom Elsie had introduced as Jared. Both men were waving their hands about something. Pat suddenly excused herself, saying she might have to referee, and went over to join her husband.

Leaning against the wall was a big, feral-looking guy with a sloping forehead. He reminded Kate of a Neanderthal.

"Is he the guest of honor?" she asked Anna.

"No. That's Cliff. He keeps to himself. Lives alone on the flat and hunts mostly. No, Clem is the guy sitting at the far end of the table. You need to watch out for him."

Anna pointed to the two hosts when they eventually came out of the liquor pantry. "Greg is the big one. Craig is a lot younger." Greg had greasy black hair and wore Levi's and a checked wool shirt. Craig looked a lot like Greg, only not as beefy. Same black hair. Different checked shirt. They were clearly brothers.

Clem Curd wasn't built as big as either of his cousins but it looked like he made up for that with ferocity. Kate watched him stand up and lurch over to Cliff. Apparently, Cliff had irritated the honored guest. Clem jabbed a finger into Cliff 's chest to drive home whatever point he was making in as aggressive a way as possible, short of fisticuffs or gunplay. Maybe it was a blessing that cousin Clem was leaving town.

After a few more drinks Clement Curd seemed to think it was time to make his parting speech. He swaggered over to the big round stove. All five couples stepped back to give him a wide berth. Clem picked up an iron poker that was leaning in the corner behind the wood burner and used it to bang twice on the stove's ornate belly. He wanted everyone's attention.

No one paid him any mind, which didn't sit too well with Clem, so he banged again, harder.

And that didn't sit too well with his cousin Greg. "Hey! Quit banging on the stove like that!" the host shouted. "That was our ma's stove. You're liable to put a hole in it!"

Baby brother Craig stayed quiet but he looked plenty steamed.

"I'll quit bangin' when folks shut up for a minute so's I can say a few words here," Clem yelled back. He banged on the stove again, more to make his point than to get folks' attention because, by this time he pretty much had everyone's attention.

"Why you son of perdition," cousin Craig growled. "Greg asked you real nice to stop bangin' on our stove."

That antique had probably been keeping the brothers warm since they were little scrub oaks. Maybe they'd even been born right there beside it. Kate edged back behind the table.

"I told you to cut that out!" Greg warned again.

"You and your kid brother can kiss my sweet behind," Clem snarled.

By now Clem was all stirred up. He began flailing at the elegant piece like there was no tomorrow. He had decided to give that round-bellied beauty the thrashing of its life and he was going at it with vicious pleasure. Clem took an extra hard swing and laid such a blow on that poor potbelly that it nearly shifted off its moorings. The strike left a big dent in the side of the heirloom.

Furious, Greg started toward his cousin, but Cliff stepped in and held him back.

"All right that's it! You can just get goin' right now! Everybody out! This party's over!" Greg announced loudly from over Cliff 's shoulder.

"I ain't had my say yet," Clem hollered back.

"And I say you're leaving!" Greg yelled. "Get out!"

"Not 'til I'm ready," Clem retorted. "And I ain't ready!" He raised the poker again.

Greg broke free from Cliff 's grip and lunged toward his cousin with fists doubled.

Clem saw him coming. He dropped the poker and bent down like he suddenly had a bad itch and was trying to scratch his ankle.

Everyone who'd lived in Sleeping Moose for any amount of time knew that Clement Curd kept a pistol in his boot. Now the crowd seemed to agree that things were getting out of hand. Something big was about to happen.

At the first sign of trouble, Craig Curd had started making his way over to the front door so he'd be ready to grab the rifle off its hooks if actions warranted. Now he was in place and reaching up for the loaded weapon.

Greg shouted out to his brother, "Get 'im, Craig! He's goin' for his gun!" That made Cliff gallop out of the line of fire, and it also made Clem turn to face Craig. The sneer on his face showed that he figured he had the upper hand. But Craig was ready for him and Craig shot first. His aim looked true but Clem didn't even blink, so Craig figured he'd missed. He fired again.

When the next bullet shot a second hole through Clement Latrice Curd, he grabbed his chest and pitched over right there in front of the belching stove.

Greg walked over and gave Clem's leg a kick. He was dead alright.

As soon as the bangs and flashes began everyone had hit the deck. Tim and Kate were wedged down between the table and the wall and Kate thought they should probably stay there for a while. But when Anna's baby woke up with a shrieking start, it got folks to breathing again and heads started popping up all around the smoky room. When they were sure that the shooting was over the celebrants started standing up and brushing off.

Discussion was sparse as people stared at the body of their recently, but not dearly departed neighbor. Greg Curd used the shortwave radio on the kitchen wall to transmit the news into town. From there, someone who had a telephone would forward the emergency message to the state troopers in Soldotna.

Cliff helped the Curd brothers carry their newly deceased cousin Clem out the door and across the clearing into the icehouse. Everyone else followed the grim procession out into the rain and watched them lay the body on a palette and throw ice and sawdust over it.

Then, as quickly as they could without making their hosts any madder, the guests started giving excuses to head for their trucks. Kate and Tim got into their rig without much in the way of goodbyes. They felt lucky to make it out of the clearing before another shot was fired.

The rain was really smashing down now and the road had turned to chocolate pudding. Kate watched sheets of rain pour over the car's windows as their rig salamandered its way home.

"That party was surreal. Did that really just happen?" Kate asked, still processing the Wild West spectacle they had just witnessed.

"I guess there's a lot we don't know about living at the end of the road," was all Tim could think to say.

"Or about the people who live there. I'm glad they taught you how to shoot in the war. Looks like we might be needing some protection from time to time," Kate reckoned.

Welcome to the neighborhood.

The "End of the Road" Gang

THREE DAYS PASSED before the rain let up enough for a trooper to get back in there to investigate.

A week later Tim and Kate were visiting with the Goodmans and the four naturally talked about the events that had transpired at Clem's party.

Neil said, "To tell you the truth, I think Craig did folks around here a favor. We was all glad to see Clem go. He was plain wicked."

Kate was silent.

"They wrote up the shooting as 'self-defense,'" Neil went on, "which is good for Craig, but it's a darned pity he shot Clem twice. If he'd o' only shot once, the fine might've been less than for shooting a moose out of season." The older man shook his head. "That Clem was bad. Still, I reckon if I get any more invites to a Curd affair, I won't go. They take their going-away parties a little too serious for me."

The friends laughed at Neil's joke. The chances of such a thing happening again didn't seem likely.

It was far too late for the honeymooners to reconsider their spur-of-the-moment decision which had settled them on that mountain. Glorious feelings about the place had already rooted and bloomed fully in their hearts. Kate was thriving in the ultra-rustic environment where freedoms abounded. If pioneering wasn't the most exciting thing a person could do, Kate guessed she didn't understand the real joys of living.

And Tim, a lifelong fan of Jack London and the movie "Jeremiah Johnson," was already in storybook heaven. By the time the two ventured over to Clem's going away party and met everyone else living on their road, they had too much work and hope invested in their dream to drag up after one rogue gunfight. Convinced that the threat was now gone they were buckling down and getting ready for winter.

But it hadn't taken more than the one social gathering for Kate to see that they were living on the Last Frontier. The Curds had made that clear. The greenhorns had unwittingly settled down with a mingle-full of misfits, and they were the newest members of an end-of-the-road gang that functioned in relative anarchy. Surprise!

Although the youthful visionaries had little in common with most of the folks in their neighborhood, they did all share the same road.

And a difficult road it was turning out to be.

* * *

The fall rains hadn't slackened, and now their only artery from the mountain to the highway was a totally useless mash of mud. When folks needed supplies, they had to walk all the way down to Sleeping Moose. Everyone's rigs were parked at the wide spot there, and would be for the next several months.

The whole gang was anxious for a hard freeze and a good snow so they could start using their snowmobiles.

One Sunday Tim and Kate were hiking down to Sleeping Moose. Kate had been itching to get out, and since they had no pressing plans, they had decided to go for pizza. This would be more of a date than a major supply run since they knew that getting a big load home would be a lot easier after the first snow.

Two walkers came around the corner. They were walking up the road as Tim and Kate were heading down. Kate recognized them. "Look Tim. That's the Myerses! They're the homesteaders from the next ridge. Elsie and Neil were talking with them at the party. Remember?"

When the four met a few yards above the bridge they stopped and reintroduced themselves, and reran the shootout at the Curds' place, which Charlie Myers assured them occurred only rarely. Charles and Augusta Myers said they had been there fifteen years and had only seen a few shootings. Mrs. Myers mentioned that they were on their way out for the year. "We've been working winters over across the inlet since the winter of

'65. You two might want to think about gettin' out o' here too, before the bad weather blows in."

Kate nodded at the advice. The woman probably knew what she was talking about.

But a minute later their new acquaintance startled Kate by saying, "If you do end up staying here all winter, be sure to watch out for any Negroes as might come nosing around, would you? They're nothin' but trouble. That's the Mark of Cain on their foreheads, you know. You send 'em packing if they look like they's fixing to settle in."

Kate was stunned and grasping for a tactful response. Come to think of it, she had yet to see a dark-skinned person anywhere on the whole Kenai Peninsula.

Tim saved the day by steering the subject back to the annual winter exodus. "So, you folks don't live here year-round?"

"No. Getting out is the smartest way to survive the winters. And it's also about the only way to make ends meet. Yup, most of us go out in the late fall and come back in the spring," Mr. Myers said.

"It sure is nice here, of a summer," Mrs. Myers allowed. "Yes, it's beautiful," Kate agreed, jumping back onto the neutral ground.

"We're going up to say 'goodbye' to Neil and Elsie before heading off to cook at the lumber camp for the winter," Charlie Myers said.

Kate had been studying Mrs. Myers. She thought the woman looked tired and maybe a little disenchanted after fifteen years on a mountaintop. She would try to cheer her neighbor by volunteering some of their own exciting plans. "We bought the back forty of the Goodman's' place. We're building our house there."

"Oh."

Not much of a reaction. Kate offered another tidbit. "We plan to be finished by next year."

Mrs. Myers pondered the optimistic information. "Well, you'd best be prepared for things to take a lot longer than you imagine they're goin' to," she foreshadowed. "If you think it'll take you a year, then you'd better figure on ten."

"Oh, I think we'll be done quicker than that," Kate said. "Tim and I are both strong and we just drug up from jobs on the Pipeline so we won't need money for at least a year. We plan to work on the place fulltime."

"So, you're not plannin' on goin' 'outside' this winter?" "Well we'll be using an outhouse this winter, of course. But hopefully we'll have our plumbing in by next summer."

Mrs. Myers raised a quizzical eyebrow but said nothing to that.

With conversation at a stalemate the four nodded their farewells, and the two sourdoughs continued up the hill to call on their friends while the cheechakos skipped off to embrace a world of seemingly unlimited opportunities. Continuing their enchanted walk, the honeymooners would not be deterred.

When they got to Sleeping Moose, they went into the post office to get the mail and then headed around the corner of the aging structure. They bought two slices at the window where the postmaster's wife sold homemade pizza, and sat and ate at the picnic table beside the store.

Kate couldn't shake her feelings after their meeting with the old homesteaders. "That Mrs. Myers seemed kind of negative, didn't she? You don't think it'll take us ten years to build our house, do you?"

"Ten years? No way!" Tim pledged.

"Good."

After a pleasant rest, they picked up two backpacks' worth of groceries and half-filled the four cans with water from the spigot outside. Tim had suggested that it would be easier to carry a balanced load if the cans weren't totally full. They were learning.

The two walked the long miles back up their mountain road, had corned beef hash for supper and went to bed.

"Maybe we should start collecting rainwater," Kate said as she lowered the lantern wick. "It'd be okay to drink don't you think?"

"Um-hum," Tim mumbled from his sleeping place along the wall.

Kate was still thinking about what Augusta Myers had said. "Tim?"

"Mmmmmm." Not much movement from his side of the bed.

"It won't take us ten years to build our house, will it?"

He mumbled something like, "If anyonk do i' wuh cahn." And then he was out.

Before she went to sleep Kate scribbled off a quick note to her mother:

September 30, 1976 - Dear Mama,

Lots of rain! I think it's rained every day this September. Our dirt road is nothing but bottomless ruts that are killers to drive in, and impossible to stay out of. We've been parking down at the turnoff, which means we walk six miles each way if we want to go anywhere. Needless to say, we don't go out much.

* * *

At three in the morning Kate tiptoed outside. The day's drizzle had stopped and the ground had turned crisp. Winter wasn't far away.

She carefully navigated the freeze-stiffened ruts until she had cleared the corner of the cabin, where she ducked and squatted down under an alder. She didn't mind this ritual. In fact, she enjoyed it. On nights with a full moon and no wind it could be otherworldly. And that was especially true if she happened to hear the crazy cackle of a loon calling out from somewhere on the flats. Heaven on Earth it was.

Just as Kate peed, the hopeful call of a loon floated up through the emptiness across the marshy flat, and she thrilled. In that perfect moment, the score for an arduous day had been evened.

Chapter Three
Late Fall, 1976

The First Privy Story

AS SOON AS they could get to it, they dug a big hole out behind Honeymoon Cottage. It was deep enough to last them until they got the house done and the plumbing in. True, the seat and the actual walls might be a while in getting built. But until then, the move was doable—if somewhat tricky. There was an alder sapling growing close to the edge of the pit. If you took hold of that, you would be able to swing your rear end out over the void.

Kate smiled as she pictured the maneuver. Yes sir, things were getting mighty fancy around there. They were practically ready for guests.

* * *

Their first visitor arrived a week or so after they'd finished digging the big pit. It was Dick, Tim's lifelong friend.

Dick told them he had parked his car below the bog and hiked up from there to see his best bud's new place. He swore he hadn't been nervous because he was "armed and loaded for bear," but he did have to admit he was tired after that long hike. Dick stopped to catch his breath and admire the view for a minute before Tim showed him around inside Honeymoon Cottage, which took about ten seconds.

He led Dick up the hill and pointed out the exact spot where the moose had slept. He indicated where the walls of their future log house would rise. Finally, he took Dick back into the alder grove, to show him where the privy pit was and line him out on the sapling-handhold trick.

* * *

At dusk, the three crowded into Honeymoon Cottage. There the two boyhood friends played some serious cards while Kate rustled up her one-pot version of corned beef hash: one can of corned beef and one onion stirred into instant potatoes. Heat. Add salt and pepper and eat.

As soon as the hash was hot, all three sat shoulder-to-shoulder on the edge of the sleeping platform and dined in the wavering lantern light.

Feeling safe and protected in the breathy glow of the lantern they talked for a long time after supper. The men exchanged memories of growing up in the Boston area and Kate got a chance to mention that she used to have a horse. That brought them to large mammals, and from there to Dick's favorite topic: bears, and the fact that a grizzly could be lurking outside right at that moment. The thought that a specimen of the family Ursus Horribilis might be close-by was both tantalizing and terrifying. The bear stories went on until everyone decided it was time to turn in.

Dick was handed a roll of toilet paper and a flashlight. His imagination afire with the evening's tales of wild beast attacks, Dick opted to take his revolver along with the other two necessities. Tim opened the door of the cabin and aimed his friend in the direction of the distant black hole.

While Dick waded out into darkness, Kate slipped into her flannel nightgown and darted out to pee under the stars. Gorgeous. She was back inside long before Dick returned. Since they'd all be sleeping in the one bed, Kate and Tim sat on the edge of the platform and waited for Dick to get back so they could get into bed with Kate on the outside, in case she needed to make a midnight run.

"Dick's been gone a long time," she finally said. "What do you think he's doing out there?"

"I don't know, but if he's not back in two minutes I'll go fish him out," Tim said.

A second later they heard hasty footsteps through soggy leaves. The door burst open and Dick bolted inside and slammed the door shut.

Tim jumped up, ready to reach for the shotgun. "Is there something out there?"

"I think so. I'm not sure. Maybe."

The three listened for ten seconds. When they were sure that nothing was prowling around outside Dick finally took a breath and told them what had happened. "The whole time I was out there I kept thinking about grizzlies rummaging in the alder. I had the flashlight and toilet paper in one hand and my gun in the other. When I got to the part about holding onto the alder branch, it took me a while to decide which one to give up."

"Well which one did you finally let go of?" Tim asked. He was finding it hard to keep a straight face.

"I'll tell you this," Dick confided. "I never let go of my gun!"

* * *

As soon as Dick left, Tim and Kate got to work on their long-overdue outhouse.

Coaling, Eating, Talking

NEIL AND ELSIE had promised to take the Peterses out on their first coaling expedition as soon as the road hardened up. The old timers had made it sound simple. "You just wait until there's a storm from the right direction, drive out west to the inlet, and sit by the pier until the tide is out. Drive through the slough the minute it's shallow enough. Pick up all the coal you can before the tide starts coming back in, and get it home."

With the Goodmans supervising, that first coal run did seem like a pretty slick way to heat your house. After they'd dropped their fresh bounty in a heap beside the door of Honeymoon Cottage Neil invited the two down for supper, which was a perfect way to end the day.

Following their meal of lamb, squash, kale, more home-canned tomatoes and biscuits with honey, Elsie brought out wild blueberries with cream, and put on a kettle for coffee and tea.

While Neil finished things off with a handful of Rolaids, Elsie set out four mugs for the final course of the evening and filled a second kettle to heat water for dishes. Digesting, the four rested heavy elbows on the table and chewed over the latest news from the neighborhood.

"Yup," Neil said, as if he'd been thinking about the story for a few minutes, "I reckon Frampton must have been pretty surprised this past spring when the Myerses showed up a few days earlier than expected."

"Oh, we met the Myerses again last week," Kate said. "They were walking up the road when we were walking down."

"That's right. They're headed outside for the winter." Neil sounded happy for them. "They told us they'd had quite a time finding a new caretaker for their place. Said they wouldn't never have Frampton back."

"Who's Frampton? He wasn't at the Curds' party, was he?" Kate asked.

"Nope. He's away to Utah; went there when Charlie Myers kicked 'im out. You gotta' understand," Neil said, seeing some explaining was needed, "Frampton Snyder, he's kind of strange. Some say he was kicked in the head by a horse, but I don't know for sure. He don't have a place of his own, so Charlie Myers had him to stay at their place while they was gone—to tend the animals and such."

The cowboy paused as if lost in thought.

"Go ahead and tell 'em what happened, Neil," Elsie prompted. "We're all waiting and the kettle's steaming."

That prod got the reminiscing fellow going again, and he went on. "Anyhow, when the Myerses showed up just a little ahead of schedule they found 'im with a litter of piglets in their bed."

"Piglets?" Both the Peterses were surprised.

"Yes sir. That's so. Fram said he was 'just keeping them pigs warm,' but Charlie Myers kicked 'im out right away. He said he didn't take kindly to no pigs in his blankets. That's when Fram took off down to Utah or Idaho, or some such place, and we haven't heard hide nor hair of him since."

"He'll be back one day, more than likely," Elsie said, finishing up the modern folktale. "There aren't many places that'll put up with him." She pushed her chair away from the table and went to fetch the hot dishwater.

"I'll never be able to think of 'pigs-in-a-blanket' the same way again." Kate said this with a half-laugh as she got up to help Elsie. "Let's just hope he finds a place down there that suits him. We don't need another problem neighbor like Clem up on this mountain."

"Oh, don't worry," Neil said. "He's not the violent sort. He's just kinda' 'simple,' you might say. But you can bet there'll be another troublemaker to come along soon. When one leaves, another one always seems to show up. That's the type as settles at the end of a road like ours. Less people around means less people to have to shoot, I expect." Sadly, Neil Goodman didn't look like he was joking.

The two women cleaned up after supper and Neil gave Tim another dose of John Birch insight about the Tri-Lateral Commission. This second analysis of a "New World Government" takeover lasted until after midnight. Finally, the Peters couple went home to their cabin so the Goodmans could get some sleep.

Yes, Kate was pretty sure Elsie would love to have a two-room house

* * *

One night, the storm they'd been waiting for swept in and started pounding the region. "We'll be coaling in the morning," Tim predicted.

Long before dawn the pioneers threw two empty five-gallon buckets into the back of the Toyota and headed for Anchor Point. They parked beside the last pier and waited for the tide to go out.

After watching the inlet recede from the tall pilings for about forty-five minutes, Tim decided the slough was low enough. "Let's go for it."

He drove straight across the draining ribbon of seawater and burst up onto the outer beach. Numerous lumps of sea-soaked coal rested half-buried in the wet sand. It was all free for the taking. As the waves continued to ebb, more and more shiny black mounds popped out on the waterlogged beach. There were chunks ranging in size from grapefruits to wheel rims. The big ones might last longer but the little ones turned out to be a lot easier to pull loose. They would fit into the stove better too.

The pair worked hard and fast, pulling the chunks free with a sucking pop and slinging bucket after heavy bucketful of coal into the back of their Land Cruiser. By the time their load reached the rig's windows the tide was starting to come in.

"We'd better get out of here now," Kate said. "The tide's coming in."

"I think we still have time to get a few more pieces. See all those big ones down by the water?"

"Please Tim. It looks really soft down there, and we don't want to swamp the car." Why not err on the side of caution?

"Okay. Okay. Get in. It would be bad to watch our nice new car float away up Cook Inlet."

"And if it got caught in the outgoing tide it wouldn't stop 'til it hit Korea," Kate added. They tossed their empty buckets on top of the load and hopped into the Toyota.

When they got back to the slough crossing it looked scarier than ever. "I think it's higher than before. Do we dare?"

"We *have* to," Tim said. He put the car in gear and burst out into the rapidly swelling stream. Kate was holding onto the dash and unconsciously lifting her feet. She hoped they'd make it across but she was ready to wade for it if their luck ran out.

As it turned out, Tim did a masterful job piloting the craft across the strait to safety. Once they were back on solid ground his co-pilot exhaled. "That was hairy."

"Hairy?" Tim sounded surprised. "Come on babe. Didn't you think that was fun?"

"Not exactly."

They decided to grab some breakfast before heading home. They strolled into the Bait Café, both feeling and looking like genuine locals, nonchalantly leaving their load of coal out front in plain view. After pancakes, ham and eggs, hash browns, toast, and coffee, they were ready to go home.

Unfortunately, they had to make one more stop—close to halfway between Footprint and Sleeping Moose—to change a flat tire. This unhappy turn of events necessitated emptying the entire load of coal out onto the side of the road so Tim could get to the jack. And they had to load every last piece of coal back into the car before they could continue their trek home.

The pair bumped over every frozen rut their mud road had ever generated all the way up to Honeymoon Cottage, where they added the new fuel to the pile under the tarp. It was nearly dark and the end of a long, long day.

After two expeditions, their stockpile of coal still looked puny. Kate looked at it and snorted. "Free fuel: You haul away." True, the price was right. But at what cost? And besides, Kate didn't like the smell that this local coal gave off when it burned.

She loved the aroma of wood smoke. It reminded her of camping trips she'd gone on when she was a girl. But this saltwater-soaked coal smelled like something dug out of a recent grave.

An image of Elsie heating her little house with coal—and looking glad of it—came into her head. Kate reasoned that if she planned on living in these woods for long, she might have to adjust.

* * *

"Will you tell me some more about riding the range?" The two women were making biscuits in Elsie's kitchen. Elsie had a lot of great stories to tell about growing up as a cowgirl in Arizona. With no brothers, she and her sisters used to help their dad round up strays right alongside the hired hands.

"Did you ever come across a rattlesnake out there?" Kate asked.

That question made the aging cowgirl put down her baking sheet and look back across half a century. "Oh, I musta' killed two or three of 'em a day."

Kate sucked in her breath. "You killed two or three rattlesnakes *a day?*"

"Yup probably." Elsie spoke low and slow, as always. "Good grief. Well did you shoot 'em, or what?"

"Oh no. My daddy wouldn't let me have a gun. I just used my reins or spurs, or whatever was handy." She picked up the pan of biscuits and slid them into the oven, then grabbed a boiling-hot potato and started peeling it with her bare hands. No doubt about it. That Elsie was some woman! Kate absolutely loved her.

Soon they were sharing another fantastic meal with the Goodmans. Then Neil and Tim sat and discussed politics while the women took up their places at the sink. That's when Kate finally gumptioned up the nerve to ask Elsie the thing she'd been wondering about since the day they'd met. "Elsie are you part Indian?"

Her question surprised the woman. "Heavens no! What makes you ask that?"

"Your hair. It's so black and you don't have any gray hair at all."

Elsie laughed at this. "Why honey, this is from a *bottle!*"

"Really?"

"Sure. I've got enough gray up there to braid a rope clear to China," she admitted candidly.

Kate was stumped. "You continue to amaze me Elsie."

"Well, I just want to look nice without takin' time out for it," Elsie said. "O' course I tried gussying up once or twice before I learned better. Around here there's mostly just enough time to get the chores done and not much time left over."

She started telling Kate about one day when she and Neil had been clearing the north meadow. "That's what you two call your front yard, now," she clarified. "Neil had a little tractor that he drove up and down that slope while I walked along behind picking up all the sticks that the plow had turned, making piles of them. After one hot and dusty morning, we walked home to rustle up dinner. We ate and Neil rested up in his recliner for a bit while I washed the dishes. Just when I'd finished cleaning up and was fixing to sit down and rest for a minute, Neil jumped up and said he reckoned it was time to get back to work—which we did. I probably should've go-mollied the dishes that time," she admitted, "but it's not my way."

She had told Kate the tale without a hint of complaint. In fact, she'd ended it with a chuckle. Yup. This gal had pulled her share of the weight around there, that was for sure. Kate considered what it would take to be a homesteader's wife. Would she have the strength and the perseverance to fill boots as impressive as Elsie's?

After those rose-colored glasses days of college in the sixties, this was a very different land and a very different era she had come to. Would she be able to control her artistic temperament enough to fit into the traditional wife's role? It might prove tricky to be both strong and demure.

Kate figured she would need to learn the ropes if she wanted to live out there with the cowboys. Luckily, Elsie and Neil were genuine "salt of the earth" folks and the cheechako knew she couldn't have found better teachers anywhere.

Wolf Tracks Behind the Cabin

WHEN THE TOMATOES in Elsie's coal-heated hothouse kicked the bucket one frosty night and berry-gorged grizzlies started heading for their favorite riverside fishing holes, Kate knew winter was nigh.

Over the next few days several layers of snow drifted in, smoothing-over Round Top's domed brow until it looked like a huge pillow at the head of their private forty-acre bed.

Nov. 20, 1976 - Dear Mamasan,

Winter's here. A wet autumn has been shoved aside. Now Tim and I sit out on our stumps to dine, and hit the sack right after the sun sets.

It's best to be under the covers before the cabin cools off. Tim likes to make us cozy by filling the stove with big chunks of beach coal.

But when the fire takes off and the cabin gets hot,

he jumps up and starts shoveling the whole shootin'- works out into the snow, and it gets cold again.

I wish he would just put in less coal or maybe

open the cabin door for a few minutes. But I remember what you once told me about picking my battles. So, I just let him do it his way. It won't kill us, I guess. Still, it seems so wasteful when getting everything up here to the top of the mountain is such a struggle.

Much love from your youngest, who is now married and is trying to be a good wife and partner.

* * *

One night, shortly before Tim's bedtime coal ritual they heard a strange noise coming from outside. It was just a low buzz at first but it grew louder as it got closer.

Tim sounded the "all clear" as soon as he'd popped his head out the door and recognized their friends. "It's Neil and Elsie on snowmobiles!"

"Howdy," Goodman called out. "We're on our way up to the top of the mountain. It's a perfect night—still and clear. We thought you two might want to come along."

"On a snowmobile? Sure! Yes. You bet! Can you wait a minute while we get into our gear?"

Tim and Kate didn't have insulated snowmobiling suits like the ones the Goodmans had on, but they donned the warmest things they owned: long underwear, insulated coveralls, Sorrels, L.L. Bean moose hide mittens, scarves, and wool knit hats with the rims pulled down. When they were zipped and snapped, they went outside, closed the cabin latch and walked over to check out the unfamiliar machines.

The rigs looked ancient, like they might have been relics from the earliest crop of snowmobiles ever produced. Their weathered yellow noses were chipped and beaten and Elsie's rig had a Bungee cord holding the seat in place. The machine Neil sat on was wider and had two black rubber tracks and one ski. Elsie's machine had just the opposite.

"This one here is a double-track. You and Kate can take it and we'll drive the single-track," Goodman said. "Oh, and here in Alaska, we call 'em 'snow-machines,'" he corrected, "because we work 'em hard. 'Snowmobiles' is what folks play on down in the Lower Forty-Eight."

Neil dismounted and demonstrated the throttle and pull start for the novices. After Tim had gotten the hang of things, the older man climbed onto the single-track and sat down in front of Elsie. The sourdoughs were ready to go.

Tim gave the rope a good pull and the crusty Skidoo started up. He stepped onto the running board and swung his leg over the seat, sat down, and took hold of both handles. Kate was still looking at a whittled wooden stopper sticking out of the double track's gas tank. Was that safe? Then, tossing concern to the wind, she boarded the bench seat behind Tim and wrapped her arms around his waist. "Tally–ho!" she cried as both mounts galloped away.

The Goodmans led as the two snow-machines followed the bear trail through the windbreak behind Honeymoon Cottage. Ducking under branches and leaning into turns, it was more like riding a motorcycle than a horse. Not scary. Just exhilarating.

When they swished past the last of the trees and broke out on the backside of the woods, there was no sign of human habitation at all—just stars and snow. "What a ride!" Kate shouted to anyone and to no one.

Both machines zipped across a wide slanting meadow that led up to the ridgeline. The antique headlights faintly illuminated the way ahead. They bounded up the ridge and soon reached the mountain's rounded top. The four riders were now on the highest point around, where no trees, or brush, or snow collected in the ever-present wind. Kate threw back her head to witness the untainted sky. An endless spray of stars sparkled above them.

Both couples got off to stand and share in the gloriousness of this mountaintop experience. Looking southwest toward Sleeping Moose, Kate could see two luminous arms stretching out to greet the highway as it passed through town. And she thought she could see a light directly east. "Is that the Myerses' place?" Kate asked Elsie.

"Yup. That's right," Elsie nodded. She turned and pointed out the silhouette of a small dark lump, barely visible in the starlight. "That's your place down there. And that light, out past the woods and over to the left of the field, that's ours."

Kate stared at the isolated signs of civilization. Shifting away from the Goodmans' and the Myerses' and their own dark and remote home, her eyes traveled northwest to where there were no signs of habitation.

"We might be the only people around for miles," Tim said, voicing his reverence and awe.

Neil spoke to that. "We may be the only people, but there's lots of black bears and wolves to keep us company out here."

His comment made the young sodbusters take an involuntary look around at both sides and behind them. They really were vulnerable out there all alone with whatever meat eaters might be watching. Kate searched the darkness for staring eyes and hoped she wouldn't see any.

The four spent a few more minutes on that wonderful, powerful spot, before whooshing back down the mountain and sweeping over the same trail they'd carved minutes earlier. Both snow-machines were aimed straight for their little hand-hewn refuge that promised safety and warmth, six miles past the edge of civilization.

When they reached the drifted meadow, Tim knew the way home from there. He increased the gas and steered over to the left so they could ride beside the Goodmans. The aging double-track died almost immediately.

"What happened?" Kate asked, astonished.

"I'm not sure. It just conked out," Tim said, confounded. The fledglings stepped off the machine into nearly waist-deep snow and stared at their inert transport. Kate felt like a mountaineer whose overloaded mule had just croaked.

Neil circled back to see why half of the party had stopped. "Are you two having trouble?"

"I don't know what happened," Tim shrugged. "It just died." He was fumbling at the frozen latches and trying to get the hood open.

"No need to lift the cowling," Neil said. He pointed to the weaving track the machine had carved into the snow right where Tim had pulled out to the left. "See that? You got off the packed trail right there. She's bogged down, that's all. There's ice packed in the tracks. Here, help me roll 'er over on her side so we can get those things cleared out."

The two frontier wives stood back as their two husbands rolled the ailing machine up onto its side and began doctoring it.

"Hey look-y there," Neil said, stopping his chipping long enough to point to a set of animal tracks that crossed the trail about six feet from where they were working. The tracks went down into a swale heading east. "That there is a wolf track," he said. "See the dragging toenail in the center? There's probably a family of 'em standing over in that gully right now listening to us. You two care to take a look-see?"

"No thanks," Kate answered quickly. Neil gave her a knowing chuckle.

The men pounded and chipped away at the frozen snow wedged between the tracks and their rollers. After a few minutes, the machine's belly was cleared and they had it righted again. Then they were off—dashing through the dark, hurtling over hummocks, and winding through woods. Finally, they arrived at sweet little Honeymoon Cottage.

Home safe.

By now everyone was ready for some cocoa and conversation. Neil and Elsie squeezed in beside Tim on the bed, and Kate pumped up the Coleman stove to make cocoa. When the water was heating, her three companions shuffled sideways so she could join them.

That night's conversation centered on wolves. Neil said they hadn't ever given him any trouble but Elsie said she'd never met a wolf she completely trusted.

After the Goodmans left Tim stoked the fire and loaded it up with coal, and he and his adoring wife climbed into bed together.

* * *

Kate awakened a couple of hours later, as Tim was climbing over her to get to the stove. She watched with one eye as he tossed all their precious red-hot coals out into the hissing snow. What a guy!

December 2, 1976 - Dear Mamasan,

Last night we rode on snow-machines up to the summit of Round Top Mountain and we crossed paths with a pack of wolves!

Don't worry. Both parties are fine.

Love, Kate and Tim

* * *

Tim loved to load up that little G.I. stove.

December 14, 1976 - Dear Mamasan,

Our road is disintegrating under all this snow. We're thinking of heading out for the rest of the winter. We can return in the spring, just like the geese. That's what people up here do. Tim hopes to go out of the Laborer's Hall and I'll go through the Culinary Union again. If we can both get Pipeline jobs, we'll have plenty of money, come spring.

Your loving, unpublished-poet-daughter, Kate

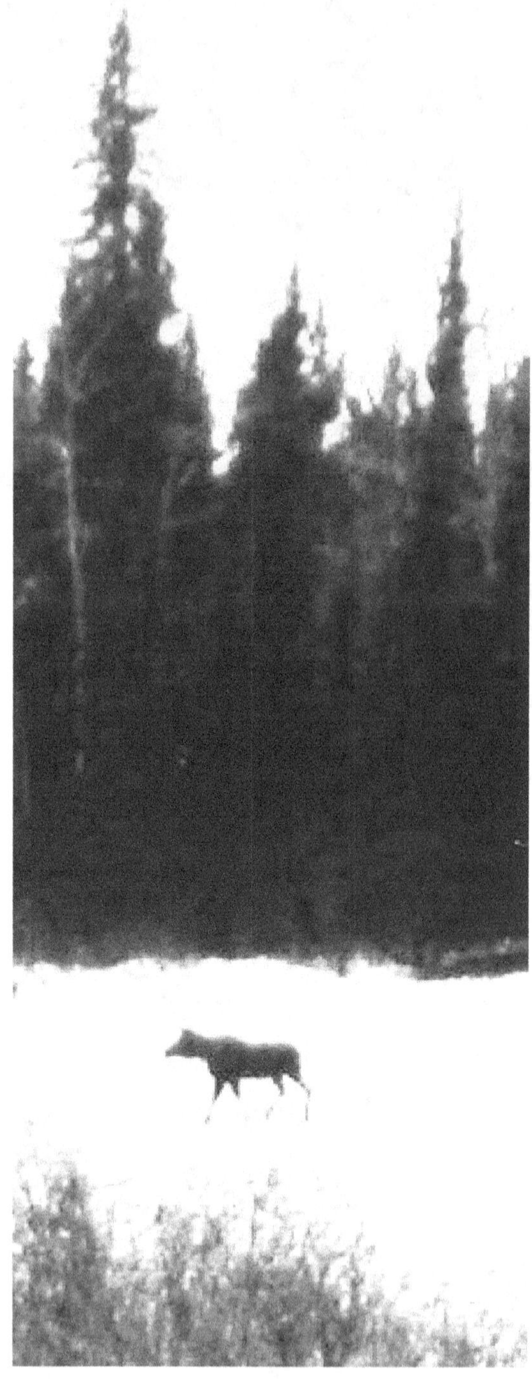

A cow moose.

CHAPTER FOUR
Spring and Summer, 1977

The Road through Spring

TIM WENT OUT right away, assigned to Franklin Bluffs, but Kate didn't fare as well. She got a temporary kitchen assignment at Pump Station #1 that lasted two weeks, and then she ended up staying in Anchorage at Dick's place, sleeping on a quilt on his living room floor and working as a teacher's assistant for the remainder of the term.

It was okay. She spent her evenings drawing house plans and her weekends cruising garage sales, and found a lot of good, used household items. Kate was stacking her bounty in Dick's carport until spring, when Tim would drag up and they could cart their goods home to the mountain.

Tim called when he could, which wasn't often. The phone lines from the camps were choked. It seemed that everyone had left someone behind.

February 13, 1977 - Dear Mamasan,

I miss Tim so much. I don't like to think of spending every winter apart for the rest of our lives. It may be the way they do it in the bush, but it's no way to stay married. One nice thing about being in Anchorage is that I can call you occasionally.

Is "collect" okay? Love, Kate

* * *

April 3, 1977 - Dear Mamasan,

I've been fine, thanks. Keeping busy; teaching and garage sale bargain-hunting. Tim was here for ten days of R&R which was heaven, but he just left.

This winter is passing much too slowly. We can't wait for spring to get here. Tim plans to hold onto his job until June. By then, our road should be good and dry. Just two more months, and we'll be heading back to our "promised land."

Love, K

* * *

June finally came. Tim quit his job and they packed all of Kate's garage sale treasures onto a flatbed snowmobile trailer that she'd also bought, and crammed the rest of the stuff into the back of the car. They made a beeline to the mountain with just about everything they'd need to set up house, including an old sink for the new kitchen.

Those Oklahoma Land Rush teamsters couldn't have driven with any more determination than Tim and Kate Peters did, the day they hauled their goods around the inlet curves and between the glaciered mountains, anxious to get to that magical place they called "home."

Before they drove down out of the Chugach Mountains, they stopped in Cooper Landing to celebrate with an ice cream cone beside the beautiful Kenai River. Now they were getting excited because they were really close.

* * *

"Dang it! Why is this road still muddy?" Kate was standing with hands on hips staring up the six-mile-long, mostly impassible driveway that led to her doorstep. "It's the middle of June. Breakup should be over by now. This road should be dry. Dang it!" she said again.

Tim had pulled the car and trailer off the Sterling Highway while Kate had walked up the road a few feet to see how hard the mud was. He eased the loaded vehicle up beside her and rolled down his window. "The surface still looks soft. I guess, at this elevation, breakup starts later and it takes longer," he surmised.

"Longer than a month?" "Apparently," he said.

"Do you think we can get in if we use the winch?" "No. Not if it gets any worse up ahead, which it will."

Kate pictured the boggy stretch that lay ahead. In here mind's eye she saw the old wooden road grader lurking along the wayside, a perennial reminder of the difficulties of a long and winding road home.

"Looks like we won't be driving up today," Tim said.

Kate nodded and looked over at their packed car and trailer. "What'll we do with all this stuff? We can't just leave it here."

"If we can get it far enough off the highway, I doubt anyone will bother it. We'll just have to take it in as far as we can and park it 'til the road's dry."

"Which will hopefully be sometime this summer," Kate grumbled.

Their plan set, they walked back across the highway to pick up a pack load of groceries and any mail that had accumulated during their long absence. There was a letter from Elsie saying that they had headed out to the logging camp at Jakalof. They would be back soon. This was an interesting bit of news. It meant that, until the homesteaders returned, Tim and Kate would be the only ones living up the road beyond the bridge.

They got back into the Land Cruiser, and Tim used low gear to fishtail the heavy load up the road as far as they could get. After the first hill, the road flattened out and followed a low ridge and they almost got to the creek. Regrettably, they had to stop there.

"We'd better park here," Tim said. "If we cross the bridge, we might not be able to turn around when we want to get back into town."

It was true. Backing out over that narrow bridge wouldn't be easy. "Looks like we're walking home from here," Kate said, disappointed. She got out of the car and started assessing what items absolutely had to come with them, and what could stay behind.

In the end, they decided to leave behind everything except the perishable groceries and half of the water. Tim poured some water out of each can before they walked across the bridge and began the hike up the mountain. Kate carried the groceries and Tim carried the two half-filled-cans of water.

They hadn't covered much ground before Tim set down his water cans. "We'd better start thinking about how we're gonna get water during breakup. Carrying it up from here won't work."

"Agreed." Kate was already panting.

"I think we should try to dig out that spring Neil showed us last year," he said.

"Sounds like a good plan to me," Kate said. She grabbed the opportunity to sit down on a fallen log.

Tim matched her move and they rested for a quiet moment in the woods. He broke the silence. "How about first thing tomorrow?"

Kate smiled. "Fine with me."

The road through spring.

They made it up the rest of the mountain in less than an hour, even though they had to struggle through the "lake" section—slipping in boot high mud and jumping around puddles that were nearly as deep as their knees. Eventually the road started to climb up out of the flat and they got a good pace going. Kate kept up with Tim better here because she now had an old song going in her head. She'd remembered her Girl Scout leader mother singing it on treks through the mountains:

"I love to go a-wandering along the mountain track. And as I go, I love to sing; my knapsack on my back. Val-deri, Val-dera, Val-deri, Val-der-ah-ha-ha-ha-ha-ha-ha-ha. . ." The tune had a great rhythm for hiking up hills.

They marched right past the Goodmans' vacant Twinkie. No one there. Now they were crossing the big flat field and taking the access road down into the woods. This was the last buffer between their private world—and the rest of the world. They were almost home.

When they cleared the last spruce, their elegant front yard blossomed before them in full color.

Kate cried out, "Look! It's Honeymoon Cottage!" She turned to Tim. "I saw it first, so I get a kiss!"

"Sure, my lady," Tim said. He gave his wife her requested reward. "The place looks good, don't you think?"

"Wonderful! Beautiful! Gorgeous!" Kate said, conveying adequately that she was more than satisfied.

They hastened a clip. A gentle afternoon breeze wafted across the alpine meadow and cooled the sweating hikers. As the two wove between waist-high monkshood and lupines, the mounds of indigo plumes nodded to them.

"Look at all these wonderful wildflowers Tim!" The girl from Hawaii was giddy. "Oh hello! Hello, you darling beautiful flowers! And hello you darling beautiful house! I've missed you all so much!"

When they finally stood at their destination, Kate set down the food and Tim swung a water can up onto the shelf outside the door. He stepped forward and opened the padlock that had been protecting their home for nearly half a year.

Lady Kate was given the honor of opening the door. And when she did, a flood of late afternoon sunshine poured in saturating the cabin with amber light.

Tim made a quick inspection of the place. The floor looked dry and there were no signs of visiting varmints. "Good. We're home."

Kate stepped in behind Tim. "Gosh I'd forgotten how small this place is. But I love every square inch of it!" She started to spread her arms with joy, but thought better of it. Still, she was thrilled to be home.

It didn't take long for them to pick up where they'd left off. Tim pumped up the stove and lantern while Kate scrounged a can of corned beef and a box of dehydrated mashed potatoes from the kitchen shelf and started cooking up her specialty.

They ate supper outside, sitting on stumps and admiring the alpenglow that washed over the landscape. How wonderful to be right there in front of their very own little handmade honeymoon house! And the view wasn't bad either.

* * *

The sun popped up over the hill at around four the next morning.

Kate trotted out to pee and stayed to greet everything outside, celebrating each moment the sun's rays kissed another cluster of blooms.

Tim emerged a few minutes later and squinted at the bright red sun. He stepped over to the alder and began scratching his stomach thoughtfully.

Kate ducked into the cabin and grabbed the speckled blue coffee pot. "Would you like some coffee?"

Tim grunted once, which usually meant "yes," so she measured out four cups of the water he had carried up the mountain the day before, and set the pot of liquid gold on the stove. As she pumped up the Coleman stove she thought about how they would have a whole can filled with fresh spring water by later that evening. Why not use two more cups and make oatmeal?

When they'd finished their breakfast, they went off to locate the source of their spring. Kate carried the shovel. Tim carried the shotgun.

They dipped down over the edge of their hill and quickly found themselves fighting much taller grass than what grew in the field above.

Kate thought about snakes. "I guess it's too cold up here for snakes," she reasoned hopefully.

Tim, who read a lot, said, "No snakes. The winters would do them in."

Reassured by that thought, Kate happily fought every jungle step because the chest-high grass hinted that water was nearby.

"Around here all we need to worry about is the occasional bad-tempered bear," Tim said. "And by the way, you'll need to learn how to use this shotgun soon."

Kate frowned. "Maybe someday."

Neil had told them there were black bears all year long. He'd said the grizzlies spent winters fishing in the lakes and rivers, and summers browsing for berries up behind the mountain. "The quickest route from salmon patch to berry patch runs right through your place," he had said.

Tim nodded. "Since it's spring, I guess we should be on the lookout for migrating grizzlies." A second later he added, "But we probably don't need to worry too much. These valleys are black bear territory, not grizzly. The grizzlies will all be up on the road."

"Why is that?"

Her brave Bostonian took a guess.

"Easier walking?"

Soon the pair pinpointed seepage beneath an extra-large spruce tree, and Tim traded in his shotgun for the shovel, and started digging. Kate held the gun, but she actually kept guard by humming a jig. After ten minutes, they switched tools and Kate dug. They alternated until midday, when they stopped digging and started resting beside their new catch basin.

The plan was to put a plywood dam across the lower end, with a shallow channel chiseled out at the top so the pool would continually rejuvenate. Kate, wary of most mechanical situations, thought it was a great design, because there would be no moving parts to break.

Satisfied so far, they hiked back up to the cabin to eat peanut butter and jelly sandwiches. Feeling confident that victory was close at hand, they used up more of their water on some powdered lemonade.

After lunch, they dug out the quarter sheet of plywood and a two-by-six they had left over from privy construction, and toted them back to the spring. Tim carried one edge of the plywood and the shotgun and Kate carried the other plywood edge and the now-empty water can. The two-by-six rode on top of the plywood.

When they dropped down into the tall grass Kate started humming again, in case any bears had come to drink, in their absence. But no wildlife had been there.

They got to work shoring up the side of the pond with the two-by-six. Tim placed the slab of plywood on its edge at the low end of the pool, and together they pressed it down deep into the mud. Next, they gathered rocks and stacked them up against the wood on either side. These would hold the board in place. The project was done.

Kate smiled. "It looks just like a miniature dam."

"If this spring has a decent flow the pool will be full by tomorrow," Tim predicted.

Meanwhile Kate was staring at a serpent of unearthed sediment that had begun sending slowly swirling tendrils up into the gathering water. "Look at all that silt. Do you think it'll settle out?"

"It should be okay if nothing disturbs it. Just be careful when you fill the cans. We'll have to get a ladle. But I'll guarantee you this water's as clean as anything you'll get out of a spigot in town."

Kate thought their first vessel of water might taste a bit earthy but she was ecstatic, nevertheless.

They passed the afternoon lounging beside their new pool. When the water was six inches deep, Tim laid the open can down on its side and they both sat back to gaze at the languid liquid as it tried to detour around, then got sucked into the vacuum of an empty can. It was a fascination.

Tim carried the water that Kate would be using to make coffee in the morning, and they happily hiked home.

Switching to an outward-sweeping summer door was a good idea.
It instantly doubled the interior space of the cabin.

June 16, 1977

Happy Birthday, Mamasan!

The road has finally hardened up and it's navigable again (if a person can survive the ruts). Our trusty little tank is able to carry us all the way home and we're parking right beside the cabin. Yay!

Our beloved neighbors, the Goodmans went out to work just like the rest of us. But we're all back home now. Recently we built a nifty dam at "Cutting Spring" so we can get our water there if we need to. But now that we can drive, it's a lot easier to get water in town.

It's shaping up to be a perfect summer. How are things in the tropics?

Aloha nui loa, Kate

Shotgun Bride

"I'VE CHANGED MY mind. I don't think I need to learn how to shoot a gun."

"Out here, everybody needs to know how to shoot a gun. If some 'no good' comes around while I'm gone, you might need to shoot him." Tim sounded adamant.

"Ha! If some 'no good' comes around I'll just run."

"Kate, really bad guys don't stand around watching blue-eyed damsels gallop away across the prairie. And besides, what if you're up in the woods and a bear comes out of the brush?"

"I'll whistle Dixie. That'll scatter the wildlife for miles." "You can't whistle, remember?" Tim lifted down the shotgun from over the door. Apparently, negotiations were over.

He put on his favorite 798er welder's hat, the yellow one with polka dots, picked up a box of shotgun shells, and ducked out under the lintel. "Oh, you might want to bring along a pillow," he called back over his shoulder.

"Okay," Kate said to the retreating form. He was right, of course. If it ever did come down to it, she would have to protect herself and any little ones they might have running around. She slung on her jacket, remembered to grab a pillow and headed up the hill to shotgun school. When she caught up to Tim, he was standing beside one of their three fifty-five-gallon drums. It was empty.

"You can use this as a target," he said.

"But we need these barrels for fuel. What good is a fuel barrel with holes in it?"

"We also need a bigger burn barrel," he said brandishing the shotgun. "Here. Shoot some air holes in it for us."

"Okay. But what if I miss? What if I hit the car behind it?" "You won't hit the car. It's too far away. This gun is for close range. You can't miss, as long as you let your target get close before you shoot."

Kate frowned. "How close would I want to let a charging bear get before I pulled the trigger?"

"About twenty feet. This triple aught buck should stop anything dead at twenty feet."

"But I don't want to kill anything. Isn't there another way to protect ourselves?"

"You mean like calling in the troopers? Remember, we don't have any way to call for help. And even if we could call, it might take days for them to get here."

"True," Kate acknowledged.

"You won't be shooting at anything unless it's charging at you, in which case you wait 'til he's right in front of you. Then you aim and fire." Her instructor paused for emphasis. "And that goes for man—as well as beast."

"I hate this," Kate muttered. But she took the gun from him and followed each one of his directions, concentrating hard, as if her life might one day depend on it.

Under Tim's watchful eye she loaded the weapon with buckshot and closed the breach with a cautious snap.

"Make sure it's closed," he corrected. "You'd better open it and close it again."

Kate complied, giving more commitment to her second attempt.

"And now you're loaded for bear," Tim said with a satisfied smile.

Kate hoped the lesson, which hadn't been too bad, was over. But that happy thought was cut short when Tim moved right on to part two of her training.

"Now you see these two hammers here?" He was pointing to a pair of levers that looked like little mouse ears sticking up out of the gun barrel. "You can cock one, or both barrels. But you'll usually just want to shoot one barrel at a time. That way you still have a second shot in case you miss with the first one." He paused and warned her again, "Remember pulling both triggers together will make one hell of a big kick and it might even break your finger."

Things were getting tricky. "Wouldn't it be a lot simpler to burst into a rousing rendition of Dixie and scare the culprit away?" Kate had lungs that fired like mortars.

Tim ignored the question, grabbed the pillow and tucked it in front of Kate's shoulder. "Remember to be ready for a wallop when you fire. Are you ready?"

"I don't think so."

"You're fine. Now cock it, and you're ready to shoot."

"I probably won't have a pillow with me," Kate said, trying once more to postpone the inevitable.

Tim cut her off. "Go!"

Resigned, Kate pressed the gun butt into the pillow while Tim held it against her shoulder. When it was seated, he stepped back and put his fingers in his ears.

Kate very carefully pulled back on the left cocking hammer and raised the weapon. She took aim on the empty gas barrel, pictured it as a charging grizzly and touched the trigger.

BLAM!!

"Ow." Her voice barely squeaked but her shoulder was singing.

"You did it! That was great," Tim was cheering.

He walked over and tapped two little holes in the side of the drum. "See? You hit the bear right here in his shoulder. But most of your shot went off to the side. Aim a little more toward the center. Aim right for his heart."

The flower child hated this whole lesson, but she knew it was something she needed to do. There really was no one close-by to help if anything threatening came up their isolated road.

"Okay," Tim said after a moment. "Let's reload. Do you think you're ready to try both barrels at once?"

"Probably not."

They reloaded, and this second time Kate cocked both mouse ears—trying to keep all fingers clear—and pulled the front trigger.

Both barrels fired. The blast nearly blew her over backward. When the smoke cleared Tim strode over to the can and pointed to a hole the size of a softball right where the charging bear's throat would have been.

"That's excellent!" he shouted. "Enough practice for one day," he said, taking the shotgun from his dazed bride.

"Good," Kate said.

1977 - Dear Mamasan,

Well, I did it! I fired a shotgun! I feel like Alaska Nellie. She's sort of famous around here: A twentieth century version of Annie Oakley. They've still got Nellie's old Pontiac "woody" parked out on the highway. I'll show it to you when you come to visit. When do you think you can come up?

Love, K and T

* * *

There weren't that many women who lived all alone out in the bush, like Alaska Nellie. You would need to be pretty good with a gun or else you would need a partner who could protect you. If you were part of a team like Elsie and Neil you could maybe make a go of it.

Kate was thankful that she had Tim and that he'd fought in the war. He would know how to protect her, if that ever became necessary. She had entrusted her life to him. In return, she'd do her full share of the labor. They would work together like a team of perfectly paired oxen.

They would probably be fine.

Kate was finally trying out her childhood Annie Oakley fantasy.

Start with a Firm Footing

BEFORE THE GOODMANS left to scout for a new place in the Lower Forty-Eight, Tim hired Neil to dig out a basement for them since he had a D-6 Caterpillar that would do the job.

When Kate showed Neil the spot where she hoped he would dig, he said they'd have a perfect view from there—one that would give them time to get the rifle ready, if they needed it.

Kate, who saw only the spectacular view when she looked out, hoped he was kidding. She stepped out of the way to let the man begin. She would try to stay close enough to fetch tools or cups of water as needed but far enough away to keep from getting backed over.

After a few swipes of the bulldozer's big blade, Kate could see that their soil was four feet of dark, smooth dirt, with a layer of sand beneath.

She smiled. They would have good drainage. And since their meadow was south-facing there would be no permafrost. That meant the ground would thaw in spring, the way it was supposed to. This was the perfect spot to grow a garden.

She watched Neil and his yellow dozer begin to carve out a bowl where the moose had bedded down.

When the excavation was six feet deep Neil climbed down off the dozer and set up an old-fashioned surveyor's transit. Kate darted in to help line up the corners. Tim, a trained mathematician, wanted everything to be square, plumb, and level.

* * *

After three days of digging and lining up corners they had a nice forty-by-fifty-foot flat-bottomed excavation. Big berms of dirt around the back and both sides formed a protective amphitheater. And the front windows of their new home would face the road so they could see any visitors as soon as they appeared on the road.

Neil lollygagged just long enough to share a cup of coffee and a couple of stories before he drove off. Then he took his Caterpillar home. Elsie would be waiting for him back at the Twinkie.

Kate suddenly felt sad. The Goodmans had lived in their little hut for nearly two decades, and now they were heading "outside."

"It's too bad they're leaving," she rued as she watched Neil's machine chug away.

"Folks live here for a while, and one day pack up and head out, the same way we drug up and quit working on the Pipeline.

He shook his head. "The rewards are nice but the battle grows old."

"Or our bodies grow old," Kate countered. "Neil says his shoulder's been bothering him for years. I guess they think they've had enough outdoor fun for one lifetime."

Tim bucked up. "But we're still young, so let's get going on our project. I say we spend tomorrow strengthening the bridge before we start working on our footing."

"Okay," Kate said, wondering what a "footing" was.

* * *

They spent the next day working on the bridge, and it looked a lot less scary by the time they headed home to Honeymoon Cottage that evening.

The newly repaired bridge.

The young pioneers sat on stumps in their outside dining room and polished off a couple of tuna sandwiches. It was peaceful sitting there watching the dusk shed its rose hue over the mountains. When the glow faded, they went inside, lit the lantern and started to make a list of the things they'd need to buy for their second phase of house construction.

* * *

By nine the next morning they were bumping down a nearly dry road, dragging their flatbed trailer behind them.

When they returned from Footprint four hours later they had a stack of two-by-tens, some rebar, several bags of cement and lime, some wooden stakes, string, a flat shovel, a trowel, five full cans of water, a shiny new, heavy-duty wheel-barrow, a framed screen for sifting sand, and a fair-sized pile of gravel.

They unloaded the trailer and stacked everything beside the big hole Neil had scraped out of the ground. Tim covered the cement sacks with a sheet of plastic in case it might rain, and they headed down to Honeymoon Cottage, tired but excited.

After hot dogs, fresh from the grocer's, they turned in for a good night's sleep. At daybreak, they would be commencing work on their worthy vision.

Up at the site early the next morning they began by lining everything out in strategic workstations. Kate helped Tim measure the lengths for each wall, and Tim used a handsaw to cut all the two-by-tens to fit. Together they laid out the shape of the house, drove stakes into the ground and fitted the lumber to the stakes.

Tim said he wanted his house to last a hundred years, so Kate held lengths of strengthening rebar as he cut them into sections with a hacksaw. She would help him make his dream come true.

They wired the long and short pieces of rebar together, forming a strong grid which they seated inside the empty frame. By sundown they had a perimeter that was secured with five-eighths-inch rods that stuck up a foot above the wood frame and down a foot into the ground. Tim told her that once they had this mold filled with cement, they would have a nice firm footing.

"Good!" she cheered. This phase hadn't been hard.

They surveyed the ten-inch-high exact footprint of their dream home. It looked huge. The structure would be thirty-by-forty feet, with a jog on each of the two long sides to accommodate the limited length of their homegrown logs.

"Tomorrow, when we start filling this trough with cement we'll have to work fast," Tim warned his assistant. "It's important to get it poured all in one day so there won't be any seams to weaken the footing."

"Luckily, it's close to the summer solstice. We'll have the advantage of a lot of sunlight.

Unless we die of exhaustion first, we can just keep working 'til it's done," Kate pledged.

They headed to bed at dusk. It was nearly midnight.

* * *

By four in the morning it was already light and they were rallying again.

"Up! Up! The sun is up! Time to rise and shine!

Today is a big day for us," Kate chirped as she started whipping up their oatmeal.

They gulped down breakfast and marched up the hill to work. Kate kept pace by humming the Seven Dwarfs' tune, "Heigh-ho, heigh-ho, it's off to work we go." It fit perfectly with their excited pace.

"You'll be the 'hod carrier,' and I'll be the mason," Tim explained. "Here's how you mix the concrete." He said it would be her job to produce unending gobs of the stuff. "You'll fetch the water and materials, and mix cement in the wheelbarrow. I'll help you drive it over and pour it into the form. I'll smooth it out while you mix the next load. We'll just repeat the same steps 'til we have this whole form filled to the top all the way around."

"That sounds simple enough," Kate said. She was a large, strong girl, and she knew she could do this. In principle, she would be providing the ground support while her incredible husband turned her penciled designs into a real house.

* * *

That first day at the rock pile turned out to be a long one for Kate. Mixing cement was tiring work and she was exhausted. Tim's job looked a lot easier. Maybe she'd try smoothing out the pour for a while, and let him mix cement.

That never happened.

If an occasional wave of resentment swept over Kate, she would think back to Elsie's story about clearing the field and stopping just long enough to cook dinner and wash the dishes. That always spurred her to return to her humble hod-carrying assignment, and wholeheartedly embrace their mutual vision anew.

They worked hard from sunup to sundown, but as it grew dark, they were still short of their goal. In the past twenty hours, they had taken only two breaks, one at two o'clock and one at eight, when they'd refueled with peanut butter sandwiches and powdered lemonade. Other than that, they had worked steadily until midnight. But they'd managed to get only a third of the footing poured.

"We'll have to stop here and continue in the morning, much as I hate to," the head mason finally said. "Hopefully these ends won't dry out too much."

He inserted extra rebar connectors into both raw ends and laid wet cloths over the unfinished pours. He wrapped them so carefully that Kate was reminded of engravings she'd seen of Civil War doctors bandaging fresh amputations.

They rinsed the barrow and shovel, stumbled down to Honeymoon, and flopped into bed, hoping that the next few hours of summer darkness would provide enough rest to rejuvenate them.

* * *

It took two more days just like the first one before they had the footing finished. When they had every last inch filled, Tim smoothed it out and stepped back to look at their work.

It passed inspection. They used a nail to scratch their names and the year, 1977, into the setting cement, washed out the wheelbarrow, rinsed off the tools, and tripped down the path to Honeymoon Cottage. This time Kate changed her tune and sang, "Heigh-ho, heigh-ho; it's home from work we go." She was ready to celebrate with a double-decker peanut butter and jelly sandwich.

* * *

Early light. After those three days of laborious mixing Kate could barely get her arms and legs moving. She painfully rolled off the bunk and slowly stood up. Pulling open the plank door she saw morning spreading its golden halo over thousands of plush flowers. That glorious sight gave her heart a kick-start and she inhaled deeply. "Oh boy! What a beautiful day!"

After splashing her eyes with a few drops of cold water from the washbowl outside, she grabbed the speckled coffee pot and filled it with water from the five-gallon can. She went back inside and started the coffee. Tim woke as soon as she began pumping up the Coleman that was perched on the kitchen shelf two feet above his head.

A few minutes later they were outdoors sitting on their stumps enjoying coffee and oatmeal. Tim lined out the plan for the day. He said Kate could take the day off from mixing cement and go into Footprint to buy a hundred concrete blocks. That didn't sound like much of a day off to Kate, but at least she'd be using different muscles. She accepted her new assignment with a brave smile.

Before sending her off on her errand Tim gave one last instruction. "Always keep both hands on the outside of the steering wheel. If you don't, and you hit a bump, you could break a thumb."

Kate started the Toyota, bumped down the rutted road through the field and disappeared into the woods. Four miles farther down the mountain she came to the bridge. This she crossed at a creep. Once safely over, she steamed ahead toward Footprint, twenty miles downhill to the west.

Two hours later she was anxiously dragging a queen-termite-of-a-tail-full of concrete blocks up the long incline back toward Sleeping Moose. Even though she was pressing her foot to the floor it still felt like the whole rig was dragging, and she couldn't figure out why. Kate took a look in the rearview mirror and saw smoke streaming out behind her load. "Holy cow! I'm on fire!"

The construction wife lurched to the side of the road, jerked the car to a stop and jumped out. She was searching for the source of the smoldering when a pickup truck slowed and pulled off the road to stop beside her trailer.

The driver got out and smiled.

"Looks like you're having some trouble," the stranger observed.

"I think I'm on fire!" the panicked woman yelled.

"It's just your tires," said the man. "They're pretty hot, but they're not on fire yet. You might want to take off some of that friction though. Your load is riding on the rubber. See here?" He pointed to one of the wheel-well covers. Kate, relieved to have someone telling her that things would be okay, looked at the tire more calmly and saw that the wheel wells were indeed rubbing on rubber.

The good Samaritan bobbed his hat and said, "Well ma'am, I just happen to have a cutting torch mounted right here on the back of my truck. If you'd like, I could whittle away at the tops of these wheel wells and give your tires a little breathing room."

This sounded like a serious alteration. Kate hesitated. Tim wasn't there to consult. It was up to her to make the call. With no other way home, she opted for emergency surgery. "Yes. Please do."

As soon as she'd spoken those words the fellow lit up his machine and started trimming away hunks of metal. After just a couple of minutes, both tires were popping up through their new sunroof vents and looking much happier. Kate thanked the kind stranger, and he got back into his truck and continued up the road, disappearing around the bend with as little fanfare as when he'd appeared.

Kate smiled, glad to know that the Goodmans weren't the only good men around. She restarted the Toyota and slowly pulled back onto the road.

Soon she was making the left turn at Sleeping Moose and goosing the accelerator for the first short climb up their roadway. So far, so good. Now she would have two miles of mud holes and bumps before the creek. After the bridge, she'd have to get through the marshy part. Once past those spots she'd nearly be home.

She saw the bridge: caution needed here. Off by a few inches and the whole load could slide forward and pin her underwater like a two-ton jackknife. Kate edged the Land Cruiser out onto the bridge. When she reached the middle she accelerated, and the rig plunged up the far side. No problems ensued.

She roared on toward the "lake" section. The old wooden grader was lurking there like a Moray eel, but Kate was too busy maneuvering through the mud and trying to keep her thumbs from getting caught in the steering wheel to even glance at it as she went by.

Up, down. Up, down. Through woods and over fields she towed her plunder home.

When she whipped her huge load around the last bend and saw Tim waving to her she nearly cried with relief.

She wanted to wave back, but she didn't dare take a hand off the wheel. Why break a thumb or an axle on that last bump in the road?

A hundred yards. Fifty yards. And done! Kate pulled the trailer up next to the new footing and killed the engine.

"Good work," Tim said. He smiled at his plucky bride. "Did you have any trouble?"

* * *

June 29, 1977 - Dear Mamasan,

Thanks for the offer, but it looks like we won't be needing a generator. Rural Electric says we should have power by July, which is two months later than they originally told us but it'll still be in time for mixing most of the cement and all.

We'll be starting our house very soon. After we get the basement finished, we'll move in there and begin working on the upstairs. We should have the whole thing done by this time next year. This is really the beginning and I'm thrilled!

Love from your daughter, a woodsman's wife

These summer days were intoxicating for Kate, especially since they were now heating with wood rather than coal. The aroma of wood smoke permeated their clothing and their hair, and Kate loved the smell of it on her man.

She was sitting on one of their "parlor" stumps out in front of the cabin breathing in the wood smoke and gazing at billions of purple and yellow flowers stretching their petals up to the sunshine. They carpeted the whole meadow. It was a lovely day and this was a divine spot, and she thought she'd like to sit here forever.

"Let's drive to the summit today." Tim had joined her to revel in the morning light. "The ground is hard enough to get up there now, and we deserve a day off, don't you think?"

Earlier, Tim had calculated the number of cinder-blocks they'd need to build the basement: around fourteen hundred. Ever since that mysterious roadside welder's help, Kate had been hauling trailer loads of blocks up from Footprint on very happy tires. By now they had six hundred blocks stacked at the site.

Kate was surprised at her mate's suggestion. It was true that the pair had been working non-stop, but now they were poised, and ready to go. Why break stride? True, it would be fun to bounce like safari travelers through the underbrush out back. Maybe this was the perfect time to take a breath. "Okay," she said, suddenly wondering what kind of wildflowers might be blooming up there.

They figured they would be back in time for lunch, so decided not to take food or water. And because they would be in the "impregnable fortress" they wouldn't need the shotgun, either.

They polished off bowls of mush with raisins, quickly saddled up, and headed out to tackle the wilderness that began behind their privy.

Their green Toyota tank plowed its way through a large alder thicket that edged the top of their meadow. Neil and Elsie had cleared the land this far, and not one foot farther.

The explorers entered the thick stand of spruce that would one day protect their home from cold north winds. After a couple of minutes, they burst back into sunshine on the far side.

Tim planned to drive through the slanting meadow up to the ridgeline. From there they would ascend the spine all the way to the top of their private mountain. They were following the exact route they'd traversed on that surprise mountaintop snow-machine excursion with Neil and Elsie last November. Kate even recognized the spot where they'd seen the wolf tracks. They would be crossing over it in a few seconds.

The little Asian bush car charged bravely into the sea of grassy lumps and almost immediately began rearing and jerking over several bigger-than-anticipated bumps. Just as they were crossing that wolves' dell, the car stopped mysteriously. It refused to proceed one more inch. The engine was still running and Tim tried gunning it, but their movable fortress wouldn't budge.

"Is there something about this particular spot?" Kate asked, only half joking.

Tim's response was, "Get out. When I give it gas you tell me what you see."

Kate climbed out of the car and looked to see what was holding them up. When Tim accelerated, she saw that the little tank's wheels were turning just fine—but they were spinning in air. Their car was straddled atop a giant lump of dead grass, flailing there like an impaled bug.

Apparently, they had just encountered that infamous foe to both man and machine—an organic obstacle that festers throughout the Alaskan backlands—the bane of the bush thwarting ease of passage to all but ptarmigan, bear, and moose. The real name for these humps of dead grass was "hummocks," but Kate had heard locals refer to them as "nigger heads." She would never be comfortable using that slur.

"We're stuck on a hummock," she reported.

"We'll have to use the winch," Tim said. He got down out of the driver's seat and went around to the front bumper. So far, the adventure had him smiling.

The plan was for Kate to run the winch mechanism while Tim walked the cable out and hooked it around the nearest tree.

He backed out twenty-five feet of cable and then stopped to look around. The loose end of the winch cable waggled limply in his hand. "Do you see anything up the hill that we could use?" he called. "I don't think we can reach the windbreak back there."

Kate looked around. "Those were the last spruce. It's all willow above here. We'll have to look for a big rock or something." She waded out among the hummocks, searching for an anchor that would be even more immovable than their heavy green rig. Once again, Kate was thankful that there would be no snakes.

But bears were a real possibility.

Meanwhile, Tim had given up on the winch idea. He went around to the Land Cruiser's back doors, opened them and started looking for the Toyota jack. He couldn't find it among all the other tools he had stored in the cargo area. Frustrated, he tossed junk out into the grass. At last he spied the undersized ratchet and wrenched it free from a set of twisted-up tire chains. He carried the frail-looking tool around to the passenger's side and jammed it in under the frame.

As soon as he'd fitted the three mini-handle sections together he started turning the thin bent-steel crank. On its third revolution, the insubstantial jack base sank down into soft ground.

Tim unearthed the tiny foot, reset it and turned the crank arm again. The base sank again. Tim was disgusted. "This thing is useless," he grumbled.

Her man wasn't happy anymore. Kate wisely stood at a distance to report her findings and await further instructions.

Tim was loath to admit it. "We're in some trouble here. We need to go back to the cabin and get something to put under this stupid base."

"Like what?"

"Something big and flat. The G.I. stove lid might work." Tim glanced up at the mountain to the other side of which lay twenty-thousand-gazillion square miles of wild land. There were grizzlies out there.

"I wish I'd brought the shotgun," he muttered to himself. "It's okay," Kate offered. "My turn to be the hero. I can sing, and that should get them out of the way."

Tim grunted and picked up the jack handle for whatever protection it could provide, and the pair started walking down the hill toward the woods through which they had just come. As they got closer to the trees Kate began singing at full volume. The important thing was to be loud. She started blurting out the Habanera aria from Carmen. "L'amour est un oiseau rebelle, que nul ne peut apprivoiser. . ."

"Easy there!" Tim said. "You don't wanna piss 'em off."

"I just wanted to give all bears fair warning," Kate said. But she softened her voice in deference to her partner's wishes.

At last their sweet little Honeymoon Cottage stood in plain view just ahead of them. There wasn't a bear in sight.

∗ ∗ ∗

Half an hour later they were hiking back up to the car, toting both the stove lid and the shotgun.

Unfortunately, their flat metal stove lid didn't do the trick either and they had to hike back down again. This time Kate didn't sing, since Tim had lost all patience and he was holding a loaded gun. On this third trip, they went right past Honeymoon and didn't stop until they got to the Goodmans' place.

When Neil and Elsie returned from town, they found the cheechakos sitting on their doorstep waiting for Neil's help. After he'd heard about their misadventure, Neil smiled and said, "You two are always into something. Let's unload these groceries before we go up there and get you out."

After unpacking the food and before they left to tackle the tow job, the four sat down for a quick piece of cobbler. Then Neil, Tim and Kate climbed into the Jeep pickup and bumped all the way up to the spot past the end of the road, where the Peterses' wilderness cruiser was stuck. With backroads expertise Neil wound up to within fifty feet of the high-centered rig and they used his truck as an anchor to winch from. It took about fifteen minutes.

Before leaving, Neil told them they should get a "Handyman Jack," as soon as possible. "Nothing else'll work up here like a good old American-made high jack."

Kate and Tim promised they would buy one the next time they were in town.

* * *

That night as they curled together inside their honeymoon hut, Tim suggested an alternate expedition for the following day. "Since we can't drive up to the top of the mountain right now, why don't we head across the creek bottom and check out the far corner of our property, instead? We can try summiting Round Top after we get a new jack."

Satisfied with the alternate plan, Tim went to sleep right away. Kate lay awake listening to the patter of a summer rain. It started softly, increased to a steady tapping on the tarpaper roof and eventually lulled her to sleep.

* * *

Sun up. Birds singing. Rain showers over, the morning rays on wet grass were making mini-rainbows that twinkled and danced everywhere. Today they would explore beyond the creek.

Kate hummed as she rinsed out the oatmeal bowls from breakfast. When it came to water economy, she was the queen. By specializing in meals that used only one pan, Kate could usually clean up the whole thing with two cups of water. Soon the dishes were done.

Tim took the rifle, Kate grabbed the stove lid, and they both climbed into the Land Cruiser. Tim started the engine, and they headed west over a lip of the hill and down a steep bank to the bottom of the valley. Lush spruce lined both sides of a little creek that ran there. With so many trees around, they could be sure the winch would pull them out of any soft spot.

To the left Kate spied the sagging barricade of intertwined alder and spruce branches that she had erected, hoping to dissuade any bears from coming through the area while they were logging. Neil had laughed when she told him about her simple plan. "It won't keep a bear from coming in if that's what he's of a mind to do. He'll just go over it or through it." The sourdough was probably right.

"Here we go," Tim announced. They had arrived at the uncharted bottomland of their purchase. He steered the little green machine down into the water and pointed its nose toward a bench of dry land about twenty feet distant. Ten feet into its valiant run, the tank rolled on its side and sank into the mud, coming to rest with Tim's side facing the sky and Kate's side half-buried.

Tim cantilevered out his window and slid down into thigh-deep sludge. He stood there for a moment with hands on hips surveying the damage.

Kate climbed out of his window after him.

"Hmm," Tim mumbled, appearing to think bad thoughts. "It's lucky we have both the shotgun and the stove lid with us today." Kate's attempt at humor fell flat so she decided to just watch and wait.

"Cuss it!" Tim hissed. "The winch is buried nose down in the creek and the stove lid will be useless in this muck. It looks like we're gonna have to get Neil to help us again."

It might have been funny if it hadn't been so darned humiliating.

After a few tense minutes Tim started feeling a little better. They helped each other out of the creek and started the hike up and over the hill toward the Twinkie.

This time Neil fired up the D-6 and beckoned the youngsters aboard. Sitting way up on top as they headed into battle, Kate's smile was a yard wide. So was Tim's. She couldn't see the driver's face but she figured he was probably grinning too.

When they got to the scene, Neil beat the muck with just one yank of the dozer. He suggested for the second time in as many days, that they ought to get themselves a better jack.

That afternoon they drove into Footprint and bought the biggest, meanest, longest-handled Handyman Jack on the face of the earth. Next time they *absolutely would be ready.*

After that second failed attempt, the pair postponed further explorations, and concentrated instead on building a house together. The project was turning out to provide a fantastic footing for two newlyweds to build upon.

Fair Play

IN AUGUST, ELSIE and Neil took Kate to the Alaska State Fair down in Ninilchik. On the Kenai Peninsula, this was the biggest shindig of the year and everyone in the entire borough would be there to admire the best of the best. Everyone, except Tim. Since there was only room for three people in Neil's truck, and since Tim wasn't much of a livestock fan, he begged off and stayed home.

When they got to the fairgrounds Neil parked the truck out in the pasture with a lot of nearly identical farm rigs, and the three headed directly for the hubbub.

Inside the ticket gate, the place was hopping. One tent was packed with excited cooks displaying delicious-looking baked goods and 'secret family recipe' pickles. In another tent, there were taciturn farmers showing off their fattest pigs, all shined up and squealing. Cowboys with big hats and oversized belt buckles strutted around between the various riding events, and little boys tagged behind them like stable puppies.

Kate was surprised to see so many of the local foreigners, dressed in their brilliant prints and satins, cruising among all the traditional-looking American farmers.

"Why are all the 'Russians' here?" she asked.

"They live just down the road in Nikolaevsk," Elsie said. "They're farmers mostly, so they always come to the fair."

"Are they sort of like the Amish?"

"I don't know much about the Amish," Elsie admitted. "But most of these folks have been here for some years. A group came up from Oregon when they ran into some trouble down there. They stick to their traditions and stay pretty isolated. Most of them only speak Russian."

"You've probably seen their cars in town," Neil told Kate. "Bright orange or green?"

"I sure have. Over in Soldotna in front of the feed store." "Yup. If you keep your eyes peeled, you'll see quite a few of 'em around."

The milling clusters of cotton candy-eating Russians were everywhere. Dressed in pinks and greens of near iridescent intensity, weaving in between all the denim overalls and cowboy hats, they looked positively gorgeous.

The little community was well represented that day and one of the scheduled events was even a demonstration of dances from their Motherland. Like lots of other sects they didn't seem to appreciate being stared at, but this dancing was a great opportunity for curious onlookers to observe the swirling immigrants in all their flamboyant colors.

Kate was having a hard time dragging her eyes away from their stunning Cossack shirts and flowered skirts.

"Well, these 'Nikolaevskites' sure get the prize for the most colorful clothing."

"All their houses are painted like that too. They just seem to love those brilliant colors," Elsie said. "One day you two should take a drive over there to see it."

"Maybe after we've finished the house. Right now, we don't take many days off. In fact, I haven't laid eyes on anyone from our road except Anna and Brian Tanner and you two, in the past year."

"And you probably won't see many of 'em, either. Everybody up this way keeps pretty busy."

"How do most folks on Round Top Mountain make their living? Do they hunt?"

"Jared farms all summer and drinks all winter. Cliff hunts," Neil said.

For a moment Kate flashed back to her adopted ptarmigan family. She had watched the little flock of Alaskan darlings out her squirrel window and been amused by their antics, until Cliff came by a few days later to ask if she would clean three ptarmigan hens in exchange for one of the dead birds hanging from his belt. That's when she realized she would never be a hunter.

"Does everyone else go 'outside' every winter to work?" "Not the Curd brothers. They have a slaughterhouse up at the end of the other fork of the road. Late fall and winter are the best times to butcher and haul the meat out, so they stay around on the mountain pretty much all year around."

Kate hadn't thought about those two black haired bulls for months—not since Clem's party. "The Curds are a little rough for me," she admitted. "But I guess they perform a good service for the Sleeping Moose community."

"Ranchers around here couldn't make it without 'em," Elsie confirmed.

When the Russian dancing and rodeo roping demonstrations died down, Neil said he was going over to look at the bulls. The two women went their own way, heading into the main tent to study some pickles.

Jostling through the crowds—admiring the cakes and pies up close—was tiring, and when the ladies eventually came to the end of that long tent and spied a pair of recliner chairs looking for a couple of tired women to sit down in them, Kate and Elsie gladly sat.

Right away a furniture salesman swooped down like a big barn spider. He started talking earnestly to Elsie, who looked interested in what he was saying. Kate couldn't hear a word he said over the din, so she just sat back and watched people pass by. Meanwhile Elsie was listening and smiling and apparently taking in everything the fellow was saying.

He flipped a switch on the side of her armchair and it began to move in little undulating waves up and down, which made Elsie whoop in genuine surprise. Happy with her reaction, the salesman whipped out a fabric swatch board and showed her the colors this style of furniture came in. She seemed to like what she saw, and once she even reached out and touched the green herringbone sample. Encouraged, the salesman talked on and on to Elsie and she continued to tilt her ear toward him and nod occasionally. When he showed her a catalog of interior styles, she pointed to the one labeled "Town and Country" and he brightened even more.

Neil finally located the two women at the far end of the busiest tent. "Are you ready to go?" he asked.

Elsie nodded, and she and Kate rose from their chairs, thanked the hovering salesman and escaped with Neil to the big pasture that served as parking for the event.

They stopped and looked around for their Jeep that was grazing with a herd of other pickups.

"There it is!" Elsie said. Neil and Elsie opened both doors and aired the hot truck out for a minute before Kate slid into the middle of the bench seat. The two seniors piled in on either side of her. They were all ready to head home.

Neil steered slowly around the parked vehicles until he could pull out onto the pavement. They turned northeast and headed for Sleeping Moose.

Once out of the fairground, Kate gave Elsie a nod. "I thought that chair salesman about had you convinced, especially when he offered to bring up a chair to match your 'Town and Country' décor."

"Is that what he said?" Elsie asked, looking surprised. "You mean you missed that part of his spiel?"

"To tell you the truth Kate, I missed pretty much all of it. It was so loud in there I couldn't hardly hear a word he said."

This was getting comical. "But you were nodding and smiling the whole time," Kate said.

"I was just trying to be nice. He was working so hard." "Now that is funny!" Kate laughed out loud, and that started Elsie laughing too.

By this time Neil was looking concerned. "You didn't sign anything, did you?" he asked Elsie.

"Oh heavens. No, I didn't sign anything. I doubt we'll ever see the poor fellow again."

Of course, Elsie knew what she was talking about. No furniture salesman in his right mind would drive a truck full of recliners over that bridge to match it with the furnishings in her house. And besides, she already had plenty of chairs tucked up in the barn loft.

But that conversation prompted Neil to tell Kate his secret about the bridge. "Well girl, I'd been thinking maybe I ought to mention how the old bridge might not be able to handle the weight of all those cinder blocks you've been dragging over 'er." He paused. "The truth is, every time I make it over safely, I figure I've cheated death just one more time. She's about ready to fall in, you know!"

His revelation gave Kate pause. "You've just confirmed my suspicions," she said. "And I'm thankful you didn't say anything earlier, because I'm sure my life is that much fuller for having accomplished that task."

* * *

Near the end of August, Neil and Elsie departed for parts unknown, having decided the time had come to move "outside" for good. Claiming that they were getting too old for this kind of life, they were pulling up stakes. The announcement hadn't been a total surprise. They'd said from the get-go that their plan was to subdivide the homestead and sell off parcels to fund a startup cattle operation down south.

Kate was glad that Elsie would finally be getting her two-room house, but she sure would miss her friend. She loved Elsie. Elsie was the only woman who lived within easy walking distance. Once the Goodmans left, their nearest neighbors would be Anna and Brian—five miles one way—and Pat and Bill—four miles, and forty years—the other way.

But best to take the departure in stride. Besides, the Goodmans would be back. Neil had said that, as soon as they found a place, they'd come back to Alaska to pack up everything and say "goodbye."

Soon they would be on their own on the mountain.

Leaving All the Bull Behind

OCTOBER. THE GOODMANS were back. They'd found a piece of ranch land in Colorado and Neil planned to start the new herd, come spring. He wanted to get out before the road fell apart, so the next two weeks were a hurried, emotion-packed time.

By the end of that month, the Goodmans were ready to head south. All their livestock—the cattle, the sheep, the hogs and the chickens—had been redistributed across the region. Only one bay horse remained on the farm. This was Neil's favorite cow pony and he'd be taking him along.

The settlers had passed down a lot of machinery to their heirs-apparent, the Peterses. The newcomers had also bought the barn full of furniture, several hand tools, and a big standup freezer packed with steaks and chops. The two hundred dollars they'd paid for the whole deal would barely cover the cost of gas for the sourdoughs' drive down the Alcan.

Neil was taking along everything he thought he would need to start the new cattle operation. He'd even dismantled the calving barn and packed that. But he said there wasn't room for Elsie's canned goods, so she gave Kate her cases of prepared vegetables, some rhubarb jam, and a dozen jars of bull meat she'd put up.

When Kate saw the beef, she joked that Neil and Elsie really were "leaving all the bull" behind.

After their very last breakfast together, Elsie handed Kate her aluminum teakettle and the moth-eaten green sweater that had kept the homesteader warm for the past twenty years. Kate received them with the respect due a cloak and scepter. Neil gave Kate a brand-new cowboy hat, and that almost made her cry.

Tim handed the aging pioneer the Handyman Jack, and Neil told Tim to, "Take both snow-machines, and treat 'em good."

The cowboy walked down to the corral, opened the gate, and led his horse over to the waiting cattle trailer, where he added the hesitant pony to the back end of the load. The bay's nostrils flared at being stuffed between a calving barn and a set of branding irons, but he went in without a scuffle.

Neil took one more look around and announced it was time to go. All four shook hands, and Kate topped things off with hugs for her beloved friends.

The two old timers climbed up into their overstuffed cargo truck, and the two greenhorns stood their ground. Neil started the engine.

After one deep breath all around, the big silver truck began slowly moving forward. There was a lot of hand waving, and Kate kept calling out good wishes for the trip and "happy trails" to them both. And she wanted to cry as she watched the hooked and bulging vehicles make their way down the bumpy, slushy road.

Kate's final view of the Goodmans was that bay gelding's rear sticking up over the back door of the packed stock trailer. She watched the brown rump sway sideways and jostle up and down as the truck bumped away.

And then they were gone.

. . . For a long moment Tim and Kate stared at the empty spot where their dear friends had just driven out of their lives. After a suitable season of mourning, Tim turned and said, "Well babe, are you ready to head home?"

Kate dragged her eyes from the vanishing point. "I guess so."

"Don't look so lost," Tim said. "We'll be fine. Remember, if anyone can do it—we can."

"So, you say." Kate took a last look down the road. "It's gonna be lonely around here without them."

"Come on, don't worry. If it gets hard you can hold onto my back pockets and I'll pull you through."

"Okay," she said. "Are they double stitched?"

* * *

They wanted to start toting their bounty up the hill right away, but the house wasn't ready to receive any goods yet. When the basement had a roof, then they could start hauling the new stuff home.

The classic old couch and chair, the sleigh bed, and an assortment of books would have to wait in the safety of Goodmans' barn until the big new place was covered. Then they could come to live in their new home at the top of the old homestead. Elsie's home canned tomatoes, green beans, rhubarb jam, and jars of beef would be stored on shelves in the root cellar, as soon as the root cellar existed.

The two old Skidoos would stay where they were until winter. Tim and Kate could walk down and ride them home when the snows began to fly. Tim thought those snow-machine relics might turn out to be the most valuable thing in that $200 outfitting package from Neil. Once they were alone on the mountain, transportation would be paramount.

The young settlers had also inherited several antique pieces with interesting shapes and mysterious uses, such as the washing machine Neil had bequeathed to Kate. She hadn't yet figured out how to use the cone-on-a-stick tool, and she wasn't sure she even wanted to. It looked like it could double as a torture device.

Neil and Elsie had left a rusted iron bed leaning against the back wall of the sawmill. Kate sanded it and painted it red, and it looked great. When it was set up in the basement, she planned to spread her old black and pink quilt on it so that it would exude a cheery greeting each time they walked in. And it would look especially friendly if they'd just had a hard journey home.

* * *

"Tim?"

It was some days later, and they were both lying in bed after another killer day.

"Do you want to hear a funny story about Elsie?"

"Um-hum." He would be happy to listen, as long as he didn't have to move.

"Do you know why Elsie never wears a dress?"

"I didn't think she even owned one. In fact, I guess I assumed they both slept in their boots."

"Ha! Ha! No, she owned one alright. She said she brought one up when they came to Alaska. She told me that Neil used to get after her every once, in a while, pestering her to put it on. But she always begged off because there was just too much work to be done."

"Hmm. I can see her point."

"Well, one day she finally decided she would surprise him by putting on her dress. While he was out with the livestock, she got all slicked up, fixed her hair, put on her dress, dusted off her patent pumps, and all. When he came in, she sashayed around in front of him for a turn or two. But he was fiddling with a metal loop and never even looked up. 'I'm gonna need your help for a minute,' is all he said.

"Elsie said she was disappointed he hadn't even noticed her getup. But they were a team—like you and me—and he needed her help. So, she said, 'Should I change first?'

"And this is what really frosted her, because Neil said, 'No, don't bother. I just need you to hold down that new hog while I put a ring in his nose.'"

Kate paused, waiting for a reaction from her mate. But Tim was quiet. So, she went ahead and finished the tale. ". . . And that's the last time Elsie ever put on a dress!"

Tim lay there, thoughtful. "I guess this is no place for a woman," he finally said.

"Not one that likes to get gussied up, anyway," Kate qualified.

Tim rolled over and kissed his wife. "So, will you help me cut some firewood tomorrow?"

"Sure. Shall I put on a dress?"

CHAPTER FIVE
Summer, 1977

Lettuce Alone

THE PROMISE OF someday having a beautiful home in an ultra-private spot with a million-dollar view kept Tim and Kate working in earnest toward that tantalizing vision. By now, the pair had established a good daily routine. After a breakfast of oatmeal, they packed up the chainsaw and axe, grabbed the shotgun and some water, and drove down into the woods. The goal was to have five logs cut and limbed by dusk.

Whenever the rain decided to let up for a minute so the ground could harden, they carried the rough logs out of the woods, chained them behind the little Land Cruiser, and dragged them up to the house site. It felt just like when they were building Honeymoon Cottage, only this time it would be two hundred logs they were hunting: not just a few.

Kate loved working with her husband. He looked so dashing in his red-and-black-plaid wool shirt and his brown canvas pants. It inspired her confidence when he stopped to assess the direction of each tree's plunge to earth before he cut the pivotal wedge. He worked with a cigar clenched between his teeth—and it, along with the chainsaw exhaust, the wild roses, compressed leaves, and damp earth—all swirled together to create a sweet elixir that she had come to enjoy, and which she knew would forever conjure up fond memories.

July 1977, Dear Mamasan,

Ah! Logging in Alaska; what could be more fun? After Tim cuts and "limbs" a tree, I move in to clear the brush away and help lay out the log for future transport. I do my best to keep up with him, but he's a powerhouse. At dusk, we head back to our little honeymoon home a few trees closer to the completion of our dream. In the evenings Tim sometimes tells me I'm the other half of his team.

We're working hard and you should see the progress we're making. We can't wait to sit in our hand-hewn lodge and soak in the beauty.

I'm glad you fed us all those hot dogs when we were growing up. I think that's what made me strong.

With love, from your youngest

The house site (white rectangle near center of picture) would provide a great natural windbreak, with nothing but empty space around it.

They logged every day, except when it was raining so hard that there was no point in going out. If it was super soggy, then they stoked up the little wood stove, and read or talked, building a collection of shared memories and imaginings, yet to come.

One morning Kate gazed out the open door at a steady rain. "Looks like we won't be logging today," she said over her shoulder.

Tim rolled away toward the log wall to catch some more shuteye. She guessed she should let him sleep. "This might be a good day to try cooking something that uses more than one pan," she mused. "I could rustle up a special breakfast and show him that I know how to make pancakes."

She started to whisper her way through the process. "Step one, get the water from the can outside. Pump up the Coleman stove and start the coffee. Heat some sugar with maple flavoring to make syrup. Dust off the griddle. Stir all the flapjack ingredients together. Set out the plates. Build a stack of flapjacks on each plate. Adorn with butter and syrup. Roust the prince."

Finally finished, Kate took extra care as she applied the syrup so she wouldn't knock the plates off the narrow shelf they'd nailed to the inside of the door. This shelf was their dining table.

"Wake up sleepyhead," she said with a cheery good morning face. "Look what's here."

Tim groaned, rolled over and opened his eyes. "Ah! What a pleasant surprise!" He scooted over to the edge of the bed, dropped his feet onto the dirt floor, and scratched his head, his back, and his stomach. Her lover rubbed his hands together with glee, as if he hadn't been aware of the whole process, from the minute she'd started pumping up the stove. Such a sweet ruse. He reached out and gingerly lifted a plate off the ledge. "These flapjacks smell great Kate!"

His praise pleased the backwoods bride. She sat down on the bed beside him, took a mental snapshot of the grand moment, and reached up to take the other plate from the slender rack. Her unbuttoned cuff brushed the rim of the tin plate as she did so, and sent the pile of deliciousness hurtling to the floor. The whole thing landed face first in the dirt. Kate stared down at the devastation lodged between her boots.

"Here, you can have mine," Tim offered, hoping to head off a tempest from the former actress.

Kate stamped her foot and roared, "No! I'll eat these!" And with that she scooped up the whole sticky wad of dough and rammed it into her mouth. The nightmare was gone in one gritty, grotesquely-huge bite.

Tim watched her melodramatics for a moment before diffusing the situation. "Hey Kate, do you know what's in a 'honeymoon' sandwich?"

"No!" she snapped.

"Lettuce alone." Tim leaned back against the rough log wall and patted the bed. "Come and sit beside me, my wonderful wife."

Kate, who was finding it hard to hold a pout when he was being so sweet, stoically piled all the dirty dishes, and pans, and anything that showed a sign of ever having been a pancake, into a stack and set them on the ground outside. She shut the door on the ugly episode and flopped down on the bed beside her partner.

"Let's take a little nap to digest," Tim suggested. "And we can start the day all over again."

Kate liked his suggestion, and she curled up and laid her head on his arm. He stroked her hair while they both studied the new map of the Kenai Borough that Kate had recently nailed to the ceiling.

Tim couldn't help but notice the nails she'd used. They were extremely large. He pictured them sticking out through the plywood-and-tarpaper roof like bayonets into the sky. Wisely, he said nothing. This woman was a treasure just to be willing to rough it with him out there, and he knew it. No need to make her feel worse. He could fix the roof later. "Why don't we look for a kitten next time we're in town?" he suggested. "This is perfect cat territory."

"Okay," Kate sniffled.

As Tim gently rubbed her temple, she shut her eyes on the world and eventually drifted off to sleep.

The next thing she knew there was a squirrel rattling the stack of dirty plates outside. When she opened the door of the cottage, the squirrel was gone and the sun was out.

Laying the first blocks.

* * *

On their next trip to town they adopted a kitten. Tim named him Sabretooth Tiger Cat. "Tooth" had very big feet. "Those two extra toes on each front foot will give him an advantage in deep snow," Tim said. He also liked the fact that Tooth could sleep right beside a running chainsaw and it didn't seem to bother him. That made him a perfect working companion for the craftsman.

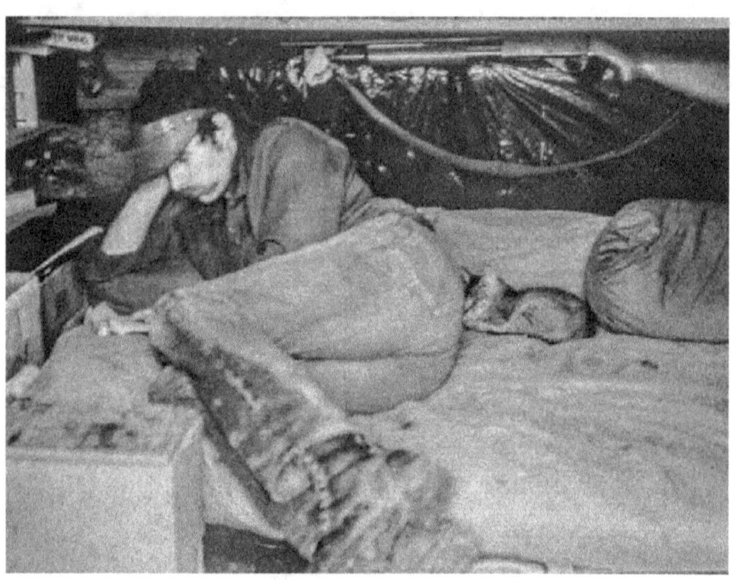

The two settlers and their little cat toiled together all day, every day. They all retired for a short rest before the sun came up and another day of labor began. The foot of the bed right next to the stove often got too hot for Tooth, so he slept on the couple's boots and socks, right there under the food shelf.

They were laying the walls now—that is to say, Tim was laying the walls. He'd started with two blocks at the southeast corner of the footing and was working outward from there. Meanwhile Kate mixed mortar and carried blocks in from the stack outside over to the mason's corner. She was dying to try laying some block. It looked like fun, and Tim wasn't even breaking a sweat. She watched him work and wondered if he would ever give up his masonry job and let her have a whirl.

When she asked to try, he told her it was vital to keep the walls straight and even. Obviously, he thought that he was the better man for the task.

Well at least she knew how to mix up a good batch of mortar and that was half the job.

Tim the mason, Kate the hod-carrier, and Tooth with twenty-four toes.

Invaders!

KATE PUT DOWN her shovel when the big livestock truck stopped just twenty yards west of their work site. She started to weigh the first question that popped up whenever an unexpected visitor came around the bend: coffee pot or shotgun? As soon as the driver climbed out, she felt herself leaning towards the shotgun choice. There was just something about him.

Where had he come from and why was he here?

The stranger stretched and unabashedly slid his hand down into the front of his overalls to give his bunched skivvies a loosening tug. When he was comfortable, he walked over to the curious couple.

Kate watched him approach. He was trampling right through her beloved lupines. Did he not care that he was crushing these beautiful flowers? She already didn't like him. First impression, he had just flattened a ton of wildflowers. Second, he looked dirty. As he got closer, Kate saw that his lip curled up unnaturally, creating an expression that almost looked like a sneer.

When the stranger reached Tim, he spoke. "Howdy. The name's Snyder. Frampton Snyder." He offered his hand—the same one he'd just used to adjust his briefs.

Tim avoided shaking the extended hand. "Tim and Kate Peters," he said.

As soon as Kate heard the name Frampton she snapped to alert. Frampton? As in "Pigs-in-a-Blanket" Frampton? Her mind was racing. Could this be the Frampton?

The visitor smiled at Kate, and she returned a small nod.

Snyder started the conversation. "You folks are new around here, ain't you?"

"Yup," Tim said. "We bought this land from the Goodmans last year."

The man wore a baseball cap and cowboy boots, and his overalls were caked thigh-high with something that looked and smelled like cow manure and axle grease. He had a pronounced scar tugging at his top lip, which Kate realized was what gave his face that nasty twist. The start of a dark beard sprouting from his cheeks and neck added to his general lack of appeal.

Kate mulled over the unlikelihood that the infamous "P-in-a-B" Frampton could be back in town.

The man jerked his thumb over his shoulder, indicating a woman who sat waiting in the truck. "That there's my wife," he said. Kate looked and saw a woman and two boys peering back at her from the front seat. One boy looked prepubescent.

The other was older, maybe sixteen or so. The crew looked like they'd all been squished together in the old truck cab for a long time.

Seeing that this fellow had a whole family with him helped Kate to relax some. "Pigs-in-a-blanket" Frampton couldn't have come up with a wife and kids so fast. She guessed maybe there might be a whole slew of "Snyders" living on the Kenai, for all she knew.

"Yes sir," the bloom-buster was saying, "Me and my little woman is just back from Idaho. That's where I picked her up. Ain't she a dandy? Even comes with two helpers," he added.

Good grief, it was him! An ice storm had just blown in across their prairie. Her heart froze.

Not seeming to notice the look of consternation on Kate's face, Snyder kept up a seamless monologue about his big ranch right up there up on Round Top, as well as a general prowess in all things animal.

Meanwhile Kate wondered where his ranch was. She hoped it wasn't close.

Now Frampton was telling them about the herd he wanted to breed, using artificial insemination. He went into a lot of detail on the topic.

"I got me a thermos full of Beefalo semen right in there." He gestured toward the truck again. "You ever heard o' Beefalo?"

No. Tim and Kate Peters hadn't.

"It's a cross 'tween a cow and a buffalo," he said. "Very ex-*pen*-sive. Them Beefalo can graze on anything. You don't need to feed 'em hardly nothin' at all."

He told the two how his special herd was gonna make him and his woman rich. He'd teach the boys how to do the chores, and Ruth could do the cooking and the cleaning, and he'd maybe have him a son or two more, while he was at it.

Tim didn't say much. He nodded, took off his visor, wiped some sweat out of the brim and slipped it back on. Snyder kept right on telling them what a great rancher he was. When he called out, "Ruth! Get over here!" the new bride responded obediently.

"You boys stay put," he ordered. And the two boys stayed put.

Ruth was attractive. She had big eyes and a nice figure, but poor Ruth looked tired. Kate figured that must have been some trip up from Idaho. The long-suffering woman had to be running from an even worse situation than what this fellow had offered her. What hellish scenario had she escaped?

The four stood awkwardly and tried to exchange small talk for a couple of minutes.

Finally, the mud-caked man turned and started walking up the hill toward the Peterses' windbreak. Ruth followed her husband with head down, trotting behind him like a nervous pack animal.

Tim and Kate stood still and watched them go.

"That guy seems mighty proud of his semen," Kate observed.

"I wonder what he's up to," Tim said. "Hmmmm," Kate cautiously agreed.

Frampton Snyder poked around near the stand of trees for a few minutes. He was no more than seventy yards from the bewildered pioneers and their nearly firm footing. Suddenly the farmer looked up and put his hands on his hips like he'd just had a great idea. He called for his woman to follow, then headed at a fast clip back down the hill toward Tim and Kate. When he reached the perplexed pair, he stopped and stood elbow-to-elbow with Tim, who was gazing at the view in uneasy silence. They stood there like two strangers in a small glass elevator. Suddenly the virgin territory that flooded out in all directions didn't feel big enough for Kate. A troubling presence had just entered their perfect world.

At last Tim broke the silence. "We don't get that many visitors up this way, Mr. Snyder. Is there something in particular that you wanted?"

"Oh, you don't have to call me 'Mr. Snyder.' Neighbors here all calls each other by their first name. You can just call me 'Fram.'"

Neighbors?

That's when Frampton Snyder lifted one muddy boot and planted it on Tim's curing threshold. Posing there with thumbs slipped under his suspenders, he suddenly proposed to Ruth, "What say we build right up there, Ruth?"

A visceral reaction blew out of Kate like volcanic ash. "Over my dead body!" she exploded, startling everyone, including her.

Kate and Tim didn't want close neighbors. That's why they'd bought land at the back of an old homestead. And they certainly didn't want this man or his herd of open-range Beefalo plopping down right on top of them. Kate looked desperately at Tim and waited to see what would happen next.

After a long pause and a slow blink, Fram spat. Then he said, "Well I don't rightly see you've got much to say about it. Your land ends just short of them trees, there. You know the Goodmans hold all them grazing leases up in back. More'n a year ago Neil Goodman told me I could pick me out a place to settle. And that's what I just done!"

"It's not going to happen!" Kate countered.

The invader's neck puffed out like a bull's, and like a bull he gave her a long, hard glare. He spat again—this time narrowly missing the settlers' new block work—and snorted his displeasure. "Come on Ruth. We're leaving!" He spun on his heel and marched back to his livestock truck. Fragile-looking Ruth hurried behind him.

The livestock truck flattened another wide swath of purple blooms as Frampton charged down the hill in a rage.

Kate felt sick. "There's no way he's gonna move in next door," she vowed. "Look what he just did to the lupines!"

July 29, 1977 - Dear Mamasan,

We're working hard up here, building the basement walls now. Still no electricity yet so we can't use the cement mixer that the Goodmans left. But we're making do. Neil also left us some big creamery cans and that means we can get fifty gallons of water up here at a time.

A bit of unsettling news: it looks like we might be getting a neighbor. And I can already tell you he's no lover of nature. He drove right through the middle of our field and didn't even try to miss the flowers. He just steamrolled right over them.

Love, your slightly-distressed flower child

* * *

After a week of hanging on tenterhooks, the young homesteaders learned that Frampton had changed his mind and was setting up camp down at the bridge. Apparently, Goodman's earlier suggestions of water and better shelter had influenced the stockman's decision. Whew!

Tim considered it a victory. But Kate still preferred the days when they'd been alone on the mountain. She regretted having been so unwelcoming—but to have that fellow living so close would have been unacceptable.

Not long after Frampton's return to the area, some folks from the local church pitched in to build him a shack right there beside Moose Creek. Tim ventured a guess that the church fathers had probably voted to set him up as far away from town as possible. Whatever the case, they were nearly falling over each other to help their newest church brother get set up on the mountain.

The photo above was taken from the spot where Frampton intended to build.

Just as soon as they'd driven that last nail into those four windowless walls-with-a-roof, Frampton moved Ruth and the boys into their new home. The church folks told Ruth it would be another day or two before anyone could get back with a door.

Fram told them there was no hurry. "Just come up with the door, anytime you get to it." If Ruth was worried about visits from the local wildlife, Frampton didn't seem to care about such concerns.

Meanwhile his precious Beefalo sperm was still waiting unattended out in the truck. It got tired and died, and another good soul at the church furnished him with a little startup herd of regular beef cattle. This way he could get established up there before the snow flew.

The arrow on the right was the Peterses' place.
Frampton's proposed location would have been the arrow on the left.
A travesty, given all the open territory he had to choose from.

As soon as that latest benefactor had bumped away out of sight, Frampton threw down a bale of hay on the bridge and turned his herd loose.

* * *

When the Peterses headed into town a few days later and came upon the new setup at the bridge, they stopped to inquire about the steers in the road. Was this to be a permanent fixture?

When asked, Fram stated his well-thought-out philosophy to them. "I don't mess with building fences to keep my animals in. Any critter'll find its way home when it gets hungry enough."

Now, in addition to the ruts and bumps that Tim and Kate already endured, they would have to contend with a dozen head of cattle living on the bridge. Not a pleasant prospect.

Fram's laissez-faire style of ranching quickly disseminated garbage in all directions. Within a week, the area around the bridge had turned into an array of overturned jugs and crates lying half-buried in cow-patty slime. And the collection of junk grew bigger in scope and size, with each passing day.

Within two weeks, the older lad had run off. Smart kid. That left long-suffering Ruth, and Jimmy the younger to deal with Frampton on the farm. Those two were in, way over their heads. But it didn't look like Ruth had much recourse. Poor Ruth and Jimmy.

In less than a month, the area around the creek had become a twenty-yard-long sluice run of ruts, guts, and bovines. It was now an issue every time the Peterses wanted to get into or out of their place.

Usually the little herd stood packed in a tight bouquet around the hay on the bridge. But sometimes they preferred to bask in the little patch of sunshine that sprayed across the turf at the corner. Either way, a person had to go between them, if they couldn't get around them. Many times, Tim and Kate had to stop and wait for two dozen indolent eyes to take notice and forty-eight lethargic hooves to shuffle out of the way. These immobilizing moments caused angst, not because of the cows—or even the manure—but because Frampton might want to saunter on over for a little chit-chat. Frampton Snyder had come to think of this area as his private domain. He loved playing a benevolent Ben Cartwright to anyone who traveled through. If they lasted longer than a nod of hello those visits tended to be awkward.

* * *

One day, Kate and Tim were headed into town. Snyder's cattle were out sunning on the last turn before the creek and

Tim slowed the car to a stop so Kate could jump out and herd the cows off the road.

Here came Frampton, aiming straight for them. He strode right up to Kate's side of the car and rested a shitty boot on the running board. This effectively blocked her from getting back to her door. He looked in the window and nodded at Tim. "Howdy." Then he turned and winked at Kate, who had stopped short and was maintaining some distance.

Whenever he got too close—close enough for a person to see leftovers in his teeth, or for him to grab a kiss if he had a mind to—Kate got nervous.

Fram, who was now in his "Cartwright" stance, began telling Tim how he'd worked out a deal with a cottage cheese factory in Anchorage. They would give him their expired dairy products in exchange for a side or two of pork, come butchering time. "Did I mention I got me some new hogs?"

Kate listened, and shifted uncomfortably as she imagined the pristine wilderness overrun with rooting pigs. Frampton, possibly mistaking her wariness for weariness, graciously slapped his knee. "Put her here," he offered.

"No thanks," she said, hedging around him and squeezing back into the car. "We're headed into town. We've gotta' get going. See you later."

Fram swooped in close before she could get her window rolled up. He smiled, and then asked Kate one of the most challenging questions she'd ever had to answer. "What do you say, pretty girl? Not bad for a 'harelip,' eh?"

Now what was she supposed to say to that, since she had long since realized that what affected Frampton's mouth was indeed, a harelip?

After an agonizing moment, she decided to go with the truth. "No Fram," she said, "not bad at all."

Her answer seemed to please the farmer. He tipped the brim of his baseball cap, gave her one last wink and stepped back from the car.

Tim pulled off through the muck. Kate waited until they'd successfully crossed the bridge to ruefully admit, "That Frampton Snyder is BIZARRE! And that's what I *really* think."

Cork Pops Up

Dear Mamasan,

SURE! It would be great to have Cork come up for a while. He would love it here, and we could sure use the extra muscle.

THEY SAID THAT Cork could stay 'til he decided to leave, or 'til they kicked him out. Kate's good-natured nephew was a mechanical wizard who had just graduated from high school. He would be fun to have around, and would probably be a help to them while building their house on the mountain.

When he arrived, Cork pitched his big blue tent in a small patch of meadow between Honeymoon and the house site. It looked cheery, sitting there among the waist-high fireweed blooms.

Over the next month, that tent became their game center. It was much roomier than the little cabin. They held many Risk® tournaments there by lantern light. A well-aimed flashlight beam could send subliminal messages to attack, and Rasputin-like whisperings urged the breaking of treaties. Luckily, this kibitzing over a board game of world domination bonded the team together, rather than leading to war. They were "the three musketeers" who vowed to complete their block basement before the snow fell.

When it was time to work, Tim remained as mason, and Kate and Cork rotated peeling logs, mixing concrete, and carrying cinderblocks. When Tim was finished filling a section of wall, one of his underlings got to tamp down the cement around the rebar verticals. Cork and Kate both vied for that privilege since it was the frosting on the cake, so to speak.

Kate liked working with the barking spud best, sitting astride one log after another to hand peel each of the trees they'd cut and hauled up to the house site. When she got tired, she would pause in that magnificent vantage point at the top of the hill, sometimes removing her leather work gloves to stroke the freshly stripped wood. Under their bark, those trees felt as smooth as dry silk.

Unfortunately, at six every evening a swarm of reddish flies rushed in to attack her mercilessly. As soon as the first red fly zeroed in on her she would have to put on her hunter's face net. If the fair-skinned girl went without the face screening, she woke in the morning with welts the size of embedded almonds all over her face.

Lupine-loving Kate in her face net after six o'clock.

Except for those flies, the glorious location and the knightly camaraderie that infused the summer of 1977 were ideal. As the block walls rose around them, Cork, Kate, Tim, and Tooth worked together through the long days, completely comfortable and with glad hearts.

Sabretooth liked to ride on Cork's shoulder.

See Kate's Spot

ONE DAY, KATE appropriated the pickaxe and began excavating the root cellar. She wanted it to be large and accessible from inside the basement. Tim had agreed to leave an opening in the block wall and make an insulated door if she would dig out the cellar.

No problem.

After two or three days of serious labor, she had a long, narrow extension carved into the deepest part of the hillside. Tim stopped his masonry and came over to frame in a doorway and line out the footing for her new pantry.

"I want to try laying block," Kate said. "Maybe I could do a row or two in the root cellar. How about it?"

Tim hesitated. "You have to be very careful. It has to be plumb. If it's leaning in even, a little bit, the whole thing could cave in."

Promising to take care, Kate was handed the trowel and the responsibility for a small section of root cellar wall. Temporarily retired, Tim sauntered away to smoke a cigar and relax.

A while later he returned to check on his apprentice's progress. He regarded the curing blocks that he had laid earlier—straight seams rising in a staggered climb, the layers offset with mathematical precision. He studied Kate's brand-new section of wall. Here the pattern of mortared seams defied logic, as they intersected in the middle like a gift-wrapped box.

"Uh, Kate what happened here?"

"Um." She stared at her work but could come up with no explanation.

"At least we'll always be able to find Kate's spot," Cork said.

His joke made everyone smile.

After that experiment, Kate abandoned her masonry ambitions and threw in the trowel.

See Kate's spot.

Cork was turning out to be a pleasant fellow to have around, and he also had a special gift with machinery that made him a real find up in Alaska. Tim and Kate got a lot done with his help.

Tim came home one day with a lumber-making attachment for the chainsaw, and he and Cork started squaring off four sides from one of the biggest logs they'd harvested. Eight beams overlapping on four columns in a line down the center of the basement would span the distance from one side of the house to the other. If things went according to Tim's plan, these columns, along with Cork's brilliantly designed metal support jacks, would still be standing at attention and supporting the floor in a hundred years.

That was Tim's dream: his very fine dream.

Here's Cork sitting on the first beam he and Tim cut.

Sharing the barking spud, Cork and his Aunt Kate alternated peeling the two-hundred logs.

*Their rebar-re-enforced wall had two openings facing the driveway,
a wide one for the basement door and a little one to be used as a coal chute.*

*Rebar-reinforced walls and Sabretooth, a kitten with extra toes.
Tooth quickly adopted the coal chute as his own.*

Sept. 12, 1977 - Dear Mamasan,

We've been building block walls 'til the cows come home (poor choice of words). I dug out a root cellar with pick and shovel. It'll have lots of shelves so we can store lots of food.

We're all in need of showers. But we don't get into town very often, so we just stink. I love it here though. Pretty soon we'll be moving into our big new basement, which we've built right under that moose's imprint.

Still hoping we'll have running water soon. The power company promised we'd get electricity this summer, but their plans seem to have changed. We're going in for showers tomorrow. (Yay!) I'll mail this on the way.

P.S. Red flies gone for the season. Good!

P.P.S. Have you ever heard of a "huck-a-lunga" contest? The object is to spit the farthest. Cork and Tim have them sometimes, and they're both pretty good at it. I'm practicing and getting better, but it'll be a long time before I win.

(Just kidding, Mom. I'll never win!)

* * *

Two beams overlapped on each column.

Soon they'd be hauling their stuff out of Honeymoon and up the hill into the basement. Then Cork would move out of the tent and into his "bachelor" cabin.

Kate was thinking that dour old Augusta Myers, homesteading over on the next ridge had been way off in her dismal decade prediction. After all, this basement was practically done!

Root cellar done and half of the joists on.

Autumnal Equinox, 1977 - Dear Mama,

We're still not quite done, but the block work is finished. We just need to haul in plywood for the roof, roll out tarpaper, tar over all the nails, and build and hang the door. It shouldn't be long. October 8th (our 2nd anniversary) is the projected start date for our water installation project. That is, if we've got power by then. But even if we don't, at least now we'll have enough room to keep our water cans inside.

* * *

Construction was going fast now. They attached the rough-cut joists, nailed sheets of plywood on top, and rolled out tarpaper.

Poof! The basement was done.

"Hey Cork, why don't you bring your sleeping bag up and roll it out on the floor here?" Boss Musketeer suggested. "It looks like it might rain tonight."

"Good idea," the lad agreed. "I'll go get my bag."

Sure enough, on that very evening, a heavy rain pelted the place without mercy. By morning Cork's tent was flattened, but he was nice and dry inside the basement.

Cork in front of his bachelor cabin.

* * *

Now they made a quick trip to Anchorage to buy a stove. Three days later they were back with a huge new Riteway furnace.

"A good—ooof—set of steps would come in handy right now," Cork grunted. They were all three struggling to get the new furnace down to the basement door. The heavy rain had turned everything to mud, and muscles worked overtime to control the brick-lined firebox's slide down two planks and in through the door.

After they had the big stove safely inside the basement, they walked it over to the center of the big space and seated it on the dirt floor. Tim riveted a couple of stovepipe sections together to reach up through the roof. And they were in business.

Their new wood/coal-burning stove was the deluxe model. It had a special T-section joining the pipe to the firebox, with a built-in dump cap for emptying any unburnt creosote. It was reputed to give off a slow, steady heat so they'd only need to stoke it a couple of times a day. Now the hardest part of keeping warm would be gathering and hauling the coal home. And the tiny door they'd built into the basement wall would make transferring coal out of the sled or car or truck and into the basement easy.

By that evening Tim and Kate had moved all their stuff into their new subterranean home, and Cork had set himself up in Honeymoon. Both developments felt hugely satisfying. "Do you think you'll be happy here?" Tim asked Kate as they stood together in their new cavern.

"You're joking, right? It's fantastic! Once we get power and water, and a stove and fridge in here, I'll never ask for anything more!"

Painting emulsion on the root cellar walls.

They all loved the wonderful new wood and coal furnace with its removable dump cap "T."

Chapter Six
Fall, 1977

Stovetop Pie

FIRST SNOW: TIME to build a coal bin. The three co-laborers marked off a section of dirt floor and built three plywood partitions running from the block sidewall out nearly as far as the furnace. The enclosure was about the size of all of Honeymoon Cottage. As soon as they had this thing filled, they wouldn't have to worry about fuel for the rest of the winter.

Kate put the emergency fire retardant kit (a box of baking soda and a bottle of vinegar) into two special slots that Tim built onto the front of the coal bin. "Good. We should be safe now," she hoped aloud.

"If we can fill the whole bin with the next good storm," Boss Musketeer predicted, "we'll be set."

"Great!" Cork cheered. "We're going coaling!"

Kate, who already knew how tricky harvesting coal floaters from the beach could be, wasn't as thrilled as the eighteen-year-old, but it was a job to be done and she would do her best to help.

Now all they had to do was wait for a strong west wind to break chunks of coal away from the exposed seams along the peninsula. A good coaling storm could leave the western beaches of the Kenai littered with coal. As soon as one hit, locals would be there to dart out between tides and gather the free fuel, and Tim and his crew would be there too.

While they were waiting for that perfect storm Tim decided to tackle some other projects. They brought up cinderblocks, two-by-fours, two-by-sixes, and finished two-by-eights, and started laying a suspended floor across most of the basement. The kitchen, living, sleeping, and workshop areas would be planked. The area around the furnace would still be dirt.

The functional flooring didn't take long to finish and it was a huge improvement. Kate was getting her house.

Next the men outfitted a workshop area in one corner of the basement. It had a long plank workbench with enough floor space to handle any kind of machine or tool Tim might acquire.

Water cans now lined up against the end of the sink.

They built a long counter for Kate's kitchen and carried in the tin sink she'd bought at a garage sale the winter before. They set it up at a right angle to the counter to divide the kitchen from the sleeping area. At last there was enough room in the house to keep the five G.I. water cans inside so they wouldn't freeze. Kate stood the four full cans in a line at the end of the sink unit. The "in use" vessel sat on a wooden block to the left of the sink. Elevating it made pouring water much easier.

Kate taped plastic sheeting across the open back of the new kitchen centerpiece to keep their bed dry, and placed an empty bucket under the truncated sink drain to catch the spent water. Five gallons in, five gallons out. Just don't forget to check under the sink before you pour.

Washing dishes would be easy now. Kate could picture some multi-pot meals being served one day soon.

The interior work moved to the back walls of the underground home, where they built storage shelves galore for clothes and books. They lined the root cellar with shelves, and built two big bins, one on either end, for storing potatoes and carrots. The trio toiled together to replace the slippery front ramp with a set of steps leading down to the basement. This would be the last improvement.

It turned out to be quite a project. Starting at the base of the squat door, they made a drain cover out of a tin can with holes poked in its bottom. This ran to a piece of buried drainpipe that led away from the foundation. They mixed and spread a six-by-four-foot platform of solid concrete around the drain and let that dry. Next, they poured an eight-inch-deep solid concrete tread on top of the first layer, setting it back about ten inches. A third step, receding another ten inches, went on top of that, and so on. About eighty tons of hand-mixed concrete later, they had a dandy set of steps, and a military-strength pillbox emplacement, all in one.

"These should be good and strong," Tim said, admiring their sturdy creation.

"And we'll be ready in case we're attacked," Cork quipped. Always the joker.

A set of solid concrete steps now led down to their snug basement home.

Kate was overjoyed to see all the improvements the men were putting in around there. Every new development felt wonderful. She decided to express her thanks by baking a pie for them. It would be fun to make something in this spacious new kitchen, and she would prove to these guys that she really could cook.

She hummed as she measured out the ingredients and mixed them together in one of her porcelain cooking pots, and she smiled as she rolled out two piecrusts on top of her nice new counter. Kate fit one crust into the pie tin and added chunks of apple, brown sugar, butter, cinnamon, and salt. She covered the pie with the second crust and crimped the edges just the way Mamasan had taught her. When the masterpiece was fully shaped, she set her culinary effort on top of the hot furnace and waited for the firebox to do its magic. Such a remarkable burst of domesticity was sure to dazzle her workmates, because they thought she could only cook oatmeal and corned beef hash. When her companions came in from cutting wood and their cold noses sniffed the aroma of cooked apples permeating the basement, she figured they would be excited.

"Sit down at the table," she instructed when they came in sometime later. The two men slipped their arms out of their sleeves, rolled their coveralls down to their waists, and eagerly followed her order to sit. With pomp befitting this monumental occasion, Kate slid her steaming pie off the stove, carried it over to the kitchen table and set it down on a trivet. She sliced three man-sized pieces and dug the first piece out of the hot pie pan. This one went to Tim.

"Ahhhh!" He breathed in the fragrance with exaggerated ecstasy. Adapting a TV commercial for flour they'd all seen some years before, he pointed to his plate and said, "Pie like this, it's got to be scratch."

Kate was positively glowing over her first pie. Then, right before their incredulous eyes her sculpted delicacy disintegrated into a shapeless blob of simmered apple guts. It spread across the plate like a steaming pile of bear scat. Devastated by her failed baking presentation, Kate jerked the plate away from Tim's startled grasp, stomped across the room, and opened the front door. "That's the last pie I'll ever bake!" she proclaimed irrationally, hurling the abomination outside.

Both men were profoundly disappointed.

Later that evening, they all forgot the unfortunate "Stovetop Pie" incident as they played Risk at the kitchen table and laughed in the lantern light. Breathing in the blended smells of wood, dirt, motor oil, supper, and the lingering hint of apple pie, there was no place on earth that any of them would rather have been.

Meanwhile Tooth had found his perfect spot on the little sample of carpet Kate had laid beneath the furnace for him. He slept there peacefully, completely undisturbed by any hubbub about a pie.

The single-track was Cork's favorite rig.

Dead Bodies in the Garden

EVEN THOUGH TIM, Kate, and Cork were the only ones living up the road behind Frampton Snyder, it didn't take long for the other neighbors to start complaining about his free-running menagerie. Frampton and the general disruption his animals were causing quickly became the polarizing topic up both forks of Round Top Road.

One morning when Tim and Kate were outside doing chores, several sharp cracks rang out across the flat.

"That sounded like gunshots," Tim said. "I'd better go see what happened.

"I think it was at Pat and Bill's."

Kate was ready to grab her coat, but Tim held her back. "You and Cork had better stay here where it's safe. I'll go check things out."

The possibility that someone might have just gotten shot at Pat and Bill's brought back memories of the Curds' going away party. Better safe than sorry.

"Okay. I'll stay here with Cork. But you be careful."

Tim went into the basement, grabbed the shotgun off its wall hooks over the bed, and marched out to the Toyota. Kate watched him drive away, and then walked down the hill toward Cork's cabin. He needed to know about the excitement. She and Cork could sit outside on the living room stumps while they waited to get a report.

Tim was back an hour later.

"What was it?" Kate wanted the details as soon as he'd returned.

"It was Fram's pigs. They got into Pat's vegetable garden and tore it up."

"I knew those animals would cause trouble," Kate said. "I'm glad no one was hurt." She frowned. "Which way did they go when Bill started shooting?"

The answer seemed evasive. "They're gone."

"Yes, but which way did they go? Are they headed up this way?"

"No. They're gone," Tim said. "Gone for good. Gone, as in 'expired.' They've been dispatched to that big meat locker in the sky." He paused. "Bill shot every one of 'em dead."

"Now let me get this straight. Are you telling us that Bill shot Frampton's whole herd of pigs?" Kate was incredulous.

"Yup, all six of 'em. Their bodies are sprawled out in Pat's carrot patch."

"Uh-oh," Cork worried. "What'll Fram say about Bill shooting his pigs?"

"He won't be happy, most likely."

"That's an understatement," Kate said, feeling a knot swell in her gut. "You'd think he could have just shot over their heads. Why did he kill them?"

"At any rate, I'd suggest we stay out of it if anyone asks us for an opinion."

"This whole thing is getting disturbing," Kate said. "As disturbing as fresh bear shit," Tim agreed.

"I'm glad it was just pigs, and not some poor schmuck passing by," Cork volunteered. "With so many trigger-happy folks around here, it could have been a lot worse."

"It could've been us," Kate murmured.

That sobering thought resonated for a moment against the wide-open wilderness. Then Cork retreated to his cabin to write to his twin brother about the episode.

Tim went into the basement to hang up the gun.

Kate followed. "Babe, are we surrounded by a bunch of social misfits around here?"

"I don't know," Tim admitted. "They say that anti-social types tend to settle in out-of-the-way places like this. That's probably so they won't have to follow laws."

"But we're not anti-social types, are we?"

Her mountain man smiled. "No babe, we're not anti-social. We just prefer to do our gardening in the nude."

* * *

Not surprisingly, Frampton took the premature slaughter of his pig family hard, and after he'd been convinced to put down his rifle at O'Leary's, he started strutting around with a pistol strapped to his waist. Rumor had it he'd challenged Bill O'Leary to a duel. But Bill, who had a sign by his door that read "This house is protected by Smith and Wesson," didn't seem too worried.

Tim reminded the other musketeers to avoid trouble by keeping their opinions to themselves. It was hard enough to get along with Nature here, let alone Man.

Kate tried extra hard to be civil to her least favorite neighbor. She even offered him coffee and took his picture once, when he came by.

* * *

A few weeks later Frampton started sitting down by the bridge for hours at a time. Hunched there in the rain with a rifle on his knee, he looked scarier than ever.

Been Her, the Charioteer

ONE NIGHT AFTER several unfulfilled at tempts to top off their ravenous, cavernous coal bin, a particularly "good" storm blasted through. Tim figured there would be coal down at the beach in the morning and they decided that the Victory Garden crew should send representatives to collect their share. Since there would only be two seats in the Land Cruiser once the back end was filled with coal, and the electric company had promised to hook up power any day, Tim stayed home to put in wiring.

Having consulted the Farmer's Almanac tidal chart, Kate and Cork took their buckets and headed for the beach at daybreak. Pledging, "Full bin or bust," the two rode off with the sun at their backs, and a specially-modified sunroof-style trailer tagging along behind them.

* * *

". . . But when we got there, there wasn't any coal." Cork was telling Tim the story of their expedition later that day. "So, we decided to try the beach just south of Kasilof."

Kate cut in. "By the time we arrived at Kasilof, the tide was already coming back in, so of course I was nervous."

"But I kept her focused," Cork clarified. "We drove down to where the coal was, but the sand was very wet."

"It was like quicksand," Kate interjected.

"So, we worked fast." the admiring lad smiled at his uncle. "We didn't want to disappoint you, Boss. We managed to get the back end of the car loaded, and most of the trailer."

"And then I insisted on dragging up, and we tried to take off but—"

"We couldn't move," Cork finished the sentence before she could, and then he went on. "We were stuck. And the tide was coming in really fast."

Kate jumped in. "Too fast. About the time the water was lapping at the hubcaps, we decided to unhook the trailer and at least save the car."

Now Cork regained the floor. "We really needed to get it up the beach, and fast. I pushed on the gas and steered, while Auntie Kate pushed from the back, and finally we got it up out of the sand. Then I jumped in and just kept going."

"Old Cork drove all the way up to the top of the beach and saved the day," Kate reminisced fondly.

"I didn't wanna stop 'til I was above the high tide line. As soon as the car was safe, I turned it around so the winch pointed back toward the ocean and then let the cable out. Luckily, it reached just far enough."

Now it was Kate's turn again. "We hooked the winch around the rail at the front of the trailer, and I rode at the back to balance it and keep the tongue up while Cork winched me in."

Tim smiled. "That must have been something to see." "You bet it was," Cork assured him.

"And now, I really must go use the privy," Kate shared. "The whole thing was almost too exciting for me, if you know what I mean." She left the two fellows and headed for the outhouse in a hurry.

Cork watched his eccentric aunt disappear into the privy. "You should've seen Auntie Kate riding that trailer up the beach," the lad said.

Always a dramatic communicator, Cork finished off the tale with one of his signature flourishes. "She was like a real chariot driver. And it looked so fun that I was wishing she'd been the one up on the beach, and I'd been her: the charioteer." Meanwhile, Kate hadn't told Tim about how she had nearly soiled her pants in a panic as the water swirled up around her ankles, or how Cork had absolutely prohibited her from taking a dump right there. And how, when she got to the top of the dunes and saw half the town was watching their drama, she was so glad the lad had laid down the law!

* * *

Cork left Alaska soon after that heroic coal run. With this first fantastic odyssey under his belt, the young man had decided to get on with his life.

Tim and Kate drove him into Soldotna, aimed him toward a plane and kicked him fondly in the tail. "You be good!" they called out after the departing musketeer. They were sorry to see him go. This meant there would just be the two of them hauling coal and firewood, and playing Risk in the lamplight. But it also meant that they could recommence the honeymoon, which was strong consolation.

No matter how hard they worked, that coal bin never did get full.

* * *

Dear Mamasan,

Remember how I said I wanted to come to Alaska to see a winter? Well the sourdoughs say there are only two seasons here: this winter and last winter. I'm happy to report that we do have four seasons. It's just that spring is breakup and no one likes to talk about that much. And the falls go by way too fast.

* * *

By Thanksgiving, Fram's spot had grown messier than a dedicated sty. The Peterses had to crawl their Skidoo through the ever-changing obstacle course of melting manure and rusting freezer parts. A lumpy layer of foulness had slicked the approach down to the bridge, on the bridge itself, and up the other bank. This made crossing Moose Creek trickier than ever. Doubling as both barn and feeding trough, their bridge had turned into an unavoidable bottleneck of goo.

Whenever the creek was frozen-over good and solid, Tim and Kate crossed upstream to bypass Frampton and his sunning bovines altogether. The shortcut also took off nearly a mile, and the only worries were several deep snow craters around the tree trunks in the flat and one ridiculously steep hill behind Brian and Anna's farm.

But if it warmed up for a couple of days and the creek got too soft to ride a machine across, they had to start using the bridge again. There was no way to avoid it.

One day as they passed over the bridge, Kate noticed a hole in the ice just a few feet downstream. She shivered involuntarily. What if the Snyder family was getting their drinking water from that hole? The entire unfortunate arrangement had her wishing that the Snyder family had never left Idaho.

December 20, 1977 - Dear Mamasan, Greetings from the far North!

Christmas is upon us! We cut down a tree and dragged it home and stood it up in the basement. So, now we're all ready for the upcoming festivities. I decorated it with strings of popcorn, dry wild cranberries and blueberries, and six little wooden ornaments that I ordered from Italy, back when we were working on the North Slope. We even wound strands of electric lights from top to bottom, just in case a miracle should occur . . .

Kate had the basement decorated for Christmas.

Power!

TWO DAYS BEFORE Christmas, a miracle did happen when an odd-looking vehicle stepped out of the woods and headed up across the field toward their house. As soon as Tim saw it, he stopped what he was doing and ran inside.

"What is it?" Kate asked. "Do we need the shotgun?" "No. It's Rural Electric. I think we're getting power!"

Was this one of Tim's jokes? She went outside to take her own look at the approaching rig.

There it was. Walking on high, jointed legs. The visiting machine reminded her of a giant mosquito. It was walking easily over their field of five-foot-deep snow, and it was making its way straight to the house.

She saw the lettering. Tim was right. The electric company was paying them a visit! She ran down the steps and burst into the basement. "I'll put on the coffee pot!" the woman of the house announced.

"You got that right." Tim was moving stuff around on his workbench, looking for the outlet box he'd bought a while back. He found what he needed and set to work. It would be a race to see if he could finish wiring up his end before they finished wiring up theirs.

Once the coffee pot was heating on the coal furnace, Kate went back outside and stationed herself to meet the crew when they arrived. Old Neil Goodman's observation had been

dead-on. It was handy to have time to prepare for whatever came out of those woods.

As it got closer, she could see that the pachyderm-sized, insect-shaped machine was just a huge tracked-vehicle. When it came to a stop she called up. "You gentlemen sure are a welcome sight. Are you here to hook up our electricity?"

All four men smiled down at her. "Yes ma'am," the crew boss said.

"Oh, that's wonderful! My husband's inside installing a light box as we speak."

"Well that's good, because it won't take us long to get you some power. We should be done pretty quick."

Kate gushed in gratitude. "Oh, thank you so much! You can't imagine how glad we are to be getting power at last. We've been on the waiting list for a year and a half."

Even as she was saying this, Kate guessed these men were well aware of how much their service meant.

"Would you like to come in for coffee when you're finished out here?"

"We sure would. Thanks," the spokesman of the group said. After a while, the men came inside to warm up, visit with Tim and Kate, and polish off a pot of coffee.

"You folks are now 'the end of the line,'" one of the men said.

"Yay!" Kate told them this was the best day of her life. The four men sat calmly, like this was just another day at work. And she guessed that maybe for them, it was.

Half an hour later the crew buttoned and zipped their coveralls before heading back outside to finish hooking up the Peterses' line. That last part of the procedure went quickly. Before Kate knew it, she heard the huge machine starting up. She ran outside and got there just in time to hear the crew boss call out from high atop his weird-looking sleigh, "Ho-ho-ho! Merry Christmas from Rural Electric!"

The huge thing backed up, rocked to a stop for a quick gear change and began its awkward stagger back down the mountain.

After watching it go Kate went back inside. "They're gone," she said.

"Well, I'm done with the light box," Tim said. "Let's try it out and see if anyone salutes it." He plugged a "trouble lamp" into the box he'd just finished wiring. The bulb blazed with light.

Kate danced and hooted, and Tim grinned broadly. "Where's an extension cord? We need to try plugging in the Christmas tree!" the bride proclaimed.

Since they'd never—until that second—had any power to extend, finding the extension cord took some time. Tim finally found a paint-stained one in a miscellaneous box Neil had handed down. He plugged one end into the tree lights and paused to wait for Kate to get ready for the wondrous event.

"Would you care to do the honors?" he offered. "No, you go ahead. I'll just watch."

"Tell me when you're ready."

"Let the games begin!" Kate cried.

Tim plugged in the extension cord and the festooned tree shot to life.

It was a sight to behold, this glowing symbol of hope and peace. And its light would shine out through their window to temper the black of night for a century to come.

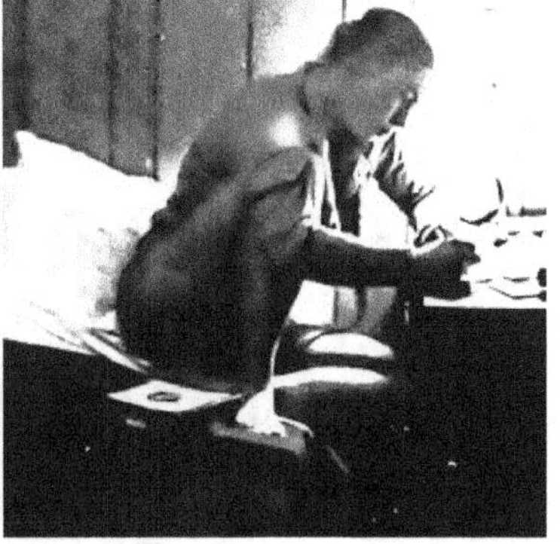

December 26, 1977 – Dear Mamasan,

News flash: Guess what! I'm writing this by light bulb. Yup. We've got electricity! It was Rural Electric's Christmas gift to us!

Late Merry Christmas and early Happy New Year to you! Thank you for the huge bowl and the wonderful blankets. We opened them yesterday, and they're perfect. I promised Tim I would try baking bread as soon as we get an oven. This bowl will be great for mixing and kneading. And of course, we can always use the blankets. Your packing job was ingenious . . .

Two days after Christmas, the pair headed into Footprint, went to the Coffee Café, and had a big celebratory breakfast. They took showers, did the laundry, bought a fancy new citizen's-band radio with a ten-foot antenna, got groceries, filled the water cans, and then headed home.

* * *

By the next evening "Victory Garden" had become the newest blip on the Sleeping Moose airwaves and Tim and Kate had started getting an insider's earful on what was happening on every farm outside of town.

Whenever Tim had the volume turned up, all sorts of cryptic messages squawked out into the kitchen.

"'Belle of the Ball' calling 'Windy Ranch.' Come in. Over." "This is 'Windy Ranch.' What's up, Dorothy? Over." "Have you seen Walter down your way? He needs to pick up those two goats before he heads home for supper. Over."

"He's over to Crestman's Ridge. I'll tell Jim to tell 'im when he gets there. Say, are you plannin' on goin' to the equipment auction at mile 108? Over."

"Not sure yet. It depends on the weather. Over."

. . . And so on.

The clipped conversations that spurted out intermittently through the long winter nights kept everyone who was connected to the rural airwaves informed, as well as entertained.

The end of the line.

At the end of the road.

CHAPTER SEVEN
Winter, 1978

Siberia Calling

TO AN ISOLATED soul, being able to call for help felt like the greatest thing since sliced bread. They weren't totally alone now and maybe they could even get to know some other neighbors by their voices and CB handles. And Kate could find out what had just happened, and what was about to happen up and down the Kenai River.

One of their earliest radio chats was with a fellow who lived up near Cooper Landing. Rumor had it that Hank Almay had struck it rich in uranium. Tim longed for details of the treasure hunt, but Hank was tight-lipped. Apparently, his fortune had been found and then lost.

Slowly they put names to all the callers out there around them and Kate began picturing sleds filled with friendly folks arriving for gala Christmases at Victory Garden. She knew their parties would be grand affairs—just as soon as they had a house to invite folks into.

Dear Mamasan,

We have a CB radio now, so you don't have to worry about us up here. We can call for help, if we need to. And you can reach us if there's an emergency, although you'd need a ham radio, and I'm not even sure you could reach us from Hawaii. Rumor has it there's a guy with a big setup on Maui who likes to serve as a go-between. I'll write with more details when (if) I get them. In the meantime, if you need to reach us in an emergency, it's still best to call the radio station in Soldotna, KSRM, Channel 920, and have them broadcast your message over the "Hi Line." Someone will get word to us, if we don't happen to hear it ourselves. Incidentally, sometimes there's an atmospheric skip, and we can hear Siberia! I wonder if they can hear us?

Love to you.

* * *

Early in the New Year, Tim came home from Footprint with a mystery box tucked between groceries in the box sled. Inside was a small black and white TV. He unplugged their tree of glory and plugged in the new icon. Kate wasn't exactly overjoyed, but a TV might be helpful for their first true winter endurance test. The tree went outside by the front door, where it rested quite happily for the next several months. The anointed TV took its place.

Tim loved his new television. His favorite show that winter was The Prisoner, which showed on Tuesday nights. That meant that if they went into town on a Tuesday, they usually ended up rushing home to catch The Prisoner. There was something about watching his hero almost get away, only to be snatched up again by some crashing reversal of circumstance, that kept Tim riveted. Kate knew "Agent Six" would never get out so she avoided the show. She found its futility depressing.

January 10 - Dear Mamasan,

I almost miss Hawaii. It's winter here and we're snowed in. Even with two snow-machines, it's tricky going into town. You never know what the weather will be like on your way home. Riding through woods on a clear quiet night is heavenly. But in a snow storm it's not that much fun.

Don't lose the trail in a whiteout!

If driving the road in perfect conditions was a dream, Goodmans' field in a total whiteout could be a nightmare.

Whiteout

IN WINTER, UNEVENTFUL runs to Sleeping Moose took nearly half an hour each way, and a trip to Footprint was more than double that. Any problem along the way could triple the time. Their sojourns to town grew less and less frequent, as each venture proved more and more arduous.

It was Tuesday, and they were returning home from Footprint. The Land Cruiser was packed full of clean laundry, water, and enough food to last them for a week.

A menacing cloud hovered overhead and Kate gazed out into the eerie cast of white that had overtaken the night. "We need to get home before this storm closes in," she said.

Tim nodded. Blowing snow was already starting to obliterate the solitary ribbon of pavement that punched through a wilderness between Footprint and Sleeping Moose. He leaned forward to see better in the thickening whiteness.

Finally, they hung a left at the post office and slithered up the first forty feet of their road. Tim parked at the wide spot next to all the other Round Top rigs. Even if it had four-wheel-drive and a winch, this was as close to home as an automobile could go at present. From here, everyone on the mountain would be snow-machining in 'til spring.

Together they heaved the forty-pound water cans up and over the high sides of the sled box and stood them in a row along its bottom, then balanced out the weight with cases of canned goods. The laundry bag sat in front of the week's-worth of water, and perishables went on top.

By the time the car was empty, the sled's cargo reached higher than its wooden sides. By now the wind was really howling. Hoping to keep the dehydrated groceries dry, the couple struggled to cover everything with a wildly flapping tarp. A pair of snowshoes went on the very top. Usually these were for emergencies, but tonight they would help to hold down the tarp. Tim took his place as captain, and his first mate sat behind. She snugged her arms around his waist.

"Ready?"

"Yup."

"Okay. Here we go!" Tim opened the throttle and used a sideways rocking motion to ease the frozen tracks loose.

Kate was looking overhead at the white sky. On a perfectly still moonlit night, snow-machining was like flying through glitter. That's when she loved the six-mile ride home, leaning with the turns, bending her knees to ease the bumps, looking ahead at a sparkling trail diving seamlessly under the double-wide ski.

But on a night like this . . .

It looked bad. The cloud above them had grown thick and solid, blotting out all hint of a moon. Too bad. There would be no glitter on their journey home tonight. Instead, a fierce white wind was now making it hard see obstacles and snags or to follow vague directions home.

Luckily, when they got to the bridge, they were able to zoom right over it with no delays. And once they'd re-entered the shelter of the woods, the giant spruce trees waving like flight-deck attendants guided Tim up the twisting road through Moose Flat.

At last the machine climbed out of the woods and passed through Goodmans' vacant farmyard. They launched out onto the all-white sea of the flat upper field. Here the snow was five feet deep and the gale was blowing full-force. With no trees to slow it down, stinging needles of frozen water flew horizontally, whipping Kate's cheeks as she craned to catch a glimpse of any landmarks. The painful effort was useless. The world had gone blank. She tucked her face back down against Tim and hoped he could see well enough to navigate.

Once they made it across this field and back into the trees, there would be one more downhill and a hundred yards of woods, before making that last turn, and getting a clear shot up the hill to the house. Of course, they would need to be able to see the house, in order to aim for it. Luckily, Kate had left one light burning inside. Now she was hoping it would be shining out through the front window to guide them home.

But first, they had to get across this field.

Tim would have to rely on the flagged marker poles they'd set up earlier to show him where the trail of packed snow led across the void. The trick was to stay on the trail. If they veered off it by more than a foot on either side, they would bog down for sure.

He searched ahead, saw not one flickering flapping fleck of a fluorescent flag, and began to blindly feel his way across the ocean.

Five seconds into the crossing, the doomed vessel veered off to the side and dove into soft snow. Tim and Kate both flew off. Neither one was hurt, but the machine's front was buried and the engine had died.

"Are you okay?" Tim shouted through the snowy rage. Kate nodded, shot him a thickly mittened "thumbs-up," and gave a shrug. Obviously, they were off the trail.

Tim unhooked the sled, and Kate tried to hold the Skidoo's back end up, to prevent it from sliding down any deeper. But the vehicle was too heavy for one woman, albeit a strong one, to lift. When it sank another foot, Kate let go.

Now they really were in trouble, with no transportation, and no direction home, somewhere in the middle of a whiteout.

"I'll hike up to the house, and come back with the other machine as soon as I can. You stay here with the sled, and wave this flashlight when you hear me coming back."

Kate looked back the way they had just come, saw that their tracks had already blown over, and nodded. Although being stranded in a whiteout wouldn't be fun, she figured fighting her way up the hill through waist-deep snow would be less fun. Plus, they'd need to be able to find their stranded supplies and get them home. She would wait like a beacon in this center of nothingness, and wait to be rescued. That was the simple plan they settled on out there, in the middle of nowhere.

Tim untied the snowshoes and started strapping them over his "bunny boots." With several layers of felt insulation, the regulation USAF rubber footwear looked like marshmallows stuck on the ends of his legs, but everyone knew they kept a fellow's feet warm and dry.

Kate watched solemnly as her partner set out on his mission. At first, she tried shining the beam ahead for him. The cone of light bounced back at her.

"Turn off the light for now. Save the batteries!" Tim shouted over his shoulder. The wind blew most of his words away, but Kate understood and switched off the torch. Her companion vanished into the white night, leaving Kate alone.

She knew that as soon as he reached the house her husband would get the single-track Skidoo and a strong rope and come back for her. She had the easy job: just sit tight and be ready to wave the flashlight when she heard him. She hunkered down on the lee side of the sled to wait, and hoped she would outlast the cold.

This was the kind of situation where one contemplated whether God is, or is not. Now Katherine Cutting Peters began doing just that. Right then, she was wishing she believed in a kind, omnipotent entity. Having grown up surrounded by scientists, she harbored some deeply-entrenched doubts. And yet, Kate was also somewhat of a mystic. A seeker. As a girl, she had once stood beside an ancient Hawaiian temple and asked God to show up. When a sudden, potent rush of wind blew in from the ocean, Kate was overwhelmed with a sense that each rock in that monument had been—and was still—laden with faith-filled power. The prayers of a thousand souls enveloped her in that wind, and the unnerved lass fled the he'iau in a hurry.

Now, waiting in a whiteout, Kate thought of a road sign she had passed once. It read, 'Some things have to be believed to be seen.' That philosophical conundrum led Kate to another, more analytically based riddle: Which came first, the chicken or the egg? She supposed the two concepts were probably ideological antitheses. Anyway, both answers were beyond her. But all the unsolvable mysteries did manage to keep her mind occupied until eventually, she saw a shaft of light bumping back toward her.

The faint sound of an approaching engine told her it was time to jump into action. Kate untucked her frozen legs and struggled to stand up. She managed to flick on the flashlight, and started waving it, and yelling, "Hello! Hello! Over here!" She hailed Tim like a maniac, relieved to know that she wouldn't be dying tonight.

When the two met up, they made quick work of tying the rope between both vehicles. They dug, tugged, and pushed until they were finally able to get the front ski pointed upward. Once it broke through the surface, Tim restarted the rescue machine and towed the bogged one back onto packed snow. They dug away the fast-growing drift that had nearly swallowed the front of their freighter, hooked the tongue back onto the freed rig and, with a lot of yanking and pushing, managed to get the loaded box sled up out of the depths and back onto the packed trail. Kate drove the lead machine, and Tim followed with the cargo load, and they retraced Tim's fresh track, one Skidoo behind the other, heading for that light in the window, and its promise of warmth inside.

Home at last, they unloaded the sled in record time, brought in the stores, and shoved their thick door shut against the wind. Tim stoked up the fire, and they both stripped off their wet gear, hung their coveralls on nails beside the furnace, and left their boots to drip down through the cracks between the floor planks and puddle in the dirt below.

Pajamas and slippers went on. There would be no trips to the outhouse on this night. Kate was glad the coffee can that she kept under the bed was nice and empty and ready to go, because she was most definitely in for the night.

Five minutes later, Tim was turning on his TV set, elated that they'd made it home just in time for his show.

Kate glanced over at the screen. Yup, there he was: old Agent Six still staring out through the bars. Kate knew he wouldn't be getting away this time either, but if Tim wanted to watch it, that was fine with her. She was just happy to be home. "Do you want some hot chocolate?" she asked her hero. "I'm having some."

Winter transportation parked out front. Privy in background.

That front door was always a welcome sight.

* * *

After any good snowstorm, fresh tracks evidenced the secret passage of all their wild neighbors. Little mice, ptarmigan and spruce hens, snowshoe hares, moose, bear, and even an occasional wolf crept silently past the farm, and each creature left its unique calling card. When the sun finally popped out after a fresh snowfall Kate liked to snowshoe around the open perimeter to note with delight each visitor's new trail. For her, snowshoeing was one of the best parts of winter.

How divine it felt to cross a virgin snow scape.

Stopping to turn and look back. Seeing your lone tracks leading to this spot, with no one else's tracks going forward was a fabulous feeling. It was exhilarating to realize that no human being had set foot there before her.

Another one of Kate's great joys of living in the woods was being able to pee outside. Although men clearly had the advantage in this arctic arena, if she was out at night squatting under the stars, and she happened to hear a pair of wolves howling to each other, Kate thrilled to be a part of this magical world. She and her man were truly living with one foot off the edge of civilization. "What a hoot!" she acclaimed with private delight.

* * *

The rest of that winter passed peacefully. The pioneers continued their honeymoon bliss, daring outside nudity and midday love on their red iron bed with the rose-strewn quilt.

Also, no one died.

CHAPTER EIGHT
Spring, 1978

The M-37

WINTER EVENTUALLY RETRACTED its brutal fist and the harsh cold finally blurred. When the ground was bare of snow, Tim went out to reclaim their trail marker flags from the Goodmans' field. He wore a mischievous grin when he returned.

"Look what I found down in the field," he said. "It was lying there glinting in the sun. I thought you might like to have it."

Kate was instantly alert. "Is it gold?"

"No . . ." Tim said mysteriously.

He whipped the treasure out of his jacket pocket, brushed it off, and held it up for Kate to see. "It's corned beef! I found this can lying exactly where we bogged down last winter. Remember that night?"

"Please shoot me if I ever forget it."

* * *

That April they purchased a Skidoo Alpine. This model was the "pickup truck" of snowmobiles. It cost them a bundle, but its load capacity and the key-start feature had Kate excited. Now she would be able to start the family vehicle anytime, anywhere. The salesman rode it right up to their door, which was some great delivery service, and Tim ferried him back down to his truck and trailer. When Tim got back, Kate began practicing, right away.

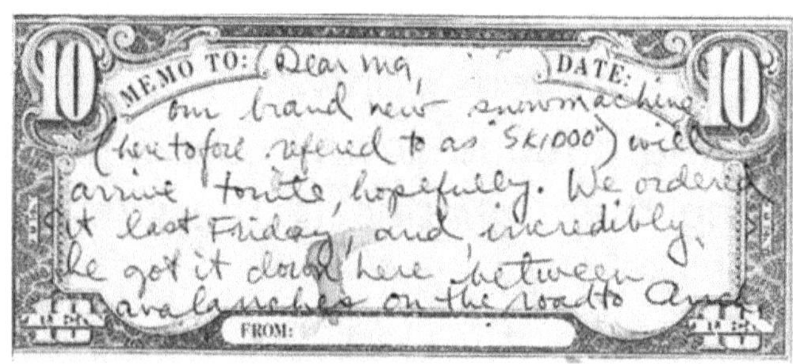

Practicing on the new Alpine.

Glad to have a snow-machine "pickup" and a covered trailer for getting supplies home.

Between the Toyota and the three Skidoos, they now had reliable access for all but twenty percent of the year, the exceptions being six weeks of breakup and half of fall. During those two seasonal transitions, folks on the mountain still had to walk at least part of the way home.

* * *

In May, they decided to solve their road problems—once, and for all—by traveling up to Anchorage to purchase a 1953 Dodge Power Wagon pickup that Tim had found through an ad in the paper.

The moment the couple saw it they both loved it.

The honorably discharged M-37 still sported its olive-drab camouflage and massive Army-issue tires with gigantic treads. The dashboard was home to tons of gauges, switches and buttons. It even had blackout lights, which was something Kate had never heard of before. And there were more levers on the floor than she knew what to do with. The giant workhorse also came with a ten-foot-long detachable A-Frame boom that Tim said would come in handy when it was time to raise the logs for the new house. After his experiences in the war, he was sure this truck would go through any terrain.

Bill Of Sale

Michael ___ ___, the SELLER, in considera-
tion of the sum of _1,500_ DOLLARS
($_1,500_) received from ___ ___
the BUYER, hereby on this _18th_ day of _May_
___, 19_78_, sells to the BUYER, the p   l
property described as: _1953 Dodge Power Wagon, M-37, 3/4 ton, Green Camoflage, PTO Winch, 10 ft Boom, As IS_

and warrants that
title to and right ___ the p___   ___ umbrances that g___
that the SELLER will defend ___   ___ed in the SELLER ___
all persons.   ___ against the unlawfu___ ___

Tim and Kate caravanned the truck home around Turnagain Arm and over the mountains. It was slow going, since the antique shook like an old lady whenever it went over thirty-five miles per hour. They parked it at the turnoff in Sleeping Moose and Skidooed home from there. One day soon they would be driving it all the way up to their door.

The M-37 still waiting to get home.

May 25, 1978 - Dear Mama,

The road still isn't drivable yet. Luckily, there's enough snow in the shady patches to travel by snow-machine.

In some spots, we need to run on mud, which isn't good for the tracks. But it sure beats walking. We've had nothing but rain for so long, I wonder if we'll ever see blue sky again.

Any day a rig could get them up to the front door was a great day.

* * *

June 10 - Hi Mamasan,

The snow is nearly gone. This might be the last time we can use the Skidoo this winter. If you don't hear from me for a while, don't worry. We're going in tomorrow to buy a ton of food and supplies. I'll mail this then. Breakup's almost here. Love, K and T

P.S. Again, I must ask you about 'seeing the elephant.' Will I know it when I see it? I'm keeping my eyes open but so far there have been no sightings.

* * *

Kate had called the doctor on their previous trip to town. She thought that she might be pregnant. The doctor had told her to bring in a urine specimen. Today they would be going into Footprint for a load of lumber, showers, laundry, water, a few groceries, and to find out if they had started a family. Kate carefully caught her first issue of the day in a mini-mayonnaise jar and stowed it in a snow bank to keep it cool 'til they were ready to go. After breakfast they gassed up, hooked the flatbed sled behind the Alpine, loaded up the laundry and the water cans, and headed to town. The spring temperatures had made the ice on the creek mushy, so they couldn't take the shortcut and would have to brave Fram's place.

Now they were entering Frampton's zone, and Tim slowed down to traverse the item-strewn area. Kate held her breath and kept the little jar as far away from herself as possible as they began slaloming through the run of nasty patches.

"Whoo-eey!" Kate gasped after they were safely across the bridge. "I sure wish he'd settled someplace else. It's a pain having his junk all over the road here."

"Better here than next door," Tim reminded her.

They got to the transfer spot and offloaded the dirty laundry and empty water cans. Kate got into the Toyota and clamped the mayo jar between her thighs, ready for the twenty-mile drive to Footprint.

Thirty minutes later, Tim deposited Kate and her jar in front of the little house that served as a doctor's office. Ten minutes after that, Kate came out with the news. "He'll have the results next week," she said. ". . . So, shall we go get showers?"

After showers and laundry at the Wash Inn they shopped for lumber and miscellaneous construction supplies before driving across town to order a dozen Rhode Island Reds at the feed store. Kate, suddenly interested in nesting, said she wanted to start with a few chickens.

Tim parked right next to an old orange compact car out front, and they both got out and entered the store.

Not surprisingly, there were two young Nikolaevskite couples shopping inside.

These "Kenai cousins" looked so foreign and so fantastic that Kate couldn't help stealing glances from the other end of the aisle, while Tim studied some fancy-looking chicken feeders.

The striking foursome made their purchases, and were getting into their orange sedan when Tim and Kate stepped up to the sales desk to purchase a feeder and order the chicks. The clerk said they would arrive in a week and that they would be coming by mail, which sounded weird. Where would they be coming from, that they'd have to be mailed? And how comfortable could it be for day-old chicks to ride in the belly of a mail plane? Or in a truck traveling up the Alcan Highway either, for that matter?

The two picked up a week's worth of groceries and filled the empty water cans. After all the usual town errands, they headed back to the Sleeping Moose turnoff, parked and unloaded the lumber, laundry, groceries, and water, and packed the sled for what would probably be the last time that winter.

Four hours of sunshine beating down since morning had done a lot of damage to the trail, especially around Frampton's. All that manure had turned nice and oozy, and a couple of times Kate had to get off to push. Breakup had arrived in southern Alaska. Anything that wasn't melting now, was permafrost.

It looked like they'd be walking when they went back in a week to hear the doctor's report and pick up their chicks.

* * *

Now that they had hens on the way, the couple needed to get going on a henhouse. Wading through ankle-deep spring mud, Tim and

Kate started building a chicken-sized barn. Sawing and hammering, and stopping for a sandwich now and again, they were both happy to be working side by side again, despite the muck of a spring thaw.

After four days of fun, they had a miniature red barn constructed for the fowl. Sabretooth had watched the project intently, and he looked ready for some baby bird playmate fun.

With two days left to go before they would be heading back into town, they figured they might as well get started on the greenhouse. The plan was to build a frame of two-by-fours and screw on the Air Force storm windows that Tim had already refurbished. They'd been leaning against the back wall of the basement for nearly a year.

The pair got half the frame up before it was time to head back into town to get the doctor's report. Tim was excited, already convinced that Kate was pregnant. Still, he guessed it would be good to get a second opinion.

Kate was almost as excited to be picking up their chicks as she was about maybe being pregnant. She was just sorry they hadn't ordered them a week earlier. "I wish we'd bought the chicks two weeks ago so we could have ridden them home on the Alpine. Carrying them up the mountain will be a pain," she admitted.

"Maybe this is the day we should see how the M-37 does in the mud," Tim said with a smile. "I think we can get all the way up to the house now. We could walk down to the turnoff this morning, and try driving home this afternoon. How does that sound?"

"That sounds good," Kate smiled.

After breakfast, they walked down the hill, ready to try driving their biggest, newest rig all the way down to Footprint, and then all the way home to their door.

As they approached the Korean War relic, its A-frame boom and the super-duty winch protruding from the front bumper made it look almost formidable. But Kate smiled when she approached, because some former owner had painted a whimsical mustache on its upper lip, just above the radiator. And that made it look friendly. They climbed up into the unadorned tin cab and closed their doors.

Once inside the truck, Kate inhaled the fabulous scent of its vintage leather bench seat. Surely, this was the sweetest-smelling car upholstery she'd ever come across. Or maybe it smelled good because she was pregnant. She didn't know.

Tim started the engine, explaining each step as he went through the convoluted procedure. They rumbled away at a conservative thirty miles an hour, and were in Footprint by lunchtime.

First stop was the doctor's office, where the nurse confirmed Tim's suspicion. The couple took a good long look at each other, and decided to celebrate the news with some six-dollar hamburgers. On to the bath house, for laundry and showers. After they'd filled the water cans and packed a month's worth of groceries in the back of the truck, they headed over to the feed store to pick up the chickens.

The Fowl Rode the Foul Road

"HERE THEY ARE," the clerk said. He shoved a shoebox-shaped carton across the counter. The box had several air holes around the top, through which a pitiful cacophony punctuated an already-dramatic day.

Kate peeked in through one of the small holes. She saw a breathing mound of feathers with a lot of wide-open, plaintiff beaks huddled in one corner. She left Tim to pay for the chicks, and carried the box out to the truck.

Their dissonant symphony continued unabated as she crossed the lot, but when she opened her passenger's side door and the loud creak of the old M-37's hinges startled the chicks, they abruptly stopped their whining.

Kate climbed up onto the running board, set the box on the seat, slid in beside it, and started humming to help her little fluffs relax. It seemed to be working, until Tim opened his own squeaky door, and the startled peepers struck up another chorus of woe. To say that it was loud inside that bare metal cab would be to downplay the unbelievability of the racket that followed the starting of that M-37's giant engine. Conversation was impossible as the two headed home.

They had traveled nearly ten miles before the hum of the truck's huge tires eventually calmed the babies, and they quieted. Kate closed her eyes and began to reflect on the doctor's news. She knew one undeniable fact about having a baby: once it was in there, it had to get out. And she'd heard that was a painful process. And then what? Living up on the mountain required a strong partnership. Would she still be able to pull her share of the load with a baby in one hand? Things were going to change, that was for sure. Kate determined she would contribute as much as she could before she morphed into a full-fledged mother. After contemplating the future for a while, she guessed everything would work out naturally.

They stopped to collect the mail at Sleeping Moose, then turned up their road. This would be the test. Would they make it all the way to the house?

When Tim stopped the truck and killed the engine at the top of the first rise, Kate was visibly disappointed.

"I thought we were driving all the way home today."

"The road's still pretty muddy," he said. "We'll need to put on chains, but I think we can make it."

He swung down out of the truck, pulled his seatback forward, and started rifling around behind it. "I'll need your help putting these on," he said as he began yanking out the long rusty links.

"Okey-dokey," his partner said, relieved that they were still on target for a drive to the front door. "What do you want me to do?"

"Help me lay these chains out in front of the tires," he said. He was fighting to separate one set of links from the twisted glob of chain.

Without hesitation, Kate lifted the carton of chicks off her lap, set it on the seat, and slid down out of the oversized vehicle. She bent and picked up a section of chain and started shaking it free. It was hard work, and she puffed and grunted as she struggled to unkink her share of the mess. At last, she got one set freed from the snarl and dragged it around to the front of the truck. Tim already had one set laid out and had started working on a second. Pregnant or not, she would need to double her efforts on this second set if she wanted to keep up.

After a lot of effort, the pair had four tire chains separated and stretched out straight, one in front of each tire.

"Now get in and drive forward slowly," Tim directed. "It's important to get all four tires centered on the chains so we can pull 'em up tight."

"Okay," Kate said, concerned that she might not be able to see the chains over the huge fenders.

"Watch for my signals," he called. "I'll guide you."

"Okay," Kate said again.

While waiting for Tim's nod to start the engine, Kate mentally ran through the sequence that would make the truck fire up, and worried that her mechanical abilities might be pushed to the limit just starting the thing.

Tim gave the signal.

She worked her way through the steps he'd shown her earlier that day:

1. Engage lever on the electrical starter knob.
2. Lift side lever to turn on ignition.
3. Press plunger on floor with left foot.
4. Pump gas pedal with right foot.

She was elated when the M-37 responded properly and sprang to life.

Of course, the jerk of the igniting engine woke the chicks and they began squawking again, but Kate ignored them and concentrated on her gassing and steering. Following Tim's cues, she edged the truck forward and back until they eventually had one gigantic wheel centered squarely on each chain. Kate killed the engine and extruded from the cab again, ready to help Tim pull the massive links up over the tires. Once those monsters were fastened, Tim tightened them with crisscrossed Bungee cords. And now they were ready to drive home.

Kate grinned at Tim when he got into the cab. "Guess what I just remembered."

"What did you just remember?"

"Now that I'm pregnant, I get to eat all the ice cream I want!"

Tim turned to her and shook his head. "Sorry babe. No freezer."

"Hmm. True. Okay, I'll just have to develop a taste for something we can keep in the root cellar."

She started to run an inventory of all her epicurean favorites that were blessed with a long shelf-life.

After a good deal of chain clanking and road-bumping they arrived at the creek. The big truck barely fit on the wooden spans, but the chains held firm and easily clawed up the far side, biting through excrement like a hot knife through double-Dutch icing. The M-37 churned through the trough of gunk at Fram's and forged a fresh set of ruts around the slippery bend. Next would be the "lake" section, where Moose Flat basically turned the roadbed into a swamp. This was where the war truck would prove itself. Kate picked up the box of chicks and held it tight against her chest, preparing for the puddles.

Splosh! The Power Wagon traveled five feet out into the bog, plunged into a mud hole, and stopped. The sudden halt sent Kate careening forward, while a surge of muddy water washed across the windshield. Luckily, the box she held to her chest lodged itself against the truck's bare metal dash, stopping her face just inches from the myriad of sharp-edged devices. "Saved by a carton of chickens," she declared.

Tim gunned the engine. A tidal wave flooded outward on all sides but the truck didn't shift from its epicenter. The sad truth was that their most reliable rig had just stopped dead in some mighty deep water.

"Are we stuck?" Kate asked, fearing the worst. "Yes dammit! I'll go see how bad it is."

"Okay. I'll take care of the little peeps here. They're all agitated again." Indeed, they had recommenced their complaining with a vengeance. So far, her first day of motherhood wasn't going the way she might have imagined. Whatever she'd been picturing, she'd been way off. Here they were, up the creek in a mega-puddle without a paddle to get home.

The ex-soldier climbed out of his military muscle car and waded around to see what things looked like in front. From the expression on his face, Kate could tell that the rig was good and stuck.

She called out, "What's the plan, 'Captain?'"

"I guess we get to try out the winch," Tim said, looking half annoyed, half pragmatic, and maybe a little jazzed at the prospect. "We're lucky this truck is so tall. The winch is still above water."

He bent down and untwisted the end of the winch cable from its figure-eight twist around the front bumper. Tim unpinned the winch drum and gave the unfamiliar cable a yank. That started the drum unwinding. He pulled steadily, unrolling stiff cable from the old spool, and aimed for a promising tree that grew on the far side of the mud hole. At sixteen feet beyond the rim of the puddle, he tugged the cable around the spruce tree and pulled it as snug as he could, taking care to insert several sticks to keep from ringing the tree. Then he hooked the winchline back onto itself.

"Okay. Now come around front and throw that lever to lock the drum," he shouted.

Kate was still holding the chickens. She put the box on the seat and slid out of the truck, landing in knee-deep water, and slopped around front to look at the lever he wanted her to throw. Clearly, it had been designed with a man in mind. She figured this thing would be hard to "throw" on the best of days, which—at the moment—this one wasn't. But in truth, she didn't feel different from any other day. And she certainly didn't feel pregnant.

It was time to apply herself the task and put this bugger-of-a-handle in its place. She wrapped both hands around the knob and pulled gamely, as hard as she could.

She was breathless by the time the lever had been lifted, shifted, and locked. But at least the winch mechanism was ready to wind.

"Okay good. Now get in and start the truck," Tim directed. "We'll wind the cable until it's tight, then use the power-takeoff to add first gear to the mix, and walk ourselves out of here," Tim explained.

She waded around the front fender, climbed up into the cab, and talked herself through the entire multi-step ignition-procedure again. As the truck roared back to life, the baby chicks renewed their cheeping sent a fresh round of deafening disharmony echoing through the cab. "Shush," Kate cooed. "You know today isn't going the way

I expected, either. Let's just work together and get the job done. Okay?"

"Depress the clutch," Tim instructed, "and put 'er in first gear. Now push the winch lever forward. It's the one beside the four-wheel-drive lever. Remember?"

Kate sort of remembered. The winch-engager lever was the long stick that looked like a gearshift but wasn't one. She depressed the clutch and pushed forward on the handle.

"Now watch me carefully," he called out. "When I raise my arm like this—he gestured—you let up on the clutch. If I put it down, press the clutch back in."

"Got it," she said. Difficult as it was, she had to get it if she wanted to be home anytime soon.

"When I say, 'engage the winch,' you push the lever forward and slowly let up on the foot pedal."

"Okay," Kate said, hoping he wouldn't add many more instructions.

"Engage the winch!" the commander called out. His first mate followed the order.

"Up-clutch!" he shouted.

Kate up-clutched, and the truck began to strain forward, hauling and crawling itself toward the tree. With both the truck and the winch in gear, they were now traveling as fast as a galloping glacier. Kate couldn't see the winch or the retracting cable, so it was up to Tim to keep the thing from crossing over on itself. If he saw it start to load lopsided, he might gesture for her to steer right or left, but other than that, she would be a passive onlooker just working the clutch.

She remembered his warning that a snapping cable end could kill a man. "You'd better stay out of reach of any flying cable ends," she whispered under her breath. But she knew that her partner would be stepping in to give the cable a tug whenever it started to tangle itself. Fighting the cable was his task, while running the machinery was hers.

Each time he needed to straighten the winding cable, Tim gave her the signal to disengage, and she depressed the inflexible foot pedal—releasing the clutch and disengaging the winch—and held her breath until he had stepped back outside of any breaking cable's lethal perimeter.

Winching took a long time. Finally, Tim shouted, "Whoa!" and Kate pulled back on the long lever. The winch drum stopped rolling. She put the truck in neutral, and winced as she retracted her foot from the clutch. It was burning after all the stops and starts she'd made with the recalcitrant pedal.

Still, this was marvelous. By using both low gear and the winch, this truck had just inched itself all the way to freedom!

Tim called out, "It's time to rewind the cable and get this baby home!"

Kate killed the engine, got down out of the truck, and went around front. She moved the obstinate lever backward to the setting that would allow the cable to rewind, returned to the truck cab and got ready to concentrate on executing all the correct steps in the correct order to restart the M-37 again, rewind the winch cable, and get home.

The rewind process took just as long as the winching and walking part had. Tim released the end of the stiff cable from around the tree and wrestled it straight. Kate thought of Kirk Douglas battling the giant squid as she watched Tim strain to keep the roiling coil from writhing over on itself, or on him. At last, Tim drew his finger across his throat. Kate pressed down on the clutch pedal for the final time, and took the M-37 out of gear.

She watched as her husband—the man with whom she had embarked upon this adventure, and now the father of her unborn child—wrapped the last ten feet of cable in a figure-eight around the bumper. After he'd slipped the end loop over a pin on the drum, he marched around to the driver's door and climbed up, ready to go. Total time elapsed, maybe three-quarters of an hour.

"Let's get home," Tim said, sounding cheery.

Kate understood. She had older brothers. She knew that nothing pleased some men more than getting stuck in a mud hole and getting out again.

Taking over the controls, Tim steered along the high edge of the road and they drove forward about ninety feet. They came to the long-embedded road grader and he veered ten degrees to the right to get around it.

SQ-LUWASH! Stuck again.

And so, it went. They progressed in leapfrog fashion all the way through the marshy area, getting stuck and winching out,

getting stuck and winching out—over and over—until Kate finally ventured a guess. "Maybe it's still too early to drive the road."

Tim wouldn't hear of it. "This thing was built for the U.S. Army. It'll go through anything."

They would persevere and conquer.

* * *

It was evening when Kate finally saw their cheery yellow-painted basement smiling to them from the top of the hill.

When they had parked by the door, the worn-out mother-to-be said, "Congratulations, 'Captain.' You got us home."

"You must be tired. Why don't you go in and lie down? I can unload the truck."

"That sounds good to me. Thanks."

The only thing Kate carried in was the box of traumatized chicks. She opened the top and set the whole thing down inside a large paper towel carton. This would be their temporary home until they were strong enough to move out into the henhouse. The big box had everything: a warming light clipped to the rim, baby bird food, a bed of dry grass, and a jar lid filled with clean water. The birds could come out of hiding when they were ready.

Tim brought in load after load of water and stuff, while Kate rested on the red bed.

"Are you okay?" he asked. "Uh-huh. Just kind of tired."

"And well you might be." He walked over to her and took her hand. "How many women do you think could have done what you did today?" He answered his own question. "Just one: my wife." He kissed her, pressing his big soft lips to hers ever so gently. "Can I get you anything?"

Kate smiled. Her moment had arrived. What did she crave? She made her decision. "Could I have a piece of cheese, please?"

* * *

It had been a hard trip for everyone.

June 17, 1978 –

Happy Birthday Grandma Tutu!

It sounds strange to call you "Grandma Tutu," but guess what? You're going to be a Tutu again! (How's that for a birthday present?) We have a baby due in January.

I know you've been talking about coming up, so may I suggest either September or March? — Unless you'd rather come in January? Ha-ha!

By September the bugs should be gone and the garden looking its best. We could probably drive you all the way up to the house, too. Of course, in March you'd have a new grandchild to see. And you might enjoy snow machining and snowshoeing. You might also see some northern lights. Take your pick, or come both times. In fact, come ANYTIME.

We love you!

With so many projects, Timber was in heaven.

June 21, 1978 – Dear Mama,

I'm just wondering, do babies ever slide out without warning? Should I hold back a little when I'm in the outhouse? What will the first stages of labor feel like? (It'll probably take us a while to get to town so I'll need some warning . . .)

Love always, your last-born.

Chapter Nine

Summer, 1978

Beaming with Pride

WHEN THEY HAD the skeleton of a greenhouse put together, Kate painted it with the most advanced anti-wood-rot-treatment known to man. The stuff gave off a wicked smell and dyed the wood such a vivid teal that it practically glowed. The expectant mother hoped it wasn't causing any damage to the child growing in her belly.

Now to attach the glass.

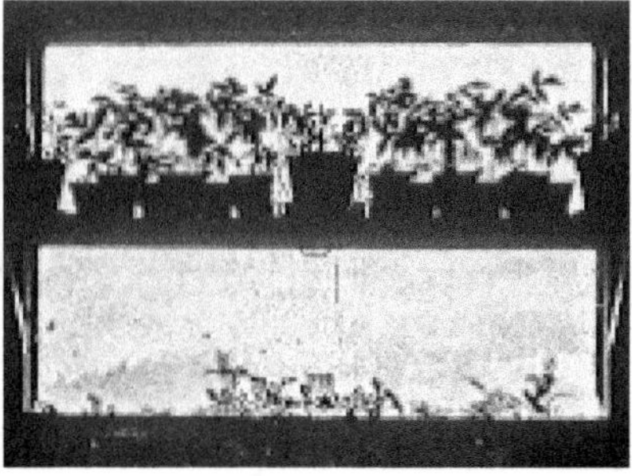

It only took one day to screw the re-glazed windows onto the drying green bones, and Kate's hothouse was ready for business.

She transplanted all the tomato and marigold starts out of the basement window and into their sunshine-filled garden home. Both Kate and her seedlings loved the new glass palace.

* * *

On the second of July, which was the first truly dry summer day to come along, the two decided to tackle a big job that had been waiting for nearly a year: moving the standup freezer out of the Goodmans' barn and transporting it up to their own basement.

This task took all afternoon. They inched the heavy load onto the back of the truck with a gear-and-pulley thing that

Tim called a "come-along," and slowly drove it up the road. It swayed crazily, but eventually their miracle of cold food storage had successfully traveled down the thick plank ramp, through the squat basement door and over to its new home in the corner of Tim's workshop. Once Tim had it plugged in, it kicked on right away and set up a subtle hum that provided a comforting counterpoint to the silence of their solitude. Tim was happy that it worked and Kate was delighted to have a place to store ice cream.

The M-37 looked content to be parked at the house, right next to the peavey hook and the burn barrel.

July 10, 1978 - Dear Mama,

I'm so excited that you're planning to come up to help. Now remember, we're talking about coming out into the wilderness in the heart of an Alaskan winter—so you don't need to come if you don't want to. Of course, we'd love it, if you did. With a light bulb and a heater, (we'll string a wire down there) Honeymoon will be a perfect little guesthouse for you. Doesn't that sound like fun? I think the baby might be almost an inch long now, but I haven't felt any movement yet. (I sure do miss being able to talk with you about babies, and about life in general.)

Love, your little girl who is living on a remote mountaintop and will soon be a mother.

* * *

When they heard that they had a little bundle on the way, they altered their log house plan and opted for an easier-to-maneuver post-and-beam design, instead. Now they just needed a bunch of beams.

Most of the trees they'd previously gathered turned out to be way too thin to make good beams, so they left the nearly two-hundred barked logs resting on their pallets and went out looking for some more substantial poles. Down the road, back in the woods there was a gnarl of large timbers that a survey team had left behind. Felled that spring, the trees were free for the taking. Tim and Kate began going down there several times a week to carve and transport their giant sculptures home.

August 1 - Dear Mamasan,

We're lumberjacking again. It's too bad the logs we already have up here are too spindly to use. Now we're harvesting some logs that a survey team left behind. They make dandy beams. We pick one out, nudge it into position with a peavey and slice off four straight sides of bark.

Picture a pair of oxen grunting and snorting, and that's what we look like when we're moving those trees around. I sit on one end of the log and pull a rope that's tied to the chainsaw handle. I just pretend I'm reeling in a marlin. Tim's nifty lumber-making attachment works sort of like an apple peeler. It takes us about fifteen minutes to slab one side. The work is hard, but the setting is divine.

I love it!

* * *

As soon as one slab of bark fell to the ground, they rotated the heavy log and started cutting a fresh side. Repeating the routine four times rendered one beam. They could usually finish two beams in one summer day. The last task was to carry the squared poles out of the woods and over to the road, straddle the eight and ten-footers across the truck's sides and make the slow drive back up the road.

They'd get home just a little before dusk and stack that day's beams with the others, which were sorted by length and dimension. Tim calculated that they would need a total of fifty-six beams, two extra-long purlins, and one fifty-five-foot ridgepole. That meant there was a lot of cutting to be done that summer, and a lot of hauling.

* * *

August 8 - Dear Mamasan,

Have you ever heard of the Lamaze Natural Birth method? That's pretty much all they do around here. The book says giving birth doesn't really hurt. It says that we call contractions "pains," because we expect them to hurt, so they do. It says I should avoid any movies depicting painful births and any wives' tales or stories about horrible experiences. I don't have a lot of ladies to share stories with around here. There was a woman down in Sleeping Moose who had a stillbirth recently. It was her first baby and she had it at home. Guess I'll skip that adventure and go see the doctor when the time comes.

Since you've had six babies, I'll trust you on this. Now tell me—and only good reports please—what's it like to have a baby?

* * *

"Since we're going up and down the road all the time now, let's use these leftover slabs to corduroy some of the muddiest sections," Tim said one day.

"Good idea," his mate agreed. "But couldn't we use rocks from the side of the road instead of wasting all these slabs? I'd like to save them for fencing. Someday I hope we can have a horse up here."

She ran an alternate plan by him. "Maybe each time we go by a soft spot, we could stop and pick up a couple of big rocks and toss them into the mud hole. Eventually it would fill up and get hard, right?"

Tim shrugged. "It couldn't hurt to try."

But it did hurt. When they tried Kate's idea, the experiment turned out to be a big mistake. Now the soggy spots were worse than ever. In addition to the usual bucking and sliding, they also endured horrid screeching sounds as their truck's underside scraped across the half-buried crags. Each scathing sound made Kate grimace, even though Tim assured her that the military truck's steel skid-plate was protecting it. After

Kate's "brilliant" idea, every trip to and from the logging operation felt less like a drive in the country and more like riding a bull 'til the buzzer sounded.

August 20, 1978 –

Dear soon-to-be Grandma Tutu,

I'll admit that carrying those beams out of the woods is hard. And when we get one out to the road we still need to tip-and-bob it home on the back of the truck. Our new house design calls for fifty-six beams plus three extra-long beams for the roof, so that means we're in for a lot of tipping-and-bobbing. Our road is the worst we've ever seen it. The thing rides like the California Trail.

* * *

August 28, 1978 - Dear Mamasan,

Tim's going up to Fairbanks to look for work in the oil fields. If there is none, he'll be back in a week. If he does get a job, he'll be back for Thanksgiving. It's hard sending your man off, but that's what a lot of women here do. I'll mail this when we go into town to put Tim on the plane. Right now, it's pouring rain, but the road should hold, so don't worry about me. Remember your great-grandpa came across the country in a covered wagon, so it's in our blood. Really, don't worry Mama. I'll be ok.

* * *

September 10 - Dear Mamasan,

Are you sure you want to come up both now, and in January? Tim came home last night, so I'm not alone anymore if that's your concern. But of course, we'd love to have you come!

So, unless you write otherwise, we'll pick you up in Soldotna on the 24th. There are two planes a day, so let us know which one you'll be on.

Love, T+K+ ?

P.S. I just found out I'm not supposed to be carrying heavy items (like forty-pound water cans or eight-foot beams.) Too bad, because I simply must. The yoga stretches should be helping though. This morning I was lying on the floor and I noticed that my belly is no longer flat. It's quite rounded, but way off-center. That's got to be baby, not pasta!

—Still no kicking yet. What does it feel like when a baby kicks?

* * *

Two weeks later Tim and Kate picked up Grandma Tutu at the Soldotna airport. Their excited visitor could hardly wait to tell them about her mini-adventure in Anchorage.

She started with the story right away: "There we were," she said, "six of us waiting to board the plane to Soldotna. About ten minutes before flight time, two pilots came through the waiting room and gave us all a nod, and we got up and followed them out to a fourteen-passenger plane parked on the tarmac."

The woman didn't pause for breath. "We loaded our bags and climbed aboard, fastened our seat belts and watched them do the whole preflight check—which was pretty interesting, since we could see right into the cockpit. But just before we started to taxi, the pilot turned around and asked, 'Is anyone here going to Haines?' And not one of us was going to Haines. 'Well then,' he said, 'you'd better get off now, because this plane is going to Haines!'"

Recounting the episode made Grandma Tutu burst out laughing.

Kate laughed, too. "Welcome to the 'Wild West,' Mamasan. You're on the Last Frontier."

Tim picked up Grandma Tutu's little case. "Is this all you have?"

"Yes, this jacket, two sweaters, new boots, every pair of socks I own, and my coat. I hope that'll be enough."

"Oh, you'll be fine. It's not cold yet, and besides we have tons of warm clothes you can wear."

The young mother-to-be paused and looked at the older, wiser one. "I'm just so glad you've come!" she said. She slipped her arm through the crook of her mother's elbow and they left the building.

When they got to the truck Kate's mother regarded the M-37 with a mixture of sentiment and curiosity.

"Hop in, Mom," Kate said, opening the door for her. The sixty-five-year-older gamely hefted herself up into the antique cab, demonstrating surprising agility. Good for her.

As Tim climbed into the driver's seat and Kate slid in on her right, Mamasan-Grandma Tutu studied all the gauges lined up on the dash, and the gearshifts and pedals on the floor. "Does this truck have blackout lights?" she asked.

Tim nodded. "It's from the Korean era. There's still quite a bit of old military equipment up here in Alaska." He pointed to the third handle on the electrical unit. "This lever operates the blackout option. Up, and you get lights. Down, and you get blackout lights."

"Goodness I haven't seen these since the war," Grandma Tutu said admiringly. She was in love with the truck, Kate could tell. Probably all those fancy gadgets reminded Tutu of her Cessna 152 training flights. She'd been taking flying lessons for a while, something she'd started after being widowed. Kate's mom was the oldest student her flight instructor had ever taught, which was one of the things that made Kate so proud of her. Mamasan had a great spirit.

"How's your flying coming?"

"I'm about to take my solo cross-country. Then just one more test and I'll have my private license."

"That's fantastic, Mama! Everyone is so excited for you. Maybe someday you'll be landing right up here on our mountain."

They got supplies and headed home. As they crossed the Goodmans' flat, upper field, Kate pointed out how it would make a good airstrip, and Tutu nodded.

* * *

"Here we are." They had just bumped to a stop beside the basement. Kate helped her mother down out of the truck, and made a sweeping gesture at the uninterrupted wildness around them. "Welcome to 'Victory Garden.'"

The tutu from Hawaii marveled at their view. "This is just beautiful, you two," she exclaimed.

"Yeah. It's a pretty nice front yard," Kate admitted with false modesty. "And now let us welcome you to our home."

They all went down the basement steps and Tim slid back the bolt. Just before pulling the latch string, he paused and smiled almost apologetically. "This is as far as we've gotten."

He opened the door and ushered his mother-in-law inside their humble underground home.

Grandma Tutu stood and looked around the open room. "Oh! This is wonderful!" she exclaimed, covering their handmade home with her seal of approval.

"You'll be sleeping down in Honeymoon Cottage. Tim fixed it up for you with a light and everything. And the outhouse is just behind the cabin. Watch out: the privy lists a little, but it has a plastic-covered window and a denim-wrapped toilet seat. I hope you won't mind."

The adventurous grandma said she'd be charmed to have her own little cabin to stay in. And she "ooh'ed and ahh'ed" when Kate took her down the trail to show her all the rustic appointments.

After a supper of corned beef hash, which their visitor claimed was the best she'd ever tasted, Kate invited her mother to come along when she went out to close the chicken house. "Do you want to meet the chickens?"

"I want to meet everything!" the matriarch said, jumping up to follow her pioneer child.

On their way to the little red hen house Kate glanced up at the sky. She was hoping the autumn sunset colors would be good, but her expectations were surpassed, by a mile. "Look, Mama!" she cried. "Northern lights!"

Both women stopped in their tracks to watch the unseasonal show.

This was no ordinary display. It was one of the best ones Kate had ever witnessed. She could imagine that they were standing under an upturned, nearly cobalt blue sundae goblet with cranberry sauce oozing out from the base of the

stem and dribbling its way down to the horizon on all sides.

And who knew what her mother was seeing?

The mysterious lights were so incredible that neither woman moved another step, until the explosions of dark red lava ribbons undulating overhead had quieted and faded away.

What a special, wonderful welcome for Tutu. And it wasn't even dark, yet. Or cold.

"Wow!" was pretty much all either of them could say following the two-minute demonstration. After that, meeting the chickens didn't seem so exciting, but Tutu "ooh'ed and ahh'ed" anyway.

They fed the hens, closed the little doors to lock them in and headed back to the cozy basement.

Mamasan said she would be happy to brush her teeth in Honeymoon's open-air washroom. The fact is, Grandma Tutu "ooh'ed and ahh'ed" over pretty much everything she saw and did during that whole rustic Alaskan visit with her pioneering daughter and son-in-law.

She volunteered for the evening trash-burning chore, saying she loved that moment of tranquility under a fading sky. And she did look peaceful out there, silhouetted against the ever-deepening pinks, guarding the glowing embers.

"If you're good, we might even take you to the dump before you go home," Kate teased. "We go over there every so often to get rid of the stuff that we can't burn or turn into compost." True to her word, on Tutu's last day they took a short detour on their way to the airport and made a quick trip to the dump.

When it was time to board her plane, Mamasan claimed she'd loved everything about her visit, including the dump. Kate thought her mama looked so happy against their Alaskan backdrop that she was sort of surprised when Grandma Tutu wanted to go back to Hawaii at all. But she did.

* * *

Two weeks later they were ready to set the first post of their wilderness-lodge dream. Tim had four beams prepared with pegged ends, ready to fit into pre-cut holes in the basement roof. It was a clean design, one which they both hoped would work.

This was it. The day had come.

Tim drove the truck over to where its boom lay in wait, and Kate held up the bottom ends, one at a time, so he could bolt them through huge screw-eyes in the truck's front bumper. Together they wrapped the cable around the roll bar. Tim hoisted the nose so that it pointed high into the air. He tied it off and drove the wobbling beast around to where the four precut beams lay. The bobbing boom made Kate think of an elephant with trunk raised, lumbering across the Maasai Mara. She watched it for a moment before trotting straight across the site to meet Tim when he arrived at the pile of pegged posts.

They hooked the first post onto the truck's chain and pulley and Tim drove it over to the front edge of the basement. He operated the pulley and lifted the ten-inch-square, eight-foot-long timber above the basement roof and set it down as gently as possible beside the first post hole. The pair scrambled up onto the low roof and stood the big beam on its end. When it rested at the edge of its fitted hole, Kate ran to get the camera. She wanted to take a picture of Tim lowering the first post home.

After that, they panted and pulled for the next month, setting post after post, and beam after beam in place.

Timothy "Jack London Jeremiah Johnson" Peters
pursues his quest.

When they got to the overhead beam work, Kate stood on the basement roof and handed tools up to Tim as he needed them. Fearless of heights, and blessed with agility, Tim scrambled over the framework, drilling holes and pounding spikes through angle iron brackets at each joint. The work progressed smoothly, except for occasional damage when someone dropped the peavey hook, or a beam slipped.

Unfortunately, these minor accidents caused gouges in the green tarpaper of the basement roof, which in turn caused a growing number of insulation-drenched leaks to trickle down into the living quarters below. This made Kate anxious to have a roof on before baby arrived. But she was sure they would beat that deadline. They still had nearly four months to get it done.

And wouldn't Augusta Myers be surprised? After all, it hadn't even been three years since they'd first laid eyes on this moose's spot.

Bear Stories

ONE BRISK OCTOBER morning when Kate was outside dumping compost, she saw termination dust powdering the nearby summits. The sight made her pause to enjoy the vista and smell the fall air. . . Was that some movement up in the windbreak?

The grizzlies would be wandering through any day now. Neil had told them this was the bears' regular trail between berry patch and fishing grounds. Kate beat a hasty retreat inside and told Tim she thought there was a bear nearby. They both went over to look through the little window beside their bed.

Sure enough, a big brown bear emerged from the woods and started making his way down into their back yard. Seemingly unconcerned about all the recent changes to his domain, he ambled right past the window, almost close enough to touch. From where they stood watching Kate could see brambles and sticks tangled in his coat.

Suddenly the migrating grizzly veered to the right and started closing in on the compost pile. There he paused to claw up scoops of rotting vegetable matter from the ripening soil. His ultra-strong arms discharged huge clods between splayed hind legs. When the hole was two feet deep, which took less than ten seconds, the bear stuck his snout down into the bottom and pulled out a mouthful of rotting vegetables. He swallowed the greens and then started moving toward the chicken house.

Tim decided it was time to turn on the radio.

When a loud, static-filled voice broke through the silence, the thousand-pound giant lifted his heavy head, snorted and trotted away.

Tim and Kate crossed over to the front window and watched the grizzly bear saunter off down their road. His breath blew out in frosty puffs and his rolling gait made the silver highlights on his shoulders shimmer like epaulets in the morning sun. Wow, what an animal!

That visit reminded Kate of the time Cliff came by and said he'd just shot a grizzly behind their place. With no hunting experience between them the Peterses were drawn by curiosity to head up the hill. They could watch and learn, and maybe even help Cliff butcher the carcass.

When they got to the scene Kate slowed her pace, in case the beast suddenly sprang back to life. When it didn't, she approached and touched the brown fur. It felt prickly and coarse, not at all huggable like a Teddy bear.

Kate observed, while Tim helped Cliff secure one end of a chain around the bear's hind feet. The hunter threw the other end over a sturdy spruce branch, and he and Tim used a pulley to hoist the bear up, until its front toenails were hanging about a foot above the ground. They stopped hoisting and tied off the chain. Once Cliff started skinning, and the fatty hide peeled down like a ripe banana, Kate decided it was time to go back to the house. Yuck! She would never relish that distasteful memory.

But she did enjoy telling folks a story about Cliff and another bear.

It seems Cliff had left some bear bait right outside his cabin door, figuring that if he lured one in close, he wouldn't have to carry it far.

While he was off hunting somewhere, a bear happened by, discovered the bait, and liked what he tasted. He polished off all the hors d'oeuvres and, with his appetite whetted, sliced through one of Cliff 's plastic-covered window holes, and climbed into the cabin. Cliff said he went hog-wild inside.

By the time the hunter got home, his quarry was gone, and the larder was empty. That bear had eaten everything in sight, including a big sack of dehydrated potatoes.

Cliff was sorry he'd missed his bear but Kate secretly felt sorrier for the bear. She figured that when he took that first drink of water and it reached all those potato flakes, he probably exploded.

* * *

". . . He's gone. I'm going back out to the shop." Tim's words broke through her reverie.

She nodded. "And I have my 'thunder mug' to empty," she said, referring to the lidded three-pound coffee can that she kept under the bed.

* * *

Over the next three months the pair toiled through every sunny break that came along, trying to beat the birthday deadline.

Kate was getting anxious, because the intense activity upstairs was taking a significant toll on the tarpaper roofing, and their basement abode was getting wet. She had an empty orange juice can set under each of the most predictable spouts, and she monitored those cans like a zealot. Kate had drawn a ring on the floor around each can to indicate the exact position for accurate replacement after emptying, which she did three times a day. Still, she was barely able to keep ahead of the water. There were now twenty-two cans peppering the pathway between their bed and the front door. This made for some tricky walking, especially at night. Concerned that it would be hard to raise a healthy baby in a damp home, she took on the duty of sweeping any rain or snow off the roof, before it could drain down into the basement. Since it rained or snowed nearly every day, this was an endless task.

Atwood Cutting and Timber

ONE NIGHT, JUST before sleep they were talking in bed and Kate was stroking Tim's hand. "You know one of the reasons I married you was because you have perfectly-shaped hands. They remind me of my daddy's hands, and that was a plus for you."

Tim held up the appendage she had been petting. "And they're 'handy' too. My mother told me so."

"And she was right."

Tim slowly elevated the "perfectly shaped" appendage, until his arm extended over and leaned slightly toward Kate's half of the bed. "Say 'timber,'" he coached.

Kate obliged. "Timber."

The long arm wavered, then tilted, and eventually toppled down onto the bed.

"Ha-ha. Very funny," Kate said.

In truth, it was sort of funny and the two pioneers had taken to playing the joke on each other often over the seasons.

"I should call you 'Timber,'" Kate remarked.

"Speaking of names," Tim began, "we need to talk about a name for the baby."

"Hmmm." She'd already been thinking about a name. "If it's a boy, I'd like to call him 'Neil Brewster,' after my grandpa, and yours, and after Neil Goodman, too."

"Hmm, I like it," Tim said.

"Well, that was easy. And what about a girl's name? Have you got anything in mind?"

"I've been thinking about naming her after you. I love your middle name: 'Atwood,'" Tim said, giving the name a singsong quality.

"I'm honored."

"And how does 'Cutting' sound for a middle name? She could be 'Atwood Cutting.'"

Tim waited for Kate to react. ". . . Get it?"

"As in timber and firewood. Yes, I get it. But will it make her feel that she has to be a lumberjack all her life?"

"If she chooses to live up here, she'll be one by default. A name like Atwood Cutting could be handy in Alaska. And besides, it would always remind her of this unique starting place," Tim argued.

Kate smiled and acquiesced. "Well okay. It does have a ring to it. And by the way, I think I will start calling you 'Timber.'"

That made Tim grin. "Okay."

"Good night, 'Timber,'" she said. She kissed his cheek and rolled away onto her side. Tim rolled onto his side too, so their backs would warm each other. Soon they were both asleep.

The clothes closet.

* * *

A moose in downtown Footprint.

November 30, 1978–Happy Thanksgiving Mama!

My due date is in six weeks. Lamaze classes are meeting weekly now. So far, it's been fairly easy getting there, but things might get interesting when we have to start going in by snow-machine.

Did you hear about Jonestown? Good grief!

Chapter Ten
Fall, 1978

Night at the Old Hotel

IT WAS TUESDAY, December 10th, and Tim had just come in from his outside shop. Another war remnant, this corrugated-steel Quonset hut made a perfect shelter for repairing vehicles. They had disassembled it and transported it up to their place during a lull in the lumberjacking. Tim had built a long work bench and installed a second G.I. wood stove in it, and he enjoyed working out there whenever bad weather put a hold on their house-building project.

"It feels like there's snow on the way," he said. "Maybe we shouldn't go in for Lamaze class tonight."

"I think we should go regardless," Kate countered. "I'd rather be a little sorry now, than a lot sorry later. If we can't make it into town when the time comes, and this ends up being a home delivery, we'll need to know what to do."

Tim looked thoughtful. "Okay. I can see that you feel strongly about it. Maybe we should take the truck, and make a coal run. We'll already be almost halfway there." He consulted the tide chart. "Low tide is at four. If we leave at ten, we can get over to Anchor Point, and still get back to Footprint in time for class."

Kate shuddered at the suggestion, but agreed to his proposal.

Tim turned and started to head back outside. Then he stopped, to add a stern order. "And you'd better not end up having a home delivery!"

The prenatal Peterses headed into town late that morning, leaving enough time to run to the beach and check out the shoreline for coal.

There was none, so they drove back to Footprint, took showers, and ate, before powering up the bluff to the midwife's little blue house. Three other dutiful couples entered along with them.

Two hours later, the class was over and everyone emerged another lesson closer to parenthood. Kate paused to wave goodbye to her co-laborers before climbing up into the cold truck.

Tim was looking at the sky. "Let's get going. I think the snow's about to hit."

Kate peered out at the night. He was right. It was pitch black and totally starless. And the air felt thick and heavy. "Yup. Let's get home."

As soon as Kate was settled, Tim gave the two electrical levers their oppositional twists, pressed the big floor plunger with his left foot, and gave it gas.

Nothing happened.

"Hmmm." Tim started fingering his mustache, which meant he was thinking. He tried flipping the light lever up. No light. He grunted and plunged the starter button to the floor again. The old Dodge refused to sputter. "It looks like we might have an electrical problem," Tim said. He rifled through the glove compartment, grabbed the flashlight, and climbed out of the truck. "Let me see if I can find the short. You stay here. I'll just be a minute."

The only thing Kate could do under a hood was hold a flashlight, and Tim was handling that part just fine. She sat tight and waited.

He searched under the hood for a few minutes. Still puzzled, he got back into the truck and looked around under the dashboard. Tim sighed. "Well babe, it looks like we're not going anywhere tonight. I won't be able to tell what the problem is until I can see this thing in the daylight." He paused. "I hope that works for you."

Kate didn't see an alternative, and said so.

They sat there in the dark truck, wordless and perplexed, twenty-six difficult miles from home.

"Well shall we get a room?" she finally suggested. "The Old Hotel is on the left at the bottom of this hill. We might be able to coast all the way down there."

Tim nodded. "Yeah I guess we should get a room—unless you think you could sleep in the truck."

"I'd rather not."

"Okay," Tim said. He released the handbrake. "Let's head for the hotel. Hold onto your hat. This might be a wild ride."

As they rolled, Kate scrutinized the uphill side of the road, calling out every hazard that jumped from the blackness. With no engine and no brakes, Tim steered the rig down the steep narrow road, careening and freewheeling all the way to the bottom.

He was right, it was a wild ride. They never lost momentum until they turned onto the flat highway. Then they barely made it over to the shoulder, before the M-37 came to a stop, fifteen feet short of the hotel's driveway. The truck was too heavy to push. Poor as it was, this parking job would have to do.

Wet snow was falling now and the road was turning white.

They got out and made their way across the lot.

Nearly Christmas, and an expectant couple far from home seeks a room at the inn. The scene sounded familiar.

The Old Hotel.

Inside, the Old Hotel landed far short of how Kate had always envisioned it. They'd driven past the place many times, and it had always looked so picturesque. But Kate now saw that the lodge had a plain white ceiling with several brown stains where the roof had leaked. The walls were flat and painted green. There was no hint of its outer log charm.

The lobby held two mismatched sofas and a couple of tables and chairs that were centered beneath a pair of blazing florescent lights. Five travelers who were drinking beer and playing cards occupied the tables. A man was stretched out on one of the couches with an open copy of the Footprint Tracker News blocking his face from the light. Check-in was over to the left.

The hotel clerk had glanced up as they entered. He'd looked, but he hadn't looked welcoming. Tim and Kate walked over to his registration desk with some reservations.

"We'd like a room for the night," Tim said. "Are you two married?"

What an odd question! This was the late seventies, after all. And since Kate was so obviously "with child," it almost seemed funny. But the clerk wasn't smiling.

"If you aren't married then you'll need to get two rooms," he explained with formidable candor.

"Oh, we're very married," Kate said, brandishing her gold wedding band.

The man wanted proof. "Do you have identification?" This guy seemed to be missing a lot of rich humor here. Too bad for him.

The couple fumbled with numb fingers and dug out their licenses. He took both cards and compared the last names before returning them.

"Okay. I guess you'll be wanting a double room?" "Yes please," Tim said, biting his lip.

"You'll need to pay in advance," the clerk said. "Of course," Tim said, counting out the cash.

Satisfied, the reticent clerk produced a key. "Welcome to 'The Old Hotel,'" he said with a perfect deadpan delivery.

Mr. and Mrs. Peters backed away from the reception desk and escaped up the stairs. They found their room and, once safely inside, they both laughed out loud.

Morning couldn't come fast enough for Kate. The bed was awful and the noise and smoke from downstairs filtered up through the floor so freely that she had to ask Tim to open the window to get some fresh air. He noted that the clouds had moved on, and predicted they'd be able to start working on the truck at first light. That was the best news Kate had heard all night.

* * *

"It's definitely something in the electrical system, but I won't know what, 'til I take it apart. We need to get it home, so I can work on it in the shop." Tim reported. It was the next morning and they'd checked under the truck's hood, first thing.

Now they were eating hash browns, eggs and sausage at a diner near the Old Hotel.

"How are we gonna get it home?" Kate asked, wishing they were already home.

"The Land Cruiser can tow it. After breakfast, I'll hitch a ride up to the turnoff and hike in. I'll drive the Toyota back here, and we'll be home by dark."

"I suppose that's as good a plan as any."

"Sure. You can wait right here. I shouldn't be too long." "How long do you think, really?" Kate was looking around the little restaurant, already feeling awkward.

"That's hard to say. If I don't have any problems, I should be back by mid-afternoon."

"Okay babe."

Kate pushed her hat across the table. "Take my hat. I won't need it here."

"No. I'm fine."

"Please take it. Just stick it in your pocket." She pressed the hat into his hands. "You never know. It might be windy on the hike up to the house."

Tim stood up, stuffed the hat into his coat pocket, kissed Kate goodbye and went outside to hit the highway.

Kate watched him through the window. Half a dozen cars passed before a rusty pickup stopped. Tim got in, and the truck putted away.

She slid out of the booth, went over and paid the bill and walked out of the warm dining room. Hesitating in the arctic entryway, the expectant woman decided she would sit right there on the empty wooden bench, to wait.

She sat down. The seat was cold and hard. She stood up, folded her canvas Carhartt jacket and sat down on top of it.

With plenty of time to muse, she started to imagine what was going on inside that farm truck right about then:

"How far you goin'?" the farmer would ask. "Sleeping Moose."

Now, unless this farmer was a brilliant self-starter, that short exchange would be followed by a twenty-mile-stretch of dead silence since Tim wasn't likely to give the fellow much of a handhold to work with. Kate figured that might be the extent of their conversation until they reached the Sleeping Moose post office, when Tim would finally speak up.

"This'll do, right here, thanks." Then he would jump out and start hoofing it up the mountain.

Kate sighed. "It's gonna be one long day, all right." She stood up, refolded her Carhartt pillow and sat down again. "At least he has a hat."

Road Rage

ABOUT SIX HOURS later, the green Toyota appeared, far up the road. Kate grabbed her pressed coat, slipped it on, and trotted out to greet Tim. They met at the hood of the comatose Power Wagon.

"How'd it go?" she asked him.

"Good. Let's get this thing home."

Tim was few words and all business as he lined out the operation. "I'll drive the car and you steer the truck. Just remember, don't let that tow rope take on any slack."

Although they had towed cars a few times before, the exercise was still a nerve-wracking one for Kate. Would the rope come loose? Or snap? Or—heaven forbid—take on slack? She climbed into the high driver's seat and prepared for that first scary tug. Sitting with lips mashed together like a wringer washer, she watched Tim tie the mammoth truck to the back of a six-cylinder car half its size.

"We'll need to have a good head of steam to get all the way up to Sleeping Moose," Tim said.

Was he talking to her, or to the rope he was tying to the back of the car? "It's lucky we're already pointed in the right direction. That means it'll be a straight shot at least," Kate offered.

Tim nodded and got into the little Land Cruiser.

From the truck, Kate could see him light the stub of his cigar and ram it between his incisors. He looked ready to go. She gripped the truck's steering wheel and heard the Toyota's engine start. A little burp of exhaust puffed out. They were about to roll.

Tim put his head out the window. "Are you ready?"

She was as ready as she ever would be. She gave a nod. "Read y."

He shot her a thumbs-up and began inching forward.

Kate saw the Toyota buck against its big load, and Tim felt the jolt. He braked and held the tension while he studied the towrope in his rearview mirror. All the connections were secure.

He wouldn't be looking look back again until they reached the turnoff. Tim was worried about all the twists and dips and steep hills they would encounter as they made their way up the long incline to Sleeping Moose. It would be vital to keep up his speed if he wanted to reach home with this load. Starting the tow in earnest Tim slowly released the clutch and began to pull the sleeping giant home. Two miles later, he was still accelerating, building up steam for the climb.

After another mile, they were getting close to the truck's speed threshold and Kate was beginning to worry. Had he forgotten that the antique truck began to shimmy at thirty-five miles per hour? She hoped he would hold it steady right where they were. But he didn't.

Sure enough, a minute later the skittish antique began to tremble. Soon it was rattling like a runaway buckboard and Kate was struggling to keep the buggy under control. What was the man thinking? Had he forgotten that she was back there?

"Hey Tim! Slow down!" she hollered.

Of course, Tim didn't hear her. He was peering forward, thinking of the cliffs and ravines ahead, oblivious to all things behind, including his wife.

Kate, held captive in a seized wheelhouse, feared the thing might shake apart at any second. She honked to get his attention. The horn was dead. She tried blinking the lights. No lights. She risked taking one hand off the wheel long enough to crank down the window. She stuck her arm out and signaled.

He didn't see her distressed waving, either. Tim's eyes were riveted ahead as he dragged the helpless woman up the road, totally oblivious of the drama going on behind him.

By Kate's estimation, she passed from agitated into frantic at around forty miles per hour. At forty-five, she started to get mad. By fifty, when the truck started gyrating, she went ballistic. Now she was shrieking, and gesticulating, and pounding on the steering wheel. Her gestures certainly would have drawn the attention of any oncoming driver—if they had met one. "Slow down you jerk! SLOW DOWN! I hate you! If we come out of this alive, I swear I'll kill you!"

"Stop, Timber!"

". . . *STOP!*"

Tim missed it all. What he knew was that they were almost there, and any minute he would be taking the turnoff and stopping, as soon as he reached the flat spot at the top of the rise. He couldn't wait to go back and check in with Kate, to see how she'd fared.

After as he'd swung his load onto the turnoff, and reached the parking spot, Tim stopped and jumped out of the car. He trotted back to the truck, and was puzzled to find his white-knuckled bride shouting a torrent of vile oaths in his direction. He approached her cautiously.

"Yes, I guess I should have warned you about the speed. No, I didn't forget that the truck shakes when it goes over thirty-five. Yes, of course I care about you and the baby." He was working hard to calm his terrified lady. Eventually Tim was able to get close enough to take Kate's hand, and finally to hold her in his arms, while she bawled.

"You aren't still mad at me, are you?" he asked when she was finally calm enough to feel more relieved than homicidal. "No. I'm not mad anymore. I'm just glad we're all alive and that we're almost home."

"This last part won't be as scary," he promised. "With any luck, we'll be crawling into our own little bed by dark."

"Let's have some luck then," she said, "because I'm whipped."

* * *

On the evening of December 15th Tim and Kate were already stretched out in their bed, poised for sleep. They'd spent all day in town, buying corrugated tin for the roof and starting to haul it home. But they'd only managed to get the load in, as far as the bridge. Kate was feeling terribly pregnant and a little bit sad. Her due date was in exactly one month, and they were still a long way from having a roof over their heads.

Tim tried his standard diversionary tactic to get her buoyed up. "Imagine you're out walking," he said, "and you suddenly fall through some sort of a time warp and find yourself dropped right here on this spot. Except, it's five hundred years ago. You have nothing with you but the clothes on your back. What would you do first?"

He loved this game. It piqued his analytical mind. Kate sometimes found the premise of being alone five hundred years ago—disturbing. But she played along, to keep him happy.

"What time of year is it?" This was always a good first question.

"It's right now: winter."

Naturally. He would have to make it difficult. "Do I have matches with me?"

"No. You just went out to feed the chickens." "But I do have my parka and boots on, right?" "Yes, and a hat."

"Oh, lucky me."

She thought for a moment. "I guess the first thing I'd do is head down toward the protection of the trees. Do I know where the spring is?"

"Yes. But there might be bears, or even Indians down there."

"I'd have to chance it. I'd head down to the spring, and if I ran into Indians, I'd try to make friends."

"Okay. There aren't any Indians. You're all alone." (It was time to introduce a second cruel twist.) "Night is closing in, and it feels like snow is on the way."

Kate nodded. "Okay. The first thing I'd do is build myself a rudimentary shelter. I'd take some spruce boughs. . ."

And so, the game went on, until they either made it to civilization, or drifted off to sleep. Usually the solution was to head south by whatever means possible. Tim favored the canoe along the coast technique, while Kate preferred an overland coastal route. Either way sounded hard.

* * *

When the next series of extra-heavy snowfalls had smoothed-over every surface irregularity for miles around, one rectangular shape remained snow free: Kate's diligently-swept basement roof. The house was leaking everywhere, and Kate was working hard to keep the downstairs from feeling like a draining colander. The unbeatable water had them both straining forward with renewed intensity. Time was running out. And still, the roof wasn't on.

December 16, 1978 – Greetings Mamasan!

How are you doing? As of yesterday, we have the tin for our roof hauled up as far as the bridge. And today we plan to cut the last half of our ridge pole. We decided to splice the ridgepole and purlins since twenty-five-foot beams are a lot easier for a thirty-six-week-pregnant woman to carry out of the woods, than fifty-footers. After we sled all six sections up to the house site and Tim has them spliced together, we'll just have to lift them into place. (That should be a trick and a half.) Our goal is to get the roof on by January 1st. There's a guy with a portable sawmill up in Cooper Landing who's cutting our rafters for us. As soon as we have a roof upstairs, we should be able to slow down a little, and putter along framing in windows and doors. Then, when I go out of commission Tim can carry on solo. It's a good plan. But, as Levi Zant said, "Man makes plans, and God laughs." So, we'll see.

We've had an unusual amount of wet weather lately. (Maybe it's not all that unusual.) Our basement ceiling is leaking badly from all the construction overhead (dropped timbers, tools, and such).

Must work fast. It gets dark at about 3:00 now. The days are short . . .

Love, K, T and ?

That evening, as Kate made her last trip outside before bed, she lingered for a moment, watching the waning moon waver like a flickering candle above the horizon.

The setting moon looked like a candle flame.

* * *

"Look, Tim. Our first egg!" Kate had just come in to show him the treasure. She thrust it forward proudly.

Tim took the brown oval, held it up high between his thumb and middle finger, and inspected it.

"Do you see this?" he asked, gazing at the marvel. "You are looking at a three-hundred-dollar egg!"

Kate's life-partner had a wonderful way of making things sound funny, even when they weren't.

A wide spot in the road.

CHAPTER ELEVEN
Winter, 1979

Racing Baby

DECEMBER 20, 1978 - Dear Mom,

I've just completed a highly successful outhouse run—and run it was, as we're having a cold snap these days. Actually, this cold is more of a blessing than a curse, since it makes walking much easier than it was, just a day ago. We've been having weird weather: snowstorms followed by above-freezing temps, which makes the snow crusty. When that happens, you don't know when you might break through and jar your back. Colder is better, if one has the choice. My hips have been killing me. The doctor says they're loosening up, getting ready to let this baby out. It was really starting to hurt, carrying those beams out of the woods. (Especially, stepping over fallen logs and ducking under branches.) But we're done, now. We sledded our last beam home, yesterday. Yay!

It looks like our lazy days are over. With my due date in less than a month, all hopes of bringing baby home to a finished mansion have been replaced with a downscaled, but fervent hope that we'll at least have a roof on, before I go into labor.

P.S. Merry Christmas in five days. And we'll be seeing you shortly after that!

* * *

January 2, 1979 - Dear Mamasan,

Happy New Year! It's an absolutely gorgeous day!

In fact, I'm sitting outside, as I write this. Tim is working on the beams, and I'm helping him when he needs me. We're a little behind schedule, trying to get the ridgepole and purlins seated today. Hopefully the two-by-eight rafters we ordered will be ready this week.

Mahalo nui loa for the Macadamia nuts. Yum! Good to have a taste of Hawaii up here in this cold, white place.

It's been snowing a lot lately. Looks like you're in for a Skidoo ride when you get here.

The nursery is fixed and waiting. We nailed up blankets to section-off a little area right next to the furnace. It should be warm and snug for baby. My bag is packed, our transportation is in working order and the roof is almost on. I guess we're about ready.

P.S. Just now this baby is climbing up the insides of my belly. It feels like the Olympic trials are going on in there. Could this be labor?

I hope not. We need at least one more week to get the roof on.

I must stop now. Baby is overpowering me, right at the moment. Will write more later.

P.P.S. It's been 24 hours since I wrote this letter, but still no baby yet. Must not be time.

Expect to see us SOON, though.

Love, Kate, Tim and ?

Nearly ready for baby
(except for two dozen juice cans scattered across the floor).

It was a sunny Sunday in early January, and the two were standing on top of the basement contemplating their greatest hurdle yet. How were they going to raise the two purlins and that fifty-five-foot ridgepole?

Those three mega-beams were now straddling a row of saw horses, waiting to be set in place. Tim's shipwright splices—with their diagonal cuts—had been elegantly executed. The hand-hewn joints looked plenty strong enough to support a roof—if Tim and Kate could just get the things up there. So far, they'd explored and thrown out several ideas. To the pregnant woman, the task didn't seem doable.

Kate had her earflaps up (it was a balmy, plus-fifteen degrees), so she was the first one to hear the approaching engine. She looked out across the field and saw a lone snow-machine rider burst out of the woods. "Heads-up, here comes someone," she warned.

Tim studied the approaching visitor for two seconds. "That looks like Brian. Do we still have coffee on?"

"There's half a pot on the furnace."

Having declared it a "coffee pot" visit, the pair struck friendly poses and waited to greet their visitor.

Brian roared up the hill, then coasted to a stop and cut the engine as he reached their basement.

They all exchanged friendly nods, and when the engine noise died away, and Tim called out the traditional greeting. "Howdy Brian. Got time for some coffee?"

"No thanks," Brian said. He smiled at Kate. "I was just in the area and thought I'd swing by to see how you two were doing." He stretched his arms forward and rested them on the handlebars.

"Looks like you're about ready to have that baby, Kate," Brian was pointing to the noticeable swell in her coveralls.

"Any day now," she confirmed. "We're just trying to get this roof on before it arrives."

"Yup, we're just about ready to raise the ridgepole," Tim seconded.

Brian was studying Tim's splice work. "You've got some nice-looking splices, there. Those are impressive beams. How do you plan to get 'em up there?"

"We're still working on that," Tim admitted.

"If you let me know when you get ready to raise 'em, I'll come up and give you a hand," their neighbor offered.

Kate felt a rush of relief. Aid had come in the nick of time.

"Thanks, but we can handle it."

Kate heard the traitorous words being spoken from a voice on her left. She whirled and stared at her husband. Had he forgotten that there were just the two of them trying to perform an impossible feat? Did he remember that she was expecting, and nearly-to-term? Why would he decline Brian's offer to help? Kate had literally been knocked speechless. Brian looked a little surprised, but he smiled and nodded.

"Okay," he said. "Just let me know if you change your mind." He turned the starter key. His rig fired up obediently, and Kate—who wanted to say they had just changed their minds and would love the help—waved weakly, and croaked out a simple, "Say hello to Anna," instead.

She watched their angel of mercy disappear into the distance and then turned to confront Tim. "What were you thinking? We definitely could have used his help!"

Tim, unmoved by her outburst, now had a vision. "We won't need his help. We won't need anyone's help. We can do this on our own."

The pioneer's wife was dubious.

"I have a plan," Tim assured her. And with that, he hatched a plot that involved daring, balance, and grunt force. As usual, he would demonstrate the first two talents, and Kate would be the grunt.

"With the help of a come-along," he explained, "you should be able to drag the beam up to the top of the house."

In another hour, they were erecting a questionable-looking-contraption of nailed-together boards that ran from the ground up to the horizontal beams topping the east wall. Their rickety scaffolding looked like the frame for an overgrown pup tent, and it was probably about as stable. Any little wind was likely to bring the whole thing down.

Tim's plan was to hoist the first purlin up the ramps, slide it over some temporary runners he'd nailed to the peak of the house, and ease the giant down the other side—where it would hopefully drop into its permanent resting place, without any major struggles or retakes. It might work, given lots of luck.

And here came the daring. As Kate gradually hauled the load upward, Tim planned to walk back and forth along the top of the house, guiding the levitating beam by tapping one end or the other with a long stick. This way, he could keep things level, and hopefully limit the meandering to a minimum.

"Okay," she said. "Let's get this show on the road."

Tim strapped a long rope around one end of the first purlin. He threaded the rope up and around a temporary stop on the scaffolding, through the come-along and pulley that was secured to a post near the center of the purlin's desired resting spot, and back through a second stop on the far end of the scaffold.

After he had secured the loose end of the rope to the other end of the beam, he checked everything once more, and then climbed the ladder to start his balancing act.

When he was in position on top of the framework, Kate started cranking. And she would keep cranking, no matter what, because this was the only way they were going to get the job done.

Kate cranked and cranked. The rope tightened, stretched, and tightened again.

Eventually she could see the beam start to move its way up the shaky rails. The progress was infinitesimal, but undeniable.

Meanwhile, Tim was performing like a tightrope walker, traveling from one end of the house to the other, guiding the beam's progress with an occasional tap from his long balancing stick—all at twelve feet above the ground. Kate watched him with feelings of dread and admiration. It was dangerous; but this was her husband, and he was performing an extraordinary feat. She was dazzled. The whole thing was amazing. "If you come down in one piece, we'll call this a success, whether we get the beam up, or not," she promised, hoping there wouldn't be any sudden wind gusts to blow the man down.

* * *

Three days later, when the ridgepole and purlins were safely secured, and Tim was still alive to tell his grandchildren about the exploit, the pair went outside to admire their accomplishment. Kate had cranked on that lever, pumping imaginary water into a bottomless pail forever, and had not gone into labor. All was well, and they were pleased.

Kate's arms and back were aching, but she was glad she'd gone along with Tim's harebrained scheme. It felt fabulous to have accomplished the task all by themselves. Standing there looking at the completed skeleton of their house being bathed in the rosy light of an alpenglow; her heart was so filled with joy she thought her overalls might pop. They had done it, without help from anyone.

"It looks fantastic," she said. "You got that right," Tim agreed.

"You were a real acrobat up there walking those beams.

You'd look good in a pair of tights, I'll bet."

Tim laughed and Kate kissed him, and they stood side-by-side admiring the silhouette of a house that had risen where a moose had once slept.

Tim put his arm around her shoulders. "You're a trooper, Kate. How-ever did I win such a spirited girl to be my bride?"

"I don't know. Just lucky, I guess." They were both beaming with pride.

Tim turned to look at her with serious blue eyes. Then he smiled. "Not bad for a couple of 'harelips,' eh?"

Driving the last spike home in one of Tim's shipwright splices.

At nine-months pregnant, Kate was mighty glad to see that last beam in place.

January 8, 1979 - Dear Ma,

Yay! We've got all the beams up! That was tricky, and scary, and exciting—and infinitely satisfying. Here's a new word for you: funambulist.

I married one!

It was baby's due date, and the race was on.

CHAPTER TWELVE
Still Winter, 1979

A Change of Plans

WEDNESDAY, JANUARY 24th, 1979. The joists were on and the homesteading honeymooners were nearly ready to attach the tin roofing. Kate had held on so far, but she was now nine days overdue. It was checkup day at the doctor's, and they were zipping along on the Skidoo, headed for town.

"Tim! Watch out!"

In a split-second they were sliding off the trail, aiming straight for the barbed wire fencing of Neil Goodman's abandoned pasture. It zoomed up to meet them, snagged the yellow cowling, and jerked the snow-machine to a halt.

Tim helped Kate up off the tilted vehicle. "Are you okay?"

"Yes, I'm fine." She dusted snow off her left leg and looked at the tipped rig. "How's the Skidoo?"

Tim gave it a quick once-over. "It looks okay. Why don't you rest for a minute while I pull it out of the fence?"

"I can help." Not wanting to hang around out there and end up having a trailside delivery like Will James' mother, Kate insisted. "I feel fine. Honestly."

Tim admitted that he could use her help, and they tugged together until the tangled machine finally broke free.

In less than five minutes, they were back on their pilgrimage to town, speeding down the slick hill with empty water cans and dirty laundry swishing behind them in the sled. Kate didn't want to alarm Tim by mentioning a strange sensation that had just started low in her belly.

* * *

When they arrived in Footprint, the doctor looked, and felt around for a long time. Usually jovial, he seemed to grow more and more serious as the exam progressed.

"You know," he said frowning slightly, "there's a good chance this might turn out to be a more complicated delivery than we'd been talking about. I think you should plan on going up to Anchorage to have this baby. They're equipped to handle emergency situations far better than we are here."

"But you said I could 'drive a truck' through there," Kate reminded him.

"Just to be on the safe side," he said, trying to sound comforting. "I think you should head to the hospital in Anchorage. I'll call ahead and get everything set up for you."

"Oh." Kate's bravado had evaporated. "Well when should I plan on going?"

"Today. You need to go today. I want you on the next flight to Anchorage."

They left that prenatal check-up quite shaken. Tim drove his wife straight to the airport in Soldotna, where the afternoon Twin Otter was just about to head north. Kate boarded and watched Tim waving goodbye to her, until he was obscured by a bank of clouds. Then she was on her own.

As soon as the plane disappeared behind the clouds, Tim beat a path home to put things in order before driving up to meet her at the hospital. He grabbed Kate's packed travel case, threw a week's worth of feed at the chickens, emptied all the orange juice cans, and stapled some emergency plastic sheeting above the crib and the bed. As a last precaution, he carried in two trashcans and placed them strategically, to catch all the water that the plastic would hopefully be funneled away from over the beds. After he'd buttoned up everything, he padlocked the basement door, and sped back down to the car.

Just as he was leaving Sleeping Moose, a monster storm closed in from the south and it nipped at his heels all the way to Anchorage. Tim drove as fast as he dared, but the blizzard made it difficult to maneuver through all the mountains and avalanche slides that rimmed Turnagain Arm.

* * *

Seven hours later, the nearly lunatic man skated across the hospital's frozen parking lot and bounded through the front door. Breathless to see his first-born child, he went straight to the admissions desk, where they told him they had no "Kate Peters" registered. Flustered, Tim called Dick to see if his pal knew anything about the missing family.

Meanwhile Kate was at Dick's, resting on a couple of pillows on the floor in front of a warm fire. The phone rang, and as soon as Dick answered it, she could hear Tim's excited voice on the other end. Dick handed the receiver to Kate.

"Hello sweetheart," she said. "I'm glad you made it up the road okay. It's bad out there."

"Where in the hell are you?" Tim interrupted. "Have you had that baby yet?"

"I'm right here where you called me—at Dick's. And no, I haven't had the baby yet."

"Well why not, dammit?"

"The doctor told me to stay here in town until I go into labor. I called the only person we both know in Anchorage, and Dick came over and picked me up and brought me back to his place. And—well, here we are—just waiting." She paused. "It was a pretty exciting ride on these city streets with all the ice out there. But we made it."

Tim didn't know how to respond.

"I'll see you when you get here," Kate said. "I think I'll lie down now." She handed the phone to Dick and sank back onto the pillows.

"Hey Tim, why don't you stop at Dunkin' Donuts on your way over here? I could use a donut."

Tim arrived at midnight. Kate was relieved to see him. She ate three donuts and then laid down again, saying she felt gassy. Tim and Dick polished off the rest of the donuts and talked.

Eventually Tim noticed that Kate's "gas" attacks were occurring at six-minute intervals. Despite the icy roads, he convinced her to let him take her to the hospital.

Four hours later, little breach-bottomed Atwood Cutting Peters was born, Caesarian.

* * *

After three days at the hospital, Titian-haired Atwood's next home was Dick's bureau drawer. Kate's mother came up from Hawaii, as soon as Tim called her, and the three generations took over Dick's bedroom, and the living room couch. They stayed there for several days, resting up before heading back to the mountain.

* * *

When Atwood was a week old, and deemed strong enough to make the trip home, Tim took off for Sleeping Moose. He wanted to have the basement warmed-up and ready for his girls, when he picked them up at the airport the next morning. That night another ice storm turned everything slicker than powdered waxed paper. Even so, Kate, baby Attie, and

Grandma Tutu all flew out the next morning, anxious to get home.

Now, as they were landing on sheer ice at Soldotna, the little plane's brakes squealed like a kid with pinched fingers. "Golly! That doesn't sound good," the pilot-in-training whispered to her companion.

Kate held Atwood close, and the blur of white runway whooshed past as the Otter ran through a full repertoire of unhealthy sounds. Gradually the screaming plane came to a full stop.

"I guess we're here," Grandma Tutu surmised.

Kate, who had been craning to catch sight of Tim, spotted him coming out of the small terminal. "Look, Attie. There's your daddy!" She lifted the newborn up so her special man could see his beautiful daughter.

When he saw them, the new father started waving excitedly. He trotted out across the runway as soon as the props stopped and the passengers started disembarking. They met up, then Tim caught their two suitcases as a young woman in coveralls tossed them from the belly of the plane. The three excited adventurers with babe-in-arms quickly headed for the warm and waiting car.

Once they were all packed into the Toyota, with poor Hawaiian Grandma crumpled up in the back, along with the groceries and five freezing cans of water, the group vamoosed out of town. Everyone was anxious to get home in the daylight.

Special Delivery

WHEN THEY GOT to the turnoff in Sleeping Moose, the Alpine and sled were dusted off, and waiting. Only one more lap, and this baby would be home.

Tim loaded the suitcases, water, and groceries into the sled, and Grandma Tutu held their little pink treasure while Kate gingerly took her seat on the Alpine. Once she was settled, Grandma Tutu handed the baby to Kate, and Tim helped their tropical visitor take her seat behind her daughter. "We'll go slow," he told his mother-in-law, as he transferred the infant back from mother to grandmother. "If you feel like you're slipping, just tell Kate to stop."

He made sure the car was empty, crunched through ice and drifted snow to the back of the sled, and grabbed the musher bar. If needed, he would help push the vehicle forward from there.

Kate turned the key, and was pleasantly surprised when the engine roared to life. She called back over her shoulder. "Is everybody ready?"

"All ready," Tim answered.

Kate looked at her mother. "Are you ready, Mamasan?" Grandma Tutu tried to sound cheery. "All ready for takeoff."

But the matriarch, who had never been on a snow-machine before and was cradling an infant in her arms, looked a little uncertain.

"Okay. Here we go!" Kate gripped the snow machine's throttle and prepared to launch.

Just before the machine started to move, Mamasan, still harboring some hesitation, leaned forward and asked, "Are you sure you know what you're doing dear?"

"*Of course,* Mother," the gallant girl assured her. And she gave it the gas.

The snow-machine tremored, and Kate rocked from side to side to break it free, while Tim pushed on the musher bar. Grandma Tutu clutched the baby, and hoped her free-spirited daughter was right.

When the Alpine broke loose, Tim jumped forward onto the footplate, and the settlers roared off on their own version of one of the greatest missions known to womankind.

Crystalized flakes flew out in wakes, as the rig charged over fresh January drifts. A frigid wind bit at their noses and stung their cheeks, but the newborn—all wrapped and swaddled—rode on without a whimper. Pounding up the trail, with their doublewide ski crashing through swell after swell, Kate was chanting a new mantra.

"I'm gonna get this baby home, if it's the last thing I do!"

When they'd rounded the last turn, their patch of yellow basement shone like a beacon at the top of the hill. Kate aimed directly for it.

There was the door. They'd made it!

The ski crunched against ice as Kate stopped at the front steps.

Tim jumped off the musher's footplate and performed the multiple handoffs in reverse order. When baby Atwood was again lying in Kate's arms, the new mother gathered her balance and prepared to carry her infant down the slippery pillbox steps.

"I got things as ready as I could," Tim said. "I hope it's okay."

"I'm sure it's fine sweetie," Kate assured him. "It's so good to be home."

She gave Grandma Tutu a kiss on the cheek. "Thanks, Mamasan. I'll bet you don't do that every day."

"That's for sure," Grandma Tutu said. She flashed her radiant smile. "I'd call this an airmail, and very special delivery."

Tim took Kate's elbow to help her carry the baby down the icy steps. The new mother was bursting with pride to be carrying their infant into the home they had built for her. "Welcome home, little one," she whispered, nuzzling her bundle-in-a-snow-covered-bunting.

Tim opened the door, and Kate, overwhelmed with hormones and happiness, swept inside. "Sweet Atwood, welcome to your new—"

Her voice trailed off as she surveyed the scene inside the house. The room looked like Gettysburg the morning after the big battle. Steam rose like a lifting fog from the damp floor. Large patches of woodwork were blackened, and all the cinderblocks were moist.

"What happened? Was there a fire?"

"Not exactly," Tim said, embarrassed. "The place was pretty wet when I got back. I had to use the propane grass burner to dry it out." He searched her face for a reaction. "It's okay now though, don't you think?"

"It'll have to be," Kate said, showing him a brave smile.

Looking slightly deflated, Tim left Kate studying the telltale battleground while he went out to help Grandma Tutu down the steps and into the house.

When they were all safe and accounted for, Kate said, "Let's put baby down in her crib and take off our gear."

That was Tim's cue. He hustled into the nursery and tapped on the plastic roofing, draining off a fresh puddle of ooze that had collected above the crib while he'd been in town picking up the ladies.

Kate was recovering from the shock. She kissed her husband on the cheek. "Warm, and almost dry: good enough! Thanks for getting things ready for us dear."

They'd all had quite a mission. And now, their baby was safely tucked into the home that her daddy and mommy had built with their own hands.

Grandma Tutu—always a cheerful soul— smiled. "You know, someday one of us is going to have to write a book about this," she said.

* * *

The next morning, the thermometer slid down to ten degrees below zero, and it stayed there for five days. That made outhouse runs more than a little invigorating. But their Hawaiian guest seemed unperturbed by this, and she happily continued to perform the daily trash burning duty, even though she couldn't deny that it was cold out there.

One day, Tim invited Grandma Tutu to go along on a water-fetching expedition, and she jumped at the chance.

"Here, you'll need this," he said, handing her an arctic face mask. "The wind chill will freeze your nose off if you don't have it covered."

Tutu obediently donned all the necessary attire, and by the time she was fully dressed you couldn't see anything but two eyes peering out from behind a stiff leather mask. She also had on a wool cap, a down vest, a scarf, and insulated Carhartt coveralls. She looked so funny that Kate took her picture.

The undaunted grandmother climbed aboard the waiting Skidoo, and was relieved to know that this time she could wrap her arms around Tim's waist and hold on. Then, she and her son-in-law zoomed away on her first sub-zero adventure.

Mamasan, dressed for minus ten degrees.

When they came back from the Tanners' (lucky Anna and Brian had running water and a composting toilet), the winter sojourners had four full cans of water, and they both wore big smiles.

"So how was the ride, Mamasan?"

"It was thrilling!" Tutu bubbled. "I can't wait to go again."

Mamasan and Mama—
the apple didn't fall far from the tree.

* * *

A week later, her visit drawn to a close, Grandma Tutu said she'd had a wonderful time helping out, and that she would never forget this very special winter vacation.

Tim had gassed up the Alpine and now he pulled the rig beside the two women who were embracing at the door. A seasoned snow-machine passenger by now, Tutu climbed on behind Tim with no hesitation, and they sped off down the hill. Kate yelled and waved to her mother until they disappeared into the woods. "Goodbye. I love you! Thank you for coming! Goodbye! Thank you for all your help!"

. . . And then, they were three.

Finally, she turned and went back inside, ready to assume her completely unfamiliar state of motherhood. After the excitement of the birth, most things would go back to normal. Kate's mother would return to Hawaii. Tim would return to the roof.

But Kate was beginning to suspect that—for her—the "simple life" might never be as simple again.

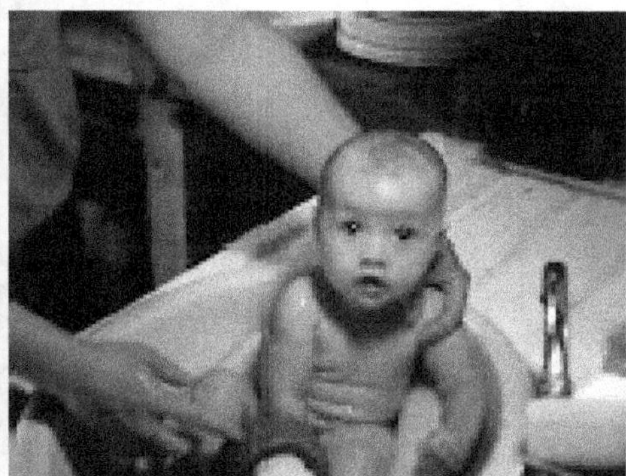

CHAPTER THIRTEEN
Spring, 1979

Trip to the Tree-Well

IT WAS STARTING to snow. The little Peters family was taking the shortcut through the woods, down to their car. Kate held three-week-old Attie tightly in her arms while Tim steered the Alpine in and out between large spruce trees.

She was thinking that Tim hadn't been as impacted by this huge change in family dynamics as she had. After all, he wore headphones at night. "You should try them," he'd suggested. "You won't hear a thing."

And he'd been serious.

But for the new mother, keeping her precious bundle safe and comfortable was her current life's work, and it required constant vigil. At this moment, she was concentrating on keeping the infant level and protecting her from the wind.

"Everything was so much easier when you were still inside," she murmured to her baby, "because I knew that conditions were just right for you." Now Kate leaned forward and called into Tim's ear. "We need-ooof-to get one of those-ooof-papoose carriers." Her words bounced out as they plowed over a deep swath of windblown snow. "I can't lean very well right now and—ooof—if we're not careful, we'll fall into one of these tree-wells."

Tim agreed right away. "Okay. We can get one today if you want to." He turned to give her a smile.

She smiled back. "I really do-oo—ooof!"

Mid-sentence, the Alpine's big ski slipped sideways and plunged down into one of the three-foot-deep craters. Tim was thrown forward off the machine, while Kate instinctively gripped the seat with her knees and let her arms rise.

Atwood hadn't gone airborne, but the jolt had awakened her and she'd begun to wail.

"Are you alright?" Tim asked, stumbling back towards them through thigh-deep snow.

"Yeah, we're okay. Luckily, I was able to hold onto 'er. But we really need to get some-kind of a baby carrier today."

"You got it," Tim promised.

Kate swept a few snowflakes from Atwood's rosy cheeks while Tim tried to pull the heavy rig up out of the well. It wouldn't budge. He turned to

Kate. "Do you think you could help me get this thing out?"

"Sure. Just let me put Attie down someplace safe." Kate looked around for a spot that would be close enough to be able to see their baby, but far enough away to keep her safe from a thrashing Skidoo. She laid her charge next to a fallen tree and waded back to help Tim yank the wallowed machine loose. The baby stopped crying and waited patiently, while her mommy and daddy heaved and pulled at the big yellow machine.

Even with both giving their all, the snow-machine was too heavy for them to drag it backwards, out of the hole. "Maybe we can drive it out," Tim said. "You get behind, and when I say, 'Go,' you shove hard."

Kate obliged.

Tim was gunning the throttle and pulling up on the machine's blunt nose. He rocked and pushed the big rig vigorously, until the buried ski-tip finally lurched out into open air. "Go!" He signaled.

Kate pushed with all her might. The heavy machine jerked, and started "walking" itself out of the hole, churning up a lot of snow, and kicking it backward as it went. Kate was showered with a spray of frosty flakes, but baby Atwood remained safe from all the commotion.

Kate brushed herself off, while Tim circled around on the machine and headed back toward them. "Good work!" he said.

That praise made Kate smile. She waded over through the snow to retrieve their child. When she untucked the blanket and checked her daughter, a remarkably calm countenance looked back at her. Relieved, the new mommy picked up her baby and warmed those little cheeks with copious kisses. "Let's go get you a papoose carrier, little girl," Kate whispered. When they got to town, the first thing they did was purchase a Snuggli© baby pouch, something that tied over Kate's chest and held Attie close. Now the infant could ride, safely tucked in her little pouch inside her mommy's coveralls, just like before she was born.

Atwood safely tucked into her Snuggli carrier.

Kate handed the tin up to Tim, but he had to roof the placet all by himself.

Bathhouse Bawl

AS WINTER NIBBLED its way through February, Tim and Kate established a workable routine. Whenever it was sunny and baby was napping downstairs, they would go upstairs and make a little progress on the roof. By early March, they had a fine tin roof completely covering their house.

As soon as the dripping had stopped, and the juice cans and plastic sheeting were taken out, walking around the basement while carrying a baby became much easier. Before she'd left, Grandma Tutu had stressed the importance of looking where you're going, and not down at your baby, when walking. Kate thought that was good advice.

Kate was transitioning into motherhood pretty well. Atwood was bathed twice a week in a dishpan filled with fresh snow that she'd warmed on the furnace in Elsie's kettle.

On nice days, the new mother took her little companion out for snowshoe excursions in the sunshine. That was a highlight for the isolated woman, and little Attie seemed to enjoy the fresh air too. If she got cranky at night, they all suited up and went for a midnight ride under the stars. The buzzing sound of the snow-machine always soothed her to sleep.

By mid-March, Attie was almost thinking about sleeping through the night, and Kate was definitely thinking about it.

* * *

Each trip to town went pretty much the same way. In the early morning, they packed all the dirty clothes into the box sled and headed to the Wash Inn. Kate would put the laundry into the washer, while Tim paid the clerk for two showers before disappearing into the men's shower room. Mother and daughter headed for the women's, shortly after.

"Let's get Mommy all clean now," Kate cooed as she set the plastic car seat down on the floor. She undressed and hung her coveralls, Levi's, shirts, and down vest on the wall hook. Time to take her weekly shower. She kissed her strapped-in baby, then ducked behind the curtain for a quick wash.

Kate had come to dread what happened next. The moment Mommy disappeared from baby's sight, Attie would break into a round of howling shrieks shrill enough to penetrate the shower walls and permeate the main laundry area. Such heartrending wails had to be giving those laundering matrons a bad impression.

Over the past month, Kate's showers at the coin laundry had become an ordeal to be endured, not enjoyed. After each screaming fit, the inexperienced and mortified mother slunk out of that shower room, shrinking away from possible public condemnation.

If Tim asked how things went, Kate would say, "Oh, we just had a bawl. Let's go. We can come back when the clothes are dry."

She couldn't get out of there fast enough.

* * *

Later that spring, Kate gladly accepted an offer to use the laundry and shower facilities down at Brian and Anna's. They were going outside for a week and they wouldn't be turning off their water. Anna told Kate she could use their washer and take a shower, if she would check on the goats while she was there. Kate was thrilled to think that she would be able to get the laundry done and get clean without everyone in town knowing about it.

On Sunday, she loaded the laundry bag in the Alpine's carrying rack, tied the baby-in-a-bag around her waist, and zipped her coveralls over most of Attie. She mounted the machine and turned the key. Varoom! It started. Kate and Attie zoomed down the hill for a private day at the spa.

When she got there, Kate threw her laundry in the washer, and then went out to check the goats. They looked up at her, turned hightail and trotted to the far end of their pen. They seemed fine. She tossed them some munchies and ducked back into the cabin, ready to take a blissful shower.

It was uncanny. All the while Kate was bathing, that baby never made a sound. Did the little imp know that, just like a tree falling in the woods, a tantrum now would go unobserved?

With the washing done, Kate repacked Attie in her baby bag, zipped her coveralls up (leaving

Attie an airway) and went out. She shut the front door, crammed the bag of wet laundry in behind her seat, and boarded the Skidoo.

When she turned key, the oppositional transport device declined to respond. It seemed that the Alpine had long ago sensed her ineptitude with all things mechanical. More often, than not, the fabulously expensive key-start feature chose to let her down.

"T-chit," Kate hissed.

She tried the key a dozen more times, but had to quit when the headlight dimmed and the battery started sounding weak. Kate would have to use the pull rope, which was always difficult for her. "Darn it!"

With little expectation of success Kate dismounted and took hold of the starter rope handle. She wrapped the cord around her hand twice, and gave what she considered to be her best yank. The sack-full of baby on her chest swung like a gong but the machine did not resonate. Kate repeated the step, with baby flopping across her belly like a bowling ball tied with elastic. She pulled three more times and the baby-bag gonged each time. "That's it. I give up. This is ridiculous! Utterly, stupidly ridiculous!" Kate was spent. "I hate you, machine! I really hate you!"

The cold-hearted machine laughed silently.

Kate lost patience, swung her leg back and kicked the machine right in the seat, the swinging baby-bag adding its own momentum to the blow. After this senseless act of violence, a fiendish idea occurred to the disturbed missus.

Maybe she should set the thing on fire. Not only might it draw Tim's attention and bring about her eventual rescue, but the revenge would be so sweet.

It was times like this that she wished they had a dog team. She related better to things that were breathing and covered with hair.

But whenever she brought up the topic, Tim always said, "A cat is plenty. Why ask for trouble?"

Kate looked down at her daughter, hanging there, totally helpless, yet perfectly composed. "Oh, don't worry little girl. It's gonna be okay. Mommy will think of something." Baby Atwood gazed up at her mother, fully believing the lie.

Out of steam, and out of ideas, Kate searched the emptiness around them. And that's when good fortune smiled. A pair of Sunday afternoon snowmobilers happened to pass by. More than rare, this was practically a miracle. The recreationing motorists stopped to exchange pleasantries, as was the Alaskan custom, and— upon seeing a panting woman standing in the middle of the woods with a baby hanging like a baboon from her front, and looking frustrated with her apparently-unresponsive transportation—one of the fellows offered his aid. "Looks like you've got your hands full. Could you use some help starting that big boy?"

"Yes please. That would be great," the exhausted mother sighed. "Thanks."

The fellow gave her machine starter cord one unencumbered manly pull, and it obediently sprang to life. Once the rig was running, Kate thanked the man, climbed aboard, and ran that baby home.

Tim was happy to see his girls coming up the hill. "Did you two have a good outing?" he asked Kate.

"No."

The "picnic pavilion" and shop, as viewed from the privy.

Walls and Windows

NOW THAT THEY had the roof on, they just needed to slap up the walls, and put in some doors and windows. Then, they could all move upstairs.

The first step was to get all the supplies in. It would be important to get everything sledded up to the house, before breakup made that feat impossible. If they had all their building materials on hand, they would be able to keep working through the next six landlocked weeks. Kate wanted to have the place baby-proofed by summer, since little Attie might be crawling soon.

"Well shall we go in tomorrow and get some siding?" Tim proposed. "I think it's about time we turn this picnic pavilion into a real house, don't you?"

"Definitely." Kate was more than ready.

They left for Footprint early the next day, and grabbed a pancake breakfast at the diner. After a feast, they purchased four-dozen sheets of oiled cellulose composite wallboard. This would serve as under-skin walls for their house. Locally cut spruce siding could follow whenever they got to it.

Sledding the thick oil-board panels home turned out to be tough. The stuff was heavy, so they could only sled a few sheets up, at a time. It took two full days of roundtrips to get all the fiberboard up from the trailer.

Nailing them up was easy. Tim fitted the panels between the post-and-beam framing, and Kate held each panel in place, while he nailed. Closing in the house, and walling out the weather took a total of two weeks.

Next, they needed some two-by-fours and sheetrock. Getting this load up the road really turned out to be a task. The monoliths of plasterboard were dreadfully heavy, and the flatbed sled cut more deeply into the trail, with each run. Despite the difficulties, they did manage to get the hundred two-by-fours and thirty fairly-dry sheets of wallboard all the way up to their place. It was a relief when they were done with that job.

Tim told Kate it might take a month to frame in all the rooms.

Nearly ready to move upstairs.

March 20, 1979 – Dear Mamasan, (Equinox)

It's spring! Yay!!!!!

We've got all the outer walls up and Tim is framing-in the rooms, and it's looking fantastic! We'll be moving upstairs, before you know it. I'm talking about upward mobility in the truest sense.

* * *

He started the interior wall project by partitioning off the big front section. The great room, a combined living-dining-kitchen, would take up half of the house, with the exposed beams and peaked ceiling creating a wonderful lodge atmosphere for them to come home to.

The rest of the house would have an insulated attic. There would be a modest-sized master bedroom, and a second bedroom that would be much bigger, and would have two doors, two windows and two closets. Kate figured it could be divided, as more children were added. That left space for a rotunda-like sewing room, a library for the book collection that they inexplicably carried around with them, and of course—a bathroom.

Every afternoon, while Attie napped below, Kate and Tim went upstairs to build another interior wall in their soon-to-be home.

Tim framed in a nice warming closet around the heat-resistant stove pipe that ran from the coal furnace up through the roof. It would be perfect for hanging up icy outerwear and drying out boots. And when they talked about how nice it would be if they didn't have to go outside to get down to the basement, they decided to add an inside stairwell. This modification was going to require carving away a big slice of the master quarters, but the convenience would be worth it.

"We'll need a lot of windows," Kate said. "I want to be able to see everything."

"Will do," Tim promised.

At the end of March, they went to the building supplier in town and ordered twenty double-glazed windows. They were told that it would be three weeks before the windows arrived in Footprint.

While they waited, Tim kept himself busy fabricating a strong east door for their castle. When he was finished, it resembled a portcullis in both weight and purpose. Made of timbers and planks, it had a foot-square, two-inch-thick, six-sided window set in it. They'd inherited it from Neil Goodman, and he'd gotten it out of a WWII fighter plane to use as a guard for his sawmill.

Unfortunately, just two days shy of the pickup date for the windows, an abnormally warm "Chinook" wind blew in.

The elevated temperatures melted deep pockets in the snow and turned the creek slushy. Going cross-country was no longer an option, and this meant that getting their new windows home had just gotten a lot harder.

* * *

After twenty-one days of waiting, the Peters family snow-machined out to the road and drove west to Footprint to pick up their new windows. When they got back to Sleeping Moose, they moved a third of the load into the box sled and towed the cargo home. By standing the fragile frames upright—with Tim mushing and holding the windows steady with one hand, and Kate (with Attie strapped inside of her mama's coveralls) skippering the Alpine up the pitted trail—they managed to surf the glass sheets home. They bumped up, and dropped down into several surprise trenches along the way, but they made it home safely, despite the treacherous snow.

The whole enterprise took four nerve-wracking trips up, from the road. Not wanting to leave the windows standing in the truck overnight, they made it a twelve-hour mushing marathon. Remarkably, not one window cracked, during transport.

The last window, and the most challenging one to handle, was their six-by-six-foot picture window. Naturally, this was the one that turned out to have a flaw in the seal.

As soon as they got it installed it started steaming up. No point in looking at their breathtaking view through a perpetual fog, so out it came. They sledded the defective window all the way back to the road, and drove it down to Footprint to exchange it. The man said it would take another three-weeks, for the new one to come in.

It was nearly breakup. The pioneers were running out of time.

While they waited for the replacement window, they carried their new Jøtul wood stove upstairs. Kate had ordered it from Sweden, and they'd been storing it in the basement for nearly a year.

Tim installed the little gem in the center of the great room. He put together several stovepipe sections and connected them to an insulated insert that went through the ceiling, twelve feet overhead, and Kate laid a decorative ceramic tile mosaic under it. The fire-preventive artwork looked pretty and it would be a warm place for Sabretooth to sleep.

They finally brought the replacement window home on the fifth of May. By this time, full breakup had arrived. The big sheet of glass would be the last cargo to come up the mountain, until summer. But they'd beaten the deadline, and they were very pleased about that.

Baking Soda and Vinegar

TIM WAS HEADING into Footprint for supplies and Kate had told him she wouldn't mind missing a trip into town. They'd learned during the past spring, that (sadly) the M-37 didn't handle their road much better than any other rig yet invented. Once again, their Toyota was parked down in Sleeping Moose and they would be walking for the duration of breakup. It was a long way to carry a baby, and since Attie's wailing ordeals at the wash house had grown in step with her expanding lung capacity, Kate didn't mind skipping an occasional laundry center experience. "You can pour a bucket of water over my head right here on the front steps," she told Tim. "That'll be fine with me."

His two girls waved goodbye as he hiked away, and then Kate carried Attie upstairs and sat down in front of the fogless, recently-replaced picture window. She sank down onto one of the low fire-tending stools she'd made from their beam scraps. The young mother would drink in their exceptional view while her babe suckled milk.

When Attie had eaten, burped, and fallen asleep, Kate carried her out through the portcullis door, down the bunker steps, and into the furnace-side nursery. Nap time for baby.

She stoked the fire, added two football-sized chunks of coal to the box and prepared to head back upstairs. The plan was to use this valuable hour to chip tarpaper off the upstairs floor. Now that the house was closed in, they didn't need to protect the basement ceiling from rain anymore. And the sooner the floor upstairs was bare plywood, the better.

Before she left the warm, safe cavern, Kate pulled back the blanket partition and looked in at her baby. Little Attie was sleeping soundly. Kate checked the furnace. The coal hadn't caught yet.

She messed around with the damper and the flue, and when she was pretty sure it was ready to catch, she checked Attie one last time, then tiptoed out the door and climbed the stairs. She couldn't wait to begin tearing away at the gritty green tarpaper that had outlived its purpose.

Using an ice chipper and a bit of finesse she started prying up the old roofing, an inch at a time.

Kate worked as fast as she could, knowing that baby would wake soon. The conscientious mother kept her ear tuned for any sounds coming from the nursery.

So far, things were quiet. Very peaceful and very quiet. Wait. What was that? A ticking?

Kate stopped scraping and listened hard, hoping to hear nothing. But she did hear something. There was a ticking sound coming from somewhere close by.

This didn't sound like an animal. She looked around and saw nothing out of the ordinary on the horizon. That's when her nose kicked in. Was that the pungent odor of burning creosote that she was smelling?

Kate put down her chipper and trotted over to check the stovepipe and knew immediately. It was the stovepipe that was ticking, and it was ticking way too fast.

She ran out the door, down the front steps and out, just far enough to be able to see over the edge of the roof. She saw flames. Sparks and flames were shooting up out of their smokestack. "Oh God, the house is on fire!"

Her first impulse was to grab the baby and run. But Kate soon realized that she had a second option. Maybe she could put out the fire. Should she grab Attie and run? Or should she stand her ground, and try to save the house? If she fled, they would lose everything she and Tim had slaved to build.

Kate tried to concentrate. "Let's see. Stack fires take off where the pipe meets the house—at the roof, not in the basement." She would probably have a few minutes to try to extinguish the flames. Then, if she failed, she would have all the time in the world to get Attie, run outside and sit on a hummock to watch their home burn down to the mud line.

Kate would have to try to snuff the thing out before it got any bigger.

All she had to work with was half a can of water and a lot of mud. No phone. No fire department coming to help. Even if she managed to get hold of someone on the CB, there wasn't enough time for help to arrive. She'd have to try the baking soda and vinegar backwoods fire cure, and hope that it worked.

Okay. Now where should she put baby while she engaged in battle with this raging beast? Outside in the grass? No. Who knew what animal might come by? She'd be safer right there in her crib.

Kate dragged the pale-yellow second-hand crib out of the nursery and rolled it close to the door, in case she lost the battle, and they had to run for it.

The sleeping babe barely startled as the wheels jerked and clacked across the plank flooring.

Once Attie was at least an arm's length from harm's way, Kate grabbed the box of baking soda and the bottle of vinegar that lived in their pockets by the coal bin door.

She'd never tried the antidote before, but she knew what she was supposed to do: shake a lot of baking soda onto those blistering-red tongues of fire, and then douse the chalky white patches with vinegar.

Kate opened the furnace door and stared into the mouth of the flame-breathing dragon. She caught her breath and plunged the hand that held the box of baking soda deep into the firebox. It was so hot inside that her arm felt like exploding. Shake, shake, shake. She used half the box, and then threw in some vinegar, slammed the door shut, and waited.

. . . Ten seconds. The hellish clicking was speeding still faster.

Desperately, she repeated the procedure: one, two, three. On her last shake of baking soda, Kate decided to save one small dose of the magic powder, in case she might need to launch a third assault. Wait and listen . . .

Tick, tick; tick-itty, tick-itty. The runaway was still accelerating. Had the time come to cut her losses, grab the kid, and run?

Kate looked around for an answer. On the back side of the stovepipe she caught sight of a glowing orange spot, right above the dump cap. That was it! The dump cap had to be filled with burning creosote. Frantically, she twisted at the nearly-melting metal cup until she managed to work the tabs loose. She quickly pulled the cap free and turned it upside down.

A pool of molten creosote poured out onto the dirt floor, but the bright orange spot above the opened pipe was still glowing hot. Kate started banging on the stovepipe, just above the ultra-heated patch. Chunks of crimson creosote clanked down out of the shaft and fluttered to the floor. Kate knocked on the pipe until a mound of glowing embers six-inches-deep snapped and smoldered at her feet.

When no new flakes resulted from the repeated beatings, she fumbled to replace the emptied cap. It was still hot, but she struggled with the stubborn piece until she finally got the tabs slipped back into their slots, and the stove was closed off.

Then she gave it the old soda and vinegar cure, a third time. After that, she was out of baking soda, so she went over near the crib, put her hand on Attie's back, and prayed.

Seemingly in answer, the clicking inferno began to reverse itself, and the terrifying ticks started to dim. Tick-itty. Tick-itty. Tick. Tick. Tick. The slowing tempo felt as reassuring to Kate, as a winter solstice sunrise must have, to the ancients.

When Kate was certain that the threat had been abated, she drew in a shaky survivor's breath. "I'll be right back," she promised the still-sleeping babe. "I just have to go outside and check the top of the stovepipe."

She went out into the bright daylight to look up at the roof. There were no more flames leaping from the smokestack. The fire had been contained. "Whew. That was close." Then she looked at her blistering fingers. "Ow."

Back inside, Kate stopped again at Attie's crib. "Sweet little babe, that was scary. We're lucky your mommy was able to handle it."

She studied the child, looking to see if she was upset or anxious, or had been adversely affected in any way, by this near-disaster. Attie appeared to be fine. She was sleeping comfortably, filled with restful trust.

It was quite some time before Kate could relax, even a little. She sat quietly rocking Attie, gazing at the now deceptively-docile-looking furnace, and remembered the story Cliff had told her about when he'd had to rip his cherry-red stove right off its moorings, and kicked it out the door. "As soon as it hit the snow, the whole thing popped wide open," he'd said.

"I never could have gotten this thing out of here," Kate told Attie.

"We're lucky we bought the deluxe dump-cap model, or there might not have been a house for Daddy to come home to tonight."

She finally allowed herself a little cry, and then she and Attie waited for Tim to come home.

Mother's Day

BY THE SECOND Sunday in May, their raw domain was totally enclosed and nearly ready to be called "home."

As the sun began to lower on her very first Mother's Day ever, Tim and Kate dragged Elsie's overstuffed couch out through the basement door and hauled it up the steps. They set it down on the bare wood floor in their glorious new great room. Tim built the first fire in their fancy new Scandinavian wood stove, and Kate went back down to get Attie.

They were a real family now, celebrating in a real house. Kate and baby sat together on the couch, waiting for Papa Tim to join them. Sabretooth, who had followed Kate inside, examined the warming stove, and then settled down beneath it.

As soon as Tim had the fire going just right, he rose from the fire-tender's stool and sat down on the couch with his two girls. The three snuggled together, watching through their picture-perfect window, as a show of spectacular sunset pinks faded away to dusk.

Kate sighed. "I've dreamed of this for so long. And it's finally here. I can hardly believe it."

Tim was quiet. He gazed up at the beams and then over at his family. The pioneer took his mate's hand in his, squeezed it, and grinned sweetly before he asked his partner, "Now that wasn't so hard, was it?"

Mother's Day, 1979
Happy in the new house.

# # #

A Note from the Author

KATE, MY MOTHER, collaborated closely with me in the writing of this book. These are really *her* stories.

Atwood Cutting and Kate Peters

Thanks for riding with us down this first section of the trail.

Best regards,

Attie and Kate

The Atwood Cutting Persona

WITH THE WRITINGS of Jack London and Ralph Waldo Emerson as inspiration, Atwood Cutting's idealistic parents chose to follow a dream and build their life together in the Alaskan backwoods.

Thus, newborn Attie was transported home from the hospital on a snow mobile. Her mother was surprised to find the nursery looking like a scene from Gettysburg—charred and steaming—but in they went, regardless.

The greatest source of material for this work of historical fiction is Kate Peters, the author's mother, who told Attie many wonderful stories about the weather, and the road, and the neighbors who lived at the end of the road.

Atwood's Grandma Tutu in Hawaii saved most of the letters Kate sent home over those twelve isolated years. All these nuggets from a remote mountain home proved to be a goldmine.

Kate also took photographs and kept journals, which shed enough light to give an accurate historical perspective for those who want to know what it was really like living in the bush before cellphones and four-wheelers had been invented.

With humor, Atwood tells these stories better than anyone else, except maybe Kate, herself.

If you enjoyed part one of this saga
you can continue the adventure with

**Part Two
The Winter of '79
&
Part Three:
Elephant in the Bush**

Book clubs and classes may download free
Sleeping Moose Saga discussion questions at:
www.atwoodcutting.com

The complete trilogy, plus a pictorial journal of
the best years of this great life adventure
can be ordered through
**your public library,
Ingram Book Distributors,
Amazon.com: atwood cutting: Books**

Also available: coffee table books
created for waiting rooms and living rooms with
photography by Atwood Cutting.

www.ingramcontent.com/pod-product-compliance
Lightning Source LLC
Chambersburg PA
CBHW070745120726
47910CB00001B/172